The Accidental Spurrt®

The Accidental Spurrt®
A Mark Fairley Mystery

Walt Pilcher

First Published 2019 by Fantastic Books Publishing

Cover design by Gabi

ISBN (eBook): 978-1-912053-20-9
ISBN (paperback): 978-1-912053-19-3

To lovers of parody and satire everywhere who never,
or hardly ever, take themselves too seriously.
You know who you are.

ACKNOWLEDGEMENTS

A book does not spring fully formed from the computer screen to the printed page or e-book file without many people assisting the writer in his or her quest to produce an eminently readable and entertaining book with few, if any, mistakes. And the best writers take the blame for any such mistakes.

The many people who assisted me in my quest to produce an eminently readable and entertaining book with few, if any, mistakes know this. They said, "If you don't acknowledge us, and your mistakes, we will not assist you ever again and you won't be among the best writers." I do want to be among the best writers. Therefore, I publicly acknowledge and sincerely thank all those listed below. I am truly sorry if I left anyone out, and the blame is mine for any mistakes.

First readers: Henry Colavita, Mariko Hara, Hamp Kenan, Susan Thompson, John Wilcox, the late John Sommer, my son Todd Pilcher and daughters Jennifer Schneier and Carolyn McAllister

- Purple Heart three-time first reader: my wife Carol Beebe Pilcher
- *Nihongo* (Japanese language) consultant: Mariko Hara, President, Method Company, Ltd., Iwaki-city, Fukushima, Japan

- Guest editors of selected sections: Steve Cushman, Coventry Kessler, Christopher Laney, Susan Thompson
- Local color advisors for passages involving UNC-Chapel Hill and Duke University: Carolyn McAllister and Jennifer Schneier, respectively
- The unsung editors and hand-holders at Fantastic Books Publishing

It's good to be a best writer, and a Fantastic one as well.

PRAISE FOR *THE ACCIDENTAL SPURRT®*

"It's a spell-binding yet side-splitting tale of mystery, danger, greed, jealousy, pathos, death and possible sex. Oh, and shadowy international forces vying for control of the multi-billion-dollar energy drink industry. I hope you'll buy it, because I'm still out of work and I need the money."
— Mark Fairley

"A cautionary tale of government overreach on steroids. Oh wait, that was *Everybody Shrugged*. We haven't read *The Accidental Spurrt* yet, but we hear it's terrific."
— *Book Week*

"Could this be the first of a new series of hilarious Mark Fairley mysteries? We hope so!"
— *Book Month*

"I love the care with which Pilcher chooses names for his characters. Zachariah Spurr II, Sheriff Seedy Belton, Detective Jake Keil, Tadashi Tanaka, Kashimoto, Nick Papadopoulos, Roberto Quinoa, and Dirk Falcone indeed, just to mention a few!"
— Durango Falcone, serial volunteer book reviewer

"… worth … reading. I couldn't … put it down."
— *Bupkis Reviews*

"In spite of Mr. Pilcher's over-the-top stereotyping of Japanese customs, culture, business practices and accents, based on having lived in Tokyo a paltry 14 months, he is welcome to return to Japan anytime as long as he brings money."
— Mariko Hara, President, Method Co., Ltd., Japanese language consultant and friend of the author

"What are you waiting for? Really, it has side-splitting mystery, danger, greed, jealousy, pathos, death and possible sex." – Mark Fairley

"See, I even wrote a cover blurb:

'I'm just an innocent consultant trying to write a history book, I thought as I surveyed the bullet-ruined upper of my down-at-heel left Bally loafer, so why am I hiding in a dumpster hoping a fake Japanese guy with a gun doesn't make me the star of the final chapter?'

Not bad, huh? Or should I just stick to churning out *résumés*?"
— Mark Fairley

"Very interesting."
— Shadowy International Forces Vying for Control of the Multi-Billion-Dollar Energy Drink Industry

Prologue

Jerry felt like a Judas. A Judas with a bad head cold.

Except he barely knew the people that he was sort of betraying. Rich folks, though, so what the heck? Besides, he was getting $30 for this gig, just to sneak around a science lab late at night with the lights out looking for … what? He wasn't sure.

He thought of the no-name guy who'd hired him as "the shadowy figure who gives me and Tom money to spy on these people." He'd read "shadowy figure" in a mystery novel. Tom had goosed the guy up from $25, so that was pretty good. Plus, gas money for the old brown Toyota Tercel they always drove, with its off-white right front fender and missing wheel cover. The only good thing about the car was it never got stopped at the area speed traps set up by cops with nothing better to do.

The no-name guy didn't say exactly what he wanted them to find, just to fill him in on whatever they saw during these little visits, sometimes to the offices of a soft drink company in Spurrville or elsewhere in town, sometimes over to a dorm at the university in Chapel Hill, and sometimes, like tonight, to the science lab at the soft drink plant, with its strange equipment, computers all over the place, and huge black tables with sinks in them, stuff he vaguely recognized from the chemistry class he failed six years ago in high school.

This was the third time sneaking into the lab and the first time Jerry was doing it alone. Even though he and Tom never found anything that rang the guy's bells the first two times, he'd told them to go back yet again. It must have been important to him, but it didn't make much sense, and it was risky sneaking around like this in the dead of night. But 30 bucks is 30 bucks. At least they also had the guy's permission to leave Chinese takeout menus here and there from the restaurant where they worked in Raleigh, even though Raleigh was pretty far from Spurrville for lunch hour takeout. And the guy always paid up.

He hadn't actually asked them to break in after business hours. That was Jerry's own idea. He was pretty proud of it. After all, how many times could you come back during the day to leave takeout menus before people became suspicious?

If Tom had come with him, of course they'd have split the $30, but Tom couldn't make it this time.

"It's Friday, Jerry. I've got a date. I haven't had a real date in a long time, so, you know …" Well, boo-hoo for Tom. But 30 bucks all for me is pretty good for poking around in the dark for a while, he thought. And the door was unlocked, so he figured technically it wasn't breaking and entering, in case the Sheriff should happen by.

Fleetingly he wondered what Tom was using for transportation tonight since he, Jerry, had the Tercel, now hidden in a small grove of trees right off the main road and within walking distance of the lab. Probably her car, he thought. Or maybe a bus, knowing Tom.

It was just as well Tom wasn't here. He had a habit of wearing too much cologne in a fragrance Jerry didn't care for and which was also dangerous since people might remember him because of it. Not smart in an espionage op, which is what this was. Shoddy "tradecraft" was what they called it in the spy novels. Also, probably why Tom had trouble getting dates. That and maybe the Tercel. No matter. He couldn't have smelled it tonight. He hadn't smelled anything all day.

Stifling a sneeze, he blew his nose into a Kleenex, the latest of many he'd used tonight and stuffed the tissue into his pocket, which was already brimming over. He didn't want to leave any evidence behind. Of course, he'd left a couple menus in the reception area and the office lobby. That was okay. Lots of restaurants leave their menus at businesses. Adding a few more of his when no one was looking wouldn't arouse suspicion. And he was wearing gloves, like the shadowy figure insisted, so he didn't have to worry about leaving fingerprints.

Man, he was thirsty! Must be the cold medicine. Dries me out, he thought, even though my nose keeps running like a faucet. Whadda they say? Drown a cold, starve a fever? Or is it the other way around: starve a cold, drown a fever? Doesn't matter. I'll be doing one or the other if I can find some water. If my nose is running, why am I dried out? Maybe I'm dried out because my nose is running? It's a medical mystery.

His flashlight casting a dim, wobbly glow, he approached one of the sinks. Finding the faucet on it, he searched around with the flashlight for a glass and finally saw something on a nearby shelf that might do. A beaker, if he remembered right from chemistry class. He put the beaker under the faucet. What the …? The faucet stuck straight out and was pointy at the end. It didn't curve down like a regular faucet so you could get a glass under it, or a beaker. Could be some new design, he figured, especially since this lab must be up to date with only the newest and best equipment, considering who owned it. Carefully, but awkwardly, he positioned the beaker, tilting it toward the faucet so it would fill up at least partially, then turned the handle. Nothing came out. Well, there was a soft whooshing sound he could barely hear over the ringing from the congestion in his ears, but no water. He turned it off. Silence. Then on again. Soft whoosh.

Must be air in the water line. He moved to another sink. Same kind of faucet. Same problem. On, whoosh. Off, silence. No water. Two dry sinks and another stifled sneeze later, he'd had enough. He hadn't found anything he thought the shadowy figure guy would be interested in, and it was time to get out before he got caught. He didn't plan on coming back, even if the guy offered more money. It was too dangerous. And he was still thirsty.

He had another idea. I'll just leave all these faucets open. When the water comes back on, won't these people be surprised when they get their water bill! Ha! They can afford it. Serves 'em right. Rich SOBs.

***

The explosion and fire that destroyed the lab and killed Elliot Spurr that night made national news and all the newspapers and TV news shows in the Raleigh area. Somehow Tom and Jerry didn't hear about it right away.

***

Twenty-four hours later a telephone rang in the plush executive office suite on the top floor of the headquarters of the Kashimoto Foods conglomerate in the Shinjuku business district of Tokyo.

"*Moshi-moshi*" (Hello?)

"*Hai, Tanaka degozaimasu.*" (This is Tanaka speaking)

"*Hai!*" (I'm listening.)

"*Aratana shintenga arimasu. Karerawa mamonaku himitsuwo hakken surudesyo.*" (There's been a new development. I think maybe they will soon discover the secret.)

"*Wakarimashita. Tsugino shijiwo matsuyoni.*" (Understood. Wait for further orders.)

"*Wakarimashita. Sayonara.*"

"*Hai, sayonara.*"

Chapter 1

The story I guess I might as well call "The Case of the Accidental Spurrt" (and get it over with) began for me with a phone call while I was in the kitchen one morning with my wife, Emily, finishing a bowl of grits left over from the night before. We'd had them with scrambled eggs and toast, as we sometimes do when we don't feel like having a big dinner. We eat what we like. After a night in the refrigerator grits are like a big glob of glue, but if you break the big glob up into small globs with a fork, add a few drops of milk and put them in the microwave for 45 seconds, they're pretty good. I like them. I have trouble deciding whether to eat them with butter and salt or with sugar, like Cream of Wheat, another favorite. Emily says we shouldn't eat butter anymore, so this time I only put on salt. Two years ago we weren't supposed to be eating salt either. But now salt's okay, apparently. Somebody must have improved it.

While Emily answered the phone, I got down a coffee mug from the cabinet. I was going to make a cup of instant and take it into the extra bedroom I use as a makeshift office. There I planned to make yet a few more minor changes in my résumé, making it absolutely perfect, again. Then I was going to mail it out with cover letters to four more potential employers I had recently looked up in the business reference section at the public library. Yes, I use the Internet for job searching from home like everybody else, but sometimes the library can be sort of a nice, quiet refuge. And good for people-watching.

I would also check my supply of the new business cards I'd

had made up over at Office Depot since the ones from my old company wouldn't work anymore. I had struggled over what to put on them. The "Mark L. Fairley" part was easy, of course. And my home address here in Greensboro, NC, my home and cell phone numbers and my e-mail address. I had no website, and my Facebook page was a joke, so those were out. Hardly anybody puts a reference to their LinkedIn page on their business cards, and especially if they're out of work, so I didn't either. No, the big question was how to describe myself on the cards. The choices were endless, starting with "Currently Unemployed" (the truth, but with a hopeful note) and running a gamut from "Retired" (in which case why would I need business cards and résumés?) to "Between Jobs" (the popular euphemism for the truth) to "Former Important Business Executive Who Hopes to Bounce Back," to "Have Mouth, Brain and Experience—Will Travel."

Unimaginatively, I settled on the first resort of all such souls as find themselves in my situation. I would re-invent myself as a Consulting Firm. The cards read "Mark L. Fairley, President, Fairley & Associates, Strategic Planning, Vinyl Siding and Storm Doors" (okay, just kidding about the siding and storm doors).

Thirty seconds into the microwave cycle, Emily said, "Mark, it's for you. I think it's Frank."

"That's odd, but I'll take a call from almost anybody these days."

Frank is my lawyer. Frank Sheldon, Esq. Not that I have a lot of legal problems, but Frank had recently done our wills, and from time to time he provides tax advice. So he knew I was, ahem, between assignments, and he had said he would throw some leads my way if he came up with any. Smart fellow—he knew the longer I remained between assignments the less need I'd have for his occasional billable hours, unless it finally came time to file for bankruptcy. He could go to dinner on that kind of work for a long time, but I guess in his view waiting for that would be like shooting the moon in Hearts—sooner or later ol' Mark *will* find a job. I took what little comfort I could in this perverse implied vote of confidence from Frank.

"Hello, Frank."

"Hey, buddy, how ya doin'?"

"Great, just great!" (I haven't had a real job in eight months.)

"Hey, that's terrific! Got anything hot?"

"Well, you know … got a few irons in the fire … should know something about one or two of them in a couple of weeks or so." (I have no "irons in the fire." Not one. I have 62 résumés out. More like barbless fish hooks in the ocean than irons in the fire. My friends with jobs won't return my calls anymore. The only good news is at least the local Amway and Nu Skin distributors have finally gotten tired of trying to recruit me. Telemarketing companies are hiring too, but I'm not ready to move to Mumbai.)

"Hey, that's the spirit!"

"I think so. Still too early to panic." (I have three kids in college, mortgage payments and a monthly blizzard of bills in spite of our attempts to cut back on spending. I'm hoping this book will bring in some income. If I can get permission to publish it. Would it help if I told you it has mystery, intrigue, danger, greed, jealousy, a possible homicide, and sex? Or is that a homicide and possible sex? Whatever, I'll be sure and put something like that in the cover blurb.)

"Listen, Mark, you remember I mentioned I had a client over near Siler City … the woman whose husband has that food company down there?"

"Spur Foods, something like that?"

"Spurr Nutritionals, with two r's. They make that Spurrt

3

stuff, sort of a healthy soft drink. Pretty popular, I guess, although I don't use much of it myself. Have you ever tried it?"

"No, Frank, I haven't. I thought it was mostly for old people."

Emily gave me the raised eyebrow look, one of her favorites. I smiled back at her.

"Our firm does some estate planning work for the family and occasionally gets involved in some liability stuff," Frank continued.

"You mean like when somebody sues them for finding mouse parts in a Spurrt bottle?"

There was an unusually long pause.

"… not funny, Mark."

"Well, excuuuse me," I said.

"Never mind. Anyway, it's not a great situation for them right now, I'm afraid. You've heard about her husband being in an accident at the bottling plant last year …?"

"No, I don't think so."

"Yeah, and he's still laid up, probably won't ever recover completely. But worse than that, her son, who was actually the president of the company, got killed recently."

"Maybe I did read about that," I said, trying to dredge it up. "A fire or something, wasn't it?"

"Right," agreed Frank. "Circumstances were a little odd, too, but I don't know too much about it. Anyway, as you can imagine, Mrs. Spurr is pretty upset right now, got a lot on her mind, especially now she's the majority stockholder and sort of running the business for all practical purposes. Last week she told me she's thinking about selling the company."

The microwave beeped four times. With the phone in one hand I opened the door with the other and took out the mug full of hot water. The mug had a picture of a microphone on it wearing a cap and gown like it was graduating and the words "WFDD – 88.5 FM Listener Supported Radio." I guess we sent in some money back when I still had a job. Tucking the phone under my chin to free my hands, I set the mug down on the counter and sprinkled a half a teaspoon of sugar into the water. The water fizzed up as if I'd dropped in an Alka-Seltzer tablet. I was making the water actually come to a boil.

For some reason, even though its temperature is way above 212°F coming out of the microwave, water won't actually boil unless something agitates it. The sugar grains do that. If you put the instant coffee powder in first, that will do it too, but it makes a sort of fuzzy foam on the surface of the coffee that never quite goes away no matter how long you stir it. I don't like fuzzy coffee, so I put the sugar in first, then the coffee powder. Still talking to Frank.

"So, Frank, what might this have to do with me?"

Emily thinks I am nuts to bother with making sure to put the sugar in first. Especially since I told her I learned this little secret tip by interpreting something I read in the children's science section on the back page of the Sunday comics in the *Greensboro News & Record*. But at least she's agreed not to tell anybody where I got it or what she thinks about it. So she says.

"Well, Mrs. Spurr told me that before she sells the company she thinks it would be a good idea to get somebody to write the company history, sort of the official story, you know, for posterity and all that?"

"Yeah …?"

"So she was asking me if I know anybody who does that sort of thing, someone she could trust. Of course, I don't know anybody like that, but I'd never admit it, so I mentioned your name."

"You mean you don't know anybody who can write, or you don't know anybody who can be trusted?"

"Come on, Mark, I've heard all the lawyer jokes already."

"Okay, seriously, I appreciate your thinking of me, and I do need some work. But it sounds like a snooze. What did she say when you mentioned me?"

"She wants to talk to you. I told her a little bit about you, just the good stuff, of course, and she said why don't I ask you to give her a call. I assume your car still runs and you can drive down to see her."

"Ha, ha to you too. Yeah, I suppose I can clear my calendar and go down there. Is she planning to pay me for this, or will I have to take it out in trade, like a trunk full of their happy juice?"

"It's a big company," Frank assured me. "They can afford to pay."

"You should know, I guess, if anybody does."

"I guess. Listen, her name is Fanny Spurr. She's a real nice lady. I've got her phone number right here. Now, I promised her you'd call."

I got the number, thanked Frank reasonably sincerely, and hung up.

"You don't look very happy," observed Emily. "What was that all about?"

I told her.

"That should be an easy job for you, and it will probably be fun," she said. "Even if it doesn't fit with your self-image, at least you'll be out of the house a lot. I can't say I'll mind that, and it will be good for you."

"Of course, I have to actually get the job first. Frank's probably not the only person she's talked to about it."

Emily rolled her eyes like an exasperated teenager. Our children would have been proud.

"Okay," I said. "You're right. I'm happy. This is an exciting day. I get to make a Long Distance Call, and then I get to count my business cards and Clear My Calendar!"

But before doing any of that, I finished my coffee, got out of my pajamas, took a shower, shaved and got dressed. After all, it was almost noon and time to get my busy day started.

6

Chapter 2

I got the job three days later, but not before a run-in with the sheriff of Lester County.

I couldn't believe it. It's less than 40 miles down US 421 from my house to Siler City, and another five miles or so to the turnoff that leads to Spurrville, where I was to meet with Mrs. Spurr at her home. Because it was my first trip there and I was unfamiliar with the route, I drove very carefully. I clearly saw the sign that said "Welcome to Spurrville," but I missed the 35-mph speed limit sign right behind it. I was still doing 55 when I saw the flashing blue lights and put on the brakes, too late.

The sheriff's car was a brown Chevrolet Caprice, festooned with emergency lights and antennas. That model Chevy is the fat, round, bulbous thing popular with police forces in the 1990s. It looks like a big jellybean on wheels, and you don't see them much anymore. I pulled over. He stopped behind me, antennas swaying authoritatively. He got out and strode toward my car. His wide brimmed campaign hat shaded his face and made him seem big. His gun was big too.

"'Preciate your stopping so quick," he said as I let my window down. "Didn't have to put the siren on you. People around here like it peaceful and quiet."

I looked around and saw nothing but farmland. Not a building within a mile in any direction. No other cars on the road.

I hadn't been stopped by the police in a long time, so I said the first thing that came to my mind.

"What's the problem, officer?" What they always say on TV.

"Guess you wouldn't have kept going so fast if you'd noticed the sign back there, huh? I'm sure you're usually a law abiding citizen."

"Sure am."

The plastic name tag on his smartly tailored brown uniform shirt said "Belton." I was now beginning to think I might actually be in real trouble. Or maybe that I had driven over a line somewhere and back into the actual 1990s. Which would also be real trouble if I couldn't find the wormhole to get me back to my own time. I used to read a lot of science fiction in my youth.

"Well, it's a nice clear afternoon, good driving conditions," he continued in his best sheriff drawl, "but there's a school about two miles on down the road, and then a little after that there's the factory. Shift changes pretty soon. Lots of traffic coming out on the highway here."

"Good thing you stopped me." What they never say on TV.

"Uh huh. Let me see your license and registration, please."

I dug them out and handed them over.

"Thank you, Mr ... uh, Mark Lamont Farley," he said.

"Fairley," I said.

"Fairley."

I sat back and tried to relax, half-heartedly looking down the road for the school Belton had mentioned.

"I see you live in Greensboro, but you're not really from North Carolina, are you?"

"Yeah, you got me on that all right; I was born up north, but we've been in North Carolina for a few years. My wife and I, I mean."

"Uh huh."

We continued sparring—him testing me, me probably not fooling him—while he wrote up my ticket. He put his tongue out a little now and then, the way some people do when they're writing. He had a small, neatly trimmed mustache, and up close he didn't seem to be as big as I had thought at first.

Maybe three pickup trucks and a couple of sedans went by the whole time I sat there. No SUVs.

As he handed me the ticket, along with my license and registration, he finally got around to asking the obligatory sheriff question.

"So, what brings you down here, Mr. Farley?"

"Fairley."

"Right."

"Actually," I sighed, "I'm here to talk to somebody about a job."

He seemed surprised I wasn't just passing through.

"Is that so? Where, if I might ask?" All politeness now. Or skepticism?

"Spurr Nutritionals. Well, actually not the plant; I have an appointment to see Mrs. Spurr at her home." (See, I belong here after all. I've been *invited*.)

"You know Fanny Spurr?"

"Never met, actually, but I've talked with her on the phone. Long conversation."

"Well, she's a nice old lady. Pillar of the community, you might say. Big supporter of law enforcement too."

"I'm sure," I said.

"But she's had a run of bad luck lately. In the family. I s'pose you know about that?"

"Well, a little. Maybe she'll tell me more." (Oops, maybe overplayed it there.)

"Well, now, why would she do that?"

"She wants to talk to me about a project to write about the company, kind of a history I think. For posterity I guess, and maybe for the grandchildren …"

9

"You wouldn't be some kind of private eye, would you?"

"Why would you think that?" I said, trying to look naïve and incompetent. "No, I'm not, but I do have some experience doing research at companies I've worked for."

"Well, it's just that we've had a few strangers poking around here, especially since the fire," he continued. "Of course, I s'pose all I have to do is call Mrs. Spurr and check it out."

This was getting ridiculous. I was on my way to be interviewed for a job. But before that, I was being interviewed for the interview. By the sheriff.

"May I go now?"

"Of course, Mr. Farley, you're free to go. Ordinarily, I'd have you follow me to the magistrate's office to pay that ticket, but seeing as you're a friend of Mrs. Spurr's I imagine we can trust you to do us the honor of mailing in your fine or appearing on your court date if you choose to contest it. 'Course, if you want to go in right now and get it over with, we do take Master Card and Visa … but not American Express, I'm afraid." He chuckled.

"Thanks; I'll mail it in."

"We do like to watch out for Mrs. Spurr, though," he said. Warning me. "Sort of keep an eye on her while she's going through this hard time."

"I'm sure she appreciates that."

Maybe she could fix my ticket. If she liked me and I got the job. Then, I don't know why, but I had to ask: "Uh, what kind of strangers?"

Sheriff Belton looked surprised, but he answered my question.

"Well, of course there's been people from the insurance company ever since old Mr. Zachariah Spurr had his accident over at the plant—maybe you heard about that—and then especially since the fire that killed their son. I've had to spend a lot of time with them that I don't really have. But besides them, there's some others, and I'm not sure who they are."

He had his hat pushed back on his forehead and was resting his elbows on my window frame. I had to lean back to keep our faces a comfortable distance apart. I'm guessing he'd had barbecue for lunch. With lots of Texas Pete sauce.

"Who do you *think* they are?" I asked, plunging ahead.

Again, the look of surprise, now mixed with suspicion.

"I don't know," he said. "There's four of them that I know of. Maybe more. Two of them look ordinary enough, except obviously from out of state."

"Obviously," I said.

"No offense," he said.

"No problem."

"And the other two look to be Chinese or something like that. And they seem to be working in pairs."

"You mean the two American out-of-staters and the two Chinese guys in two separate pairs, right? Not mixed."

"Uh … right," said Belton.

"What do they do?"

"Not much of anything we've been able to figure. They're just around sometimes, here and there."

"Why don't you ask them what they're up to?"

"Got no reason," he shrugged.

"You asked *me*."

"Had a reason with you. I caught you in the speed tra–, I mean, caught you speeding."

"I wouldn't think you'd need an excuse."

"Well, maybe not, but there are limits, even here," Belton said with an ever so slightly sheepish grin.

"I'm glad to hear it," I said, starting my engine and putting on my left turn signal. "Maybe I won't be mailing in that fine after all." I had visions of Frank Sheldon defending me in a clear case of entrapment.

11

"We'll see about that," he said, straightening up, adjusting his hat and offering his right hand. "I'm Sheriff Cecil Belton, Mr. *Fairley*. You need anything around here, you just come see me. Okay?"

"Okay. Nice to meet you. Thanks."

We shook hands, and I eased the car back out on to the highway. In the mirror I saw Belton saunter back to his jellybean cruiser, but instead of getting into it he stood there watching me drive away. I could see he had the microphone out and was talking to somebody on his radio. I couldn't tell if his antennas were still swaying.

Chapter 3

"Mr. Sheldon faxed me your résumé, Mr. Fairley, and I must say it is impressive," said Mrs. Spurr with a smile.

I didn't think anybody used faxes anymore, but I guess I was wrong.

"Thank you, ma'am." I put down my teensy spoon in my teensy saucer and took a teensy sip from my teensy teacup.

I arrived for my meeting with Fanny Spurr on time, but barely. Not that it was hard to find her house, but my dalliance with the sheriff had eaten well into the time I had planned for driving around to see the layout of the town. Now that would have to wait.

It also took me longer than usual to get dressed that morning because I put on a suit and tie, which I wasn't used to because Casual Friday had long ago turned into Casual Every Day where I had worked, and since being downsized I wore suits only at weddings and funerals. However, "Always put your best foot forward," Mom always said. I never got why one foot would be better than the other, and since there were only two of them how either one could be "best," but you don't argue with your mother. She always liked me in what she called "the preppy look," characterized by my only concession to sartorial comfort on business attire occasions: loafers. The truly authentic Southern preppy look is to wear the loafers without socks, but I didn't grow up in the South, and I've never been comfortable doing that.

The typical small town in this part of the country has one

neighborhood of nice old homes, usually on the main road, and then there is the rest of the town. The Spurr home was clearly the largest mansion in a neighborhood of mansions but was otherwise not comparatively pretentious. It was a three-story Georgian-style structure of antique brick. Well, Georgian is what Emily told me it was after I described it to her. The house sat well back on a more or less level lot I guessed to be about four acres. There was a large circular drive paved in the same brick as the house, and there were dogwood trees and several large, well-shaped magnolias on the lawn. An extension of the driveway led to a separate three-car (or two cars and a boat?) garage to one side, connected to the house by a covered walkway. I assumed correctly there was a swimming pool in the back, but when I saw it later it was covered by a tarpaulin and looked like it hadn't been used for a long time.

I parked my crystal black pearl Acura TLX in the circular drive, adjusted my tie and rang the doorbell. Mrs. Spurr herself came to the door, greeted me warmly and led me to the Florida room, where we then sat, having our demitasse.

"Zachariah agrees with me," she went on.

That startled me.

"Oh, is he …" I started, "I mean, I thought he was …"

"Oh, his mind is still sharp as a tack. It's just that even after his physical injuries healed from being flung through that … machine, he has not been able to write legibly or speak clearly. But I keep him company, talk to him a lot, and I let him read some of the important company papers and documents so I can get his opinion on things. He can tell me 'yes' and 'no' by nodding his head, and that is about all, but even that is very helpful. Heavens to Betsy, I never thought I would be running the company, you know …" She trailed off a little wistfully.

"No, I guess not," I agreed, sounding sympathetic I hoped.

"I think it's good for him too," she resumed. "I mean to have someone to talk with, important things to do. We were optimistic, at first, that he would recover completely. He was up and around within a few days after the accident, and he had lots of energy. But lately he has not been himself. He seems to be tired all the time."

I wondered why she was telling me all this so early in our conversation. At that point I had no way of knowing my encounter with Sheriff Belton wasn't the only surprise in store for me that day.

"He's upstairs now. You will meet him before you leave, I hope."

"Well, yes, I'm looking forward to it."

"Sheriff Belton likes you, too," she went on. "He says you all had a nice chat this afternoon."

I almost spat out some tea, but since it was only a teensy amount I was able to hold it in.

"He means well," she said, "and he's a nice enough man. I just wish he were a little more, shall we say, sophisticated."

As a rule, I hate Florida rooms. They're all windows, mirrors, white wicker furniture, white walls, white floors and ceilings, and odd, dangerous-looking plants with wide, spiky leaves. Like Florida but without the alligators. The furniture always looks comfortable but isn't. On a sunny day, I'm usually blinded in a Florida room, especially if I'm seated facing a window, which you always have a 75% chance of doing in a Florida room and which I was then. I was talking to Mrs. Spurr's silhouette.

But it's a nice old silhouette, I couldn't help thinking to myself. It might give me a job, even if only temporary. And fix my speeding ticket.

"You're not originally from around here, are you, Mr. Fairley?" she asked.

Where does this question come from all the time? I've decided it has to be in some kind of Southern etiquette book handed out in the sixth grade. There's a chapter on How to Talk to Foreigners. That is, anyone who's "not from around here."

"How on Earth did you know?" I played along, squinting into her solar eclipse.

"Oh, heavens to Betsy, I could just tell," she chuckled. "Besides, your résumé shows where you were born."

Mrs. Spurr was a small woman. Thin, but not frail. I'd have guessed she was at least a decade younger than the 79 I knew her to be from the newspaper articles that popped up when I Googled the company after talking to Frank Sheldon. Her own accent was one of those soft, lilting ones most often, but not exclusively, heard among women of breeding in this part of the world.

"Well, we've been in North Carolina for a while now," I said, "And we like it very much."

We went through the ritual small talk for a few more minutes. I politely declined a plate of finger foods, then relented and carefully chose two little crustless air sandwiches. I welcomed the chance to look down and give my eyes a rest. Squinting is painful after a while.

I elaborated on some points from my résumé, especially the part about why I was currently available. My standard explanation is I was caught in a "downsizing" of the company I was working for.

I remember when downsizing was called a "reduction in force," or RIF. If you were let go during one of those you were said to have been "riffed." Before that, when no one worried about political correctness, you were just "fired."

This happens in so many companies now that there's not the stigma attached to it like there used to be. I keep telling myself.

16

Actually, now they call it "rightsizing," as if the management gurus really believe if companies could only find that "right" size, no one would ever have to be laid off again. What will they do when they discover this isn't true? Say, "Oops, sorry. Guess we didn't get it quite right yet. You're out of here"? Will they call it "oops-sizing"? You can change the words but not the reality. Whatever it's called, it'll still be just as painful for those whose continued presence would push their companies over the dreaded precipice of being The Wrong Size.

Whatever happened to One Size Fits All?

Fortunately, Mrs. Spurr seemed to understand, although she somewhat proudly claimed nothing like that had ever happened at Spurr Nutritionals.

I showed her some samples of my writing, which she read carefully and seemed to like. I rested my eyes while she read.

"All right, Mr. Fairley, let me tell you what I have in mind," she said finally. "I said I was running Spurr Nutritionals, but of course that is not entirely true. We are still a privately held company, and with Zachariah's shares and mine combined, plus the support I presume I will get from my grandson, young Zachariah the Third—we call him Trey—who inherited from his father, Elliot, after he ... passed, I essentially own the business for all practical purposes."

"Are there any other shareholders?" I asked, again trying not to squint too obviously.

"My heavens, yes, there are many, including the bank, extended family members, a number of employees who have been with us through thick and thin, such as Wash Booker our sales and marketing vice president and Jim Sullivan our CFO, which I think stands for 'chief financial officer.' Or something like that. Anyway, he handles the money."

I assured Mrs. Spurr that was the correct translation of the acronym.

"And there are some outside parties, such as our attorney, Mr. Sheldon, whom you already know," she continued. "And even Sheriff Belton, now I think about it. But the total number of shares they all have is small," she explained. "In any case, although I am whom you might call 'the boss,' it is actually Jim Sullivan who is now in charge day to day. I go to the office when I can, but usually Jim comes here to see me when there are papers to sign and whatnot, because I do need to be here with Zachariah most of the time. And as I said, we consult Zachariah as often as possible, but you know even before he … before the accident … he had not been president of the company for several years. Elliot, our elder son, took over about ten years ago. And now, of course, with Elliot not … with us anymore …"

She paused and collected herself.

"So, anyway, as you can imagine," she continued, "I have had to study very hard to learn enough to feel I am living up to at least some of my new responsibilities. It has been a difficult time for all of us. Jim seems to be doing a good job, and I am certain I can trust him, so we are muddling through somehow. However, I am getting on a bit, as you can see, and I have always been told I don't have a head for figures. So I have decided it would be best to try to sell the company."

"But don't you have a younger son too?" I interjected gently. "Couldn't he possibly …?"

"I am afraid not," she interrupted, too quickly, I thought. Then she continued, but with what might have been a mixture of sadness and frustration just under the surface. "You see, Adam … that's his name … Adam really seems to have no calling for the business. No head for it, some would say. We were hoping he would, especially after working in the plant after school and in the summertime just like his brother before him, and then especially when he went off to Duke University in Durham, but … I don't know. Perhaps it simply was not to be."

"And where is Adam now? What does he do?" I asked, just to close the subject.

"He teaches chemistry at Duke," she said quietly.

"Ah," I said and took another sip of tea, or pretended to, as my little cup had been practically empty even when I had first received it from Mrs. Spurr's manicured hand.

"Oh my, where are my manners?" she exclaimed more brightly. "Would you like some more of that?"

"Yes, thank you," I said, positioning my thimble under the tilting spout for her. After all, the quantity posed little risk of sending me running to the bathroom any time soon.

"Now, then, Mr. Fairley, where was I?"

"Please call me Mark, Mrs. Spurr."

"All right … Mark."

She did not ask me to call her Fanny.

"You were talking about selling the company."

"Yes, that is correct," she said. Then she paused as if to gather her thoughts again before continuing. "This is not a happy time for any of us here in Spurrville … Mark."

I nodded, not wanting to interrupt. A dog barked, sounding like it was tied up in the back yard.

"Ever since the War, when it became apparent Spurr Nutritionals was going to be a success, and we had paid off all our debts, I suppose we all rather assumed the company would continue to be run by the family forever. First, Elliot would take over, and then his son, young Trey who is in college now over in Chapel Hill, and so on. But it is not working out that way, as you can see.

"Starting when my son took over, more than ten years ago now, the company just seemed to stop growing. Competition was heavy. Costs went up. We borrowed heavily to finance

19

investment in a major expansion of the plant building, new bottling equipment, new computers, and more efficient warehousing and distribution systems to reduce operating costs. And of course the new research laboratory which is now in ruins. We introduced a few new products, which required more investment, but they never became very successful so we discontinued them. And we never developed much of an export business. We were 'running in place,' as the business journals liked to characterize us. Stable financially and able to meet payroll every month but not growing, and slowly losing what they call 'market share.' Then too, Elliot lost some of his drive and determination for a time after his wife, Lucy, was killed in an automobile accident. He bounced back eventually, and five years ago he brought in Wash Booker, from Coca Cola I think, to create a proper marketing department. I'm told Mr. Booker seems to have some good ideas, and sales have increased somewhat, but we are still heavily in debt—bank loans and bonds—and Jim Sullivan tells me we therefore cannot afford to invest any additional funds for more new product development or advertising. Evidently, our biggest loan has what they call a 'balloon payment' that is due very soon, and I do not know how we will be able to manage it. Of course, I do not claim to understand all of these things."

"Well, you couldn't be expected …" I said.

"And then my husband had his accident, and somehow the spark seemed to go out of the company. I think the employees had gotten used to seeing my husband come to the plant almost every day, in spite of his age. He would walk around, ask people what they were doing. It made them feel important. When he could not come anymore, I think they missed him. Elliot was not as outgoing and also probably did not see the need to duplicate his father's efforts."

A telephone rang in another part of the house. Mrs. Spurr

seemed not to hear it. Finally, someone answered it, probably a maid. Probably not the dog. Mrs. Spurr continued.

"Then after the accident Elliot had so much to do, dealing with the insurance companies, the reporters, reassuring the employees, and so on."

"I guess it must have been hard for him to concentrate on the business," I offered.

"Yes. And also it seemed more people began to show interest in buying the company from us. We received calls from investment bankers at all hours of the day and night."

"You said 'more people,' Mrs. Spurr. Had there been others before?" I asked.

"Oh, yes, over the years there were occasional inquiries. There was one Japanese company that seemed quite persistent. From time to time they would send someone to call on us, but they were very polite and did not press themselves upon us unduly. Actually, I never have understood why they wanted to buy us. We were never successful in our attempts to export Spurrt to Japan.

"But we simply did not want to sell anyway," she went on, "because, as I told you, we had a vision that the company would stay in the family, although now I can see that might have been a bit too romantic and naïve a notion."

"Not at all," I said. "There are many family-owned companies that have survived the generations."

"Not ours I'm afraid. Not now that Elliot is … is gone, and poor Trey is an orphan and far too young." She said the last few words so softly I could barely hear them.

"Is the Japanese company still interested?" I asked.

"They were the first ones to call after my husband's accident, and now they seem extremely eager for us to negotiate with them." She paused again. "Why do you ask?"

"It's just that today there are not many Japanese companies

21

buying American companies," I said. "There was a lot of it in the 1980's, but not so much now."

"Well, in any case, now it does seem inevitable we must sell the company, and so I suppose we will talk to them," she said. "Jim Sullivan and our bankers are preparing a 'prospectus' to show to potential buyers so we can present ourselves in the most favorable light."

"Have you considered an IPO?" I asked, drawing on my limited experience of such things.

"IPO?" she said. "Oh, you mean an initial public offering. Creating new shares of stock to sell on the open market."

"That's right. It might be a good way to raise money to pay down the debt and provide funds for investment in new products. You could structure it so the family still retains control of the company."

"Yes, that is something we might be willing to consider, but Mr. Sullivan seems to think our prospects for raising the requisite amounts are not high, considering the financial condition of the company. And of course, we would have to make all of our financial information public, and we are not comfortable with that."

"I understand." No point in getting into an argument about it at this early stage of our relationship.

"In any case," she continued, "before we simply give up everything and abandon the company to outsiders, who might even change its name, I want to create a lasting memorial to my husband's work, and to my son's memory," she said. "I want to commission the writing of a complete history of the company. I want it to start with the early childhood of my dear husband growing up in the family of the first Zachariah Spurr, describing the events leading up to the development of our first product, Spurr's Restorative, the formation of the company, the founding and settlement of Spurrville, and our growth over the years. I want to show how Zachariah the First's dream was fulfilled and what a contribution he made. The history should come right up to the present time, so people will appreciate what they had here when it is gone. And it will be gone. I would like to have this project completed during my husband's lifetime, and mine if possible."

She had a faraway look on her face, and I was glad she stopped for breath when she did. I was becoming embarrassed. Also, my eyes were watering from the sunlight. I didn't want her to think her speech had moved me to tears, although it probably wouldn't have hurt.

"Mrs. Spurr, it would be an honor if you selected me to undertake this project," I said. "I don't know what records have been kept and how difficult it might be to reconstruct missing pieces of the story, but I'm sure with your help and that of others who have been in Spurrville for a long time, it won't take more than a few months to complete a rough draft."

She seemed pleased with this assessment. "That is good to hear. I think you will do an excellent job, Mark, and if possible, I would like you to begin right away. You will need to work with Mr. Sullivan also, of course. He will need your help in preparing a small historical section for the Prospectus too, I think."

"Of course. I'd be delighted to work with him," I said.

"I am sure there is an empty office at the company you can use. I will ask Agnes to arrange it."

"Agnes?" I asked.

"Agnes Smith. She will be an important person for you to meet. She was my husband's secretary almost from the beginning, and then she worked for Elliot. We never could get her to retire. I suppose Spurr Nutritionals is her family too, in a way. She is a very nice old lady and a walking treasure trove of the kind of information you will need. Feel free to call upon

Agnes for any secretarial help you might need as well, of course."

"I'm anxious to get started," I said. "Is this a good time to discuss the matter of compensation?"

"Why, of course," she said.

I mentioned a figure and some other details of a working arrangement, and Mrs. Spurr readily agreed to everything. I was glad, because for some reason I didn't relish the thought of having to negotiate with her.

The conversation seemed to be drawing to a close. There wasn't much more I wanted or needed to learn from Mrs. Spurr on this visit. Besides, I was desperate to get out of the Florida room. I would send her a formal proposal on the project for her signature in a few days and then be back to start my work. However, Mrs. Spurr wasn't quite finished with me.

"Mark, are you an adventurous person?" she asked.

I was caught off guard.

"I'm sure this assignment will be exciting," I lied, "but to be honest I haven't thought of it as an adventure."

"Mr. Sheldon says you can be trusted and you take your work seriously," she said.

"That's nice to hear." (Question is, can Sheldon be trusted?)

"There is another reason I want you to work on this project." Mrs. Spurr took a deep breath and sighed. "You see, I believe there are suspicious things going on around here. It may just be a mother's paranoia, but I am not satisfied with the investigation into my son's death."

I was speechless.

"I know what you are thinking," she continued. "That I believe he was murdered. Well, I do not necessarily believe that. I simply do not know what to believe. I know my son was not a careless man, Mark. That night in the research lab when the fire started … that was not the first time he had worked late at the plant. Not the first time he had spent the night there, sleeping on a cot. Many of us had observed his habits, although he would not tell any of us what he was working on during his last few weeks. We still do not know.

"The insurance people concluded it was an accident, and if anyone would have an incentive for concluding otherwise, I realize it would be the insurance company. Still, they and our local fire marshal were not able to pinpoint a cause for the fire except to say it appeared to be from a natural gas explosion. They do not know how it happened."

"Did you go to the police?" I asked, shifting uncomfortably in my wicker chair.

"Sheriff Belton *is* the police in this town. We're too small to have our own police force. He and his deputies investigated. I'm sure he did his best, but in the end he agreed with the insurance people. He is a good man, as I said, but prideful, bless his heart. I think he was in over his head and that he knew it and that he was really more concerned with getting the outsiders to go away and leave him alone. All my suggestions to him were politely ignored. 'What could an old lady know, anyway?' was what he seemed to be thinking."

"Are you saying you want me to re-open the investigation?" I asked, incredulously.

"In a manner of speaking, yes," she said calmly. "And not just the fire. Something is going on around here, and I want to know what it is. How could a fire start in a building that had all the latest smoke detection equipment? Why did our security guard miss it until it was too late? What was my son working on? Why do people have such an interest in buying our company? Who are the strangers Sheriff Belton says he has seen around town? And then there is the matter of the alleged product contamination."

"Product contamination?"

"That's right. A woman in Henderson claimed she found mouse parts in a bottle of Spurrt Lyte and has threatened to sue if we do not settle with her. A few days later a man in Asheboro claimed the same thing. Mouse parts! Mark, there is no possible way a bottle of Spurrt Lyte could have left this plant with any foreign material whatsoever in it. No possible way. And that has been verified by the FDA and Department of Agriculture inspectors time and time again."

Well, that explained Frank Sheldon's reaction when I stumbled on the contamination idea as a joke. Trust him to be holding out on me, as usual. What else wasn't he telling me?

"And to add to that," Mrs. Spurr went on, "I am told there is a hateful Facebook page called 'Boycott Spurrt' that is making all sorts of fanciful claims about the company and its products. We do not know who is responsible for it, but Mr. Sheldon, the Raleigh police and the SBI are looking into it. The Facebook page claims we have shoddy quality control, that we do not pay our employees enough, that our family is not diversified enough, and so on. Mark, our workforce is highly diversified, as you will see, but obviously it is true our family is all white. How on earth can we diversify that?"

She had a point. I began to have visions of this unfolding in a bad way as an exposé on "Sixty Minutes."

"For all I know, the answers may go all the way back to my husband's accident," she continued. "Things were fine until then. I want you to find out what is happening."

She was working herself up, and I became concerned for her. I probably sat there staring at her, squinting, for a full 10 seconds before I came up with anything to say. When I did, it was pretty lame.

"Why not just hire a private investigator?"

"But, don't you see, Mark, in a way that is what I am doing," she answered in a quieter tone. "A real private investigator could not work in secret in a town like this. If there are people out there who wish us ill, it would be a signal that I suspect their existence. Who knows what they might do then? Also, I am afraid it would hurt Sheriff Belton's feelings. Even with his limitations, I do enjoy his protection, and I do not wish to alienate him.

"On the other hand," she went on, "you can easily look into these things while you are researching the history of the company. No one will question my decision to have the history written or to hire you. I think it will work just fine, if you are 'game.' Are you, Mr. Fairley? Game?"

I must admit at that moment I felt more like "fair game." No wonder she had so readily agreed to the payment figure I had suggested. And I had been worried I was asking too much, considering how simple and easy I had thought the assignment was going to be.

"By the way," she said, as if to reveal something that would clinch the argument in her favor, "Zachariah agrees."

Well, what could I say? Later, of course, and often, as things progressed, I would think of several things I wish I had said. But I didn't say them then. I just said I would do it.

By then, it was finally time to go upstairs and meet the great man himself. Mr. Zachariah Spurr the Second.

Chapter 4

As best I could reconstruct the event after talking to eyewitnesses and repeatedly viewing the video, this is what happened on the morning of Zachariah Spurr's last day as a normal person. Reasonably normal for a very rich person anyway.

It was dark, cloudy and threatening rain. Zachariah Spurr II, 80-year-old son of the founder of Spurr Nutritionals, Inc., of Spurrville, North Carolina, retired but still chairman emeritus of the board, said good-bye to his wife, Fanny, after a light breakfast of coffee and grits. He backed his immaculate 15-year-old sable black Cadillac DeVille DTS out of the garage and drove the familiar three miles to the bottling plant that bore his name. He had done the same thing almost every working day since he had started working at the plant over 50 years ago.

He pulled off the two-lane highway and through the raised gate at the entrance to the employee parking lot. With a smile and a nod for Lonnie, the gatehouse guard, he eased the big car toward the sprawling red brick building with the sign on top reading

Spurr Nutritionals, Inc.
Home of Spurrt*
The Drink that Says 'Got a Life!'

in letters five feet high. Passing the executive parking area near the office employees' entrance, he continued around to the shipping dock in the rear. Three eighteen-wheelers were backed up to the dock taking on loads, and a fourth waited its turn nearby. Its driver waved from the cab.

"Morning, Mr. Zachariah!"

"Morning, Jimmy," answered Zachariah with a wave of his own, neither man minding that Zachariah's greeting couldn't be heard with the car windows up.

The Cadillac rolled to a stop in the space next to the building marked by a neatly lettered white sign saying "Mr. Z," and Zachariah got out. A light drizzle had begun, and he walked slowly but impatiently to the nearest door, keeping his head down to watch his footing on the damp walkway and trying not to get his suit too wet, and especially not his new silk tie, a birthday gift from his grandson, Trey. With a last look around at the gloomy morning, he opened the door and entered his familiar domain.

Midway down the No. 3 bottling line, Wendell Cox, the VP of Manufacturing and R&D, was huddled with the line operator, the first shift foreman, a couple of technicians and a young woman with a video camera. The line wasn't running. They were all grinning from ear to ear, admiring a new piece of equipment.

"Here comes Mr. Z!" whispered one of the technicians. They usually called him Mr. Zachariah or Mr. Z instead of Mr. Spurr, which was fine with him. He thought it made them feel like he was just one of them, nothing special. Of course, they knew better but were happy enough to go along with the faux camaraderie it produced. Close friends could call him simply "Z." But never "Zach."

They all straightened up and looked in the direction the technician was facing to see Zachariah shambling closer. He was rubbing his hands together almost gleefully.

"Morning, boys!" he said. "And lady. Is that thing ready to go yet?"

"Oh yes, sir!" they said, almost as a chorus.

"Okay, then. Just show me what to do first."

The gray, boxlike piece of equipment straddled the bottling line at a point between the filling operation and the bottle capping station, forming a bridge under which the bottles had to pass. There were no visible moving parts, and it appeared as though the bottles would not be touched as they passed through. The only markings on the machine, other than a control panel, were the name "ViroBactiZap 5000" and a sign saying "Danger, High Voltage."

"Don't you think we ought to wait for your son?" asked Cox.

"Elliot? What for?" answered Zachariah good-naturedly. "He's only the president of the company. I may be officially retired, but I guess I still have some say around here. Besides, it's almost nine o'clock, and we can't hold up production all day."

Not entirely sure he was kidding, and having no apparent alternative, the others nodded their assent to the old man's assertion of authority. The morning's agenda called for Mr. Z and his elder son, Elliot, the current president, to be videoed as they inaugurated a new process which promised to improve the quality and reduce the manufacturing cost of the company's leading product, Spurrt, the popular nutritional supplement and "pick-me-up" energy drink. The video would be edited and shown at employee meetings as well as provided to the sales force to show to customers in the retail trade. Shorter versions would be given to the media for public relations purposes, and the original would be stored for later use in a documentary the company was thinking of producing, or for possible use in TV commercials.

"All right, Mr. Z," said Cox, apparently adjusted to proceeding without Elliot. "All you have to do is push this green button marked 'Power' as soon as we start the line running. Any problem, just hit the big red button and the whole thing shuts off."

"And then we'll have to throw out umpty-ump gallons of spoiled juice, right?"

"Theoretically, yes, sir. But we've checked everything out already, and there shouldn't be anything to worry about."

"You mean, 'Nothing can go wrong'? Isn't that what they said in the movie where the dinosaurs ran amok?"

"I guarantee we won't see any dinosaurs today, sir."

"Tell me again how many cases will be in this first batch?"

"It's a small test batch, sir, 10 cases," answered Cox. "240 12 oz. bottles."

"Okay. Now remember, this batch is all mine. I've got plans for it, and none of it is to be sold, no matter what my son says. I want you to deliver it to my house as soon as you can."

"No problem, sir."

Zachariah turned his attention to Heidi Wilton, the woman with the video camera. Miss Wilton was a trainee in the Marketing Department.

"Is that thing ready to roll?"

"Yes, sir," she said eagerly. "Why don't you just stand there next to the machine—that's good. You can start talking any time after you see this little red light go on." She pointed to a spot on top of the camera. "Just relax, and remember if you make a mistake you can simply start over. The camera will stay on. We'll fix everything when we edit."

Zachariah drew himself up to his full height, eliminating any trace of the slight stoop with which he normally walked. The red light went on.

"Good morning, fellow employees," he began. "Today marks another milestone in the history of our company as we inaugurate the use of the ViroBactiZap 5000 in-line sterilizer machine. This machine automatically sterilizes the contents of each bottle of Spurrt right on the line. It works by sending a high-energy beam through the bottles as they pass by. I can't explain how it works scientifically, but the experts tell me the laser-like beam or ray is sort of a combination of electrical energy and ultraviolet light that kills every kind of germ that anyone would ever worry about. It beats all the government requirements. In fact, it's more effective than the current method that involves two costly and time-consuming operations. Up until today, we've had to heat-sterilize all our bottles, and we've had to bring the Spurrt mixture to a boil for ten minutes before bottling it. Now, with this new machine sitting right on the line, the need for those two operations is eliminated, saving time and money, and, as an extra-added bonus, making the product taste fresher.

"At this time, we only have one of the new machines, an experimental model set up on the No. 3 line. But by the end of the year, we expect to have them installed on all the lines and running on all three shifts. Now I know some of you may be concerned about doing away with the washing and boiling operations, but let me assure you that with the growth in sales we expect to get by investing most of the cost savings in new advertising to tell our customers about the better tasting product, no one should be worried about losing their job.

"And now I have the honor of pushing this switch that will start another new era at Spurr Nutritionals. Wendell, please start up the line."

At a nod from Wendell Cox, the line operator removed the safety cover from a control box and flipped a toggle switch. The high-speed bottling line conveyor belt instantly and noisily came to life. All the men, and Miss Wilton with the video camera, reached into pockets for small foam earplugs, which they rolled tightly between their fingers and placed in their ears.

Then Zachariah pushed the green button on the ViroBactiZap 5000 and stood back to watch. Bottles proceeded rapidly through the new machine. The video camera continued to record the scene.

"Nothing's happening!" shouted Zachariah, ignoring the camera. "Is it working? I don't see anything!"

"You're not supposed to see anything, sir!" answered Cox over the din of the machinery. "The beam is invisible."

"Then how do you know if it's working? Are you sure it's plugged in!"

Zachariah moved closer to the ViroBactiZap 5000. He bent over as if to get a better look at the bottles as they entered it with dizzying speed. Only the videotape later revealed what happened next because it happened so fast nobody actually saw it.

As Cox reached to take Zachariah by the shoulder and coax him upright to point out the digital indicators on the control panel, Zachariah's new tie fell loose and wrapped itself around one of the bottles hurtling into the tunnel. In an instant, before anyone could move a muscle, Zachariah plunged head first on to the bottling line and through the ViroBactiZap 5000. He shot out the other side, landing in a heap on the floor at the feet of one of the technicians.

Red warning lights flashed and safety klaxons sounded. Incredibly, the bottling line did not shut down. An eerie bluish glow enveloped the ViroBactiZap 5000, and inside it thousands of mini-lightning sparks played on the bottles as they continued to pass through, like a Tesla coil experiment, accompanied by a continuous zapping sound that rivaled the decibels of the line itself.

Cox sprang to the line controls and flipped the "off" switch. Almost simultaneously, a technician thrust a clipboard through the bluish glow and hit the big red button on the

ViroBactiZap 5000 with it. The sounds died away. The blue glow faded. There was deathly silence for a long moment.

On the floor, shoeless, his tie and shirt in shreds, Zachariah moaned softly and held up a trembling right hand, waving it gently from side to side as if to say to anyone who would believe it, "I'm okay."

Heidi Wilton remained transfixed behind the still-running video camera. Later, the slowed-motion video would also show the barest hint of a bluish glow fading from Zachariah's head as he raised it once, briefly, before losing consciousness. No one there could possibly have known then what it portended.

Chapter 5

"Why did you think Sheriff Belton had barbecue for lunch?" Emily asked at the kitchen table that evening as I recounted the day's events.

"Barbecue *and* over-sweetened iced tea with a lemon wedge," I elaborated. "The Southern national drink. Nonalcoholic drink, anyway."

"We're sure that wouldn't be Spurrt, I guess?"

"Pretty sure."

"So why?" she persisted.

"I think I saw barbecue sauce and lemon pulp in his mustache."

"That's really appetizing." She groaned. "Can we change the subject?"

"Ordinarily, yes," I agreed, "but there is a relationship there between him and Mrs. Spurr. He was very protective of her. Suspicious of me. Worried about strangers in town. So was Mrs. Spurr, for that matter."

"Wouldn't that be normal for a sheriff?" Emily countered.

"Fortunately, I don't have that much experience with sheriffs. I guess he'd be pretty solicitous of the town's leading citizens. They carry a lot of weight at re-election time. Mrs. Spurr seemed to like him, but she said something about wishing he were more … sophisticated. That's the word she used."

"What do you think she meant?"

"If all my sheriff did was hang around a speed trap all day,

I guess I'd wonder about his level of sophistication too," I said. "She thinks he bungled the investigation of the fire that killed her son."

I had arrived home at around 5:00 p.m., greeted Emily warmly, ascertained that no prospective employers or executive recruiters had called, went to the bathroom, checked the mail, put the bills in the growing stack on the left side of my desk, stuffed two more "thanks for sending us your résumé, we'll keep it on file" letters into the thick manila folder labeled "Job Search," tossed the advertisements, checked my e-mail (nothing), changed from my business suit into chinos, sport shirt and Top-Siders, and skimmed the comic strips in the newspaper, a treat I always save for the end of the work day. By 5:30 we were seated, and I was debriefing myself.

We were having home-delivered pizza, something quick and easy, and early, because we had to go to a Neighborhood Watch Committee meeting right after dinner.

I described my run-in with Belton and my interview with Fanny Spurr, including the part where she asked me to become a private eye. It was sobering, so Emily asked about Belton's lunch to try to lighten the mood. The break was fun while it lasted, but then we were back into the serious stuff.

Emily served us another slice of pizza each while she talked. "Wouldn't that be natural to some extent? She was his mother, after all. How could she ever be satisfied, really?"

"Yeah, I know," I said, chewing pensively, which is not easy with pizza. "But there would be no reason to suspect foul play, I hope."

"Speaking of suspicious characters," Emily interjected. "I had a strange phone call this afternoon."

"What was it?"

"A hang up."

"We have those all the time, don't we?" I said. "Charities and robo-call nonsense about lowering your credit card interest, and when it's not me who answers they just hang up because they know you'll screen the call and tell them I refuse to take it."

"This was different," she said. "It felt different."

"How do you answer the phone?"

"You mean, 'Hello'?"

"Is that what you say?"

"Actually, I usually say, 'Fairley residence,'" she said.

"And that's what you said this time?"

"Yes."

"And they hung up? They didn't say anything? No heavy breathing?"

She shook her head.

"What was different?" I asked.

"Maybe it was the sounds in the background. I thought I heard cars or trucks going by, and that thing that goes 'ding' when you pull into a gas station. I think they were calling from a pay phone somewhere."

"Not even charities and scam artists call from pay phones anymore," I mused. "In fact it's hard these days to even *find* a pay phone. Maybe it was a legitimate wrong number. Or someone calling from 1960 when they still had dingers at gas stations."

"I hope it was a wrong number," she said, "but it was odd."

I napkined some grease off my fingers and took a sip of Cheerwine, the other Southern national drink, which I like a lot. Emily did the same.

"I also met Zachariah Spurr," I said.

"What's he like?" asked Emily.

"Unfortunately, he's incoherent, so it's hard to tell. In fact, he didn't say anything the whole time I was there. Mrs. Spurr did all the talking."

Mrs. Spurr had taken me upstairs to a large combination office and bedroom. Like mine at home, except much bigger. Zachariah Spurr sat in an easy chair facing a window, dressed in a business suit and bedroom slippers. He turned around slowly as we entered the room. Mrs. Spurr introduced us.

"This is Mr. Fairley, the young man I told you about, Zachariah, dear," she said. "Mr. Fairley, this is my husband, Zachariah Spurr, son of the founder of Spurr Nutritionals."

He smiled wanly and put out his hand, but he didn't get up. "Mrfffly," he said.

"It's Mark, sir," I said, on a wild hunch. "Nice to meet you."

His handshake was, in fact, shaky. Unlike his wife, Zachariah Spurr looked every bit his age of 80 years. He could have been older. Sitting with his head jutting forward, his thin face standing out from a shock of mussed gray hair, he was the picture of a dejected old man. Yet, there was an intelligent sparkle in the eyes that looked at me briefly before he turned away to the window again.

On an end table next to his chair an empty glass stood next to a bottle of Spurrt, also apparently empty. As I looked around the room, I noticed more empty Spurrt bottles. Stacked on one side of the door by which we entered were several cases of empties, and as many unopened cases were stacked on the other side of it. Although I tried to hide it, Mrs. Spurr must have noticed a quizzical expression on my face.

"It's practically all he consumes," she explained. "The doctors and I have tried to dissuade him, to get him to eat solid food, but heavens to Betsy he simply will not listen ... will you, dear?"

Spurr nodded in the negative.

Again to me, she said, "I know Spurrt has nutritional properties, but he is losing weight."

I had observed the same thing. He looked like a business

suit with a scarecrow inside. I probably wasn't going to get much of a history lesson from Mr. Zachariah Spurr II. Too bad, as he was the only person who had been there for practically the whole thing.

"Why is he like this?" I asked, not knowing how to phrase a more specific question.

"It was the accident," she explained, giving me her version of what happened on that morning last year. "It was all videotaped by Miss Wilton of the Marketing Department. Horrible, but you should probably have a look at it."

I said I would be sure to. Mr. Spurr eased himself up from his chair, shuffled over to a case of unopened bottles, picked one up and twisted off the cap with some difficulty, dropping it into a wastebasket I could see was already half full of them. He took a long swig from the bottle and sat back down.

"It is another one of those strange things," Mrs. Spurr continued. "Before they ran the first batch of Spurrt through that … machine that almost killed him, he had asked that the fellows at the plant send the whole batch over here for his personal use. Zachariah always liked Spurrt, and the new machine was indeed supposed to make it taste fresher, and it wasn't the first time he had had large quantities of product sent over here, but it was the first time he started drinking so much of it himself. And by the way, for safety's sake until we can ascertain just what went wrong, Zachariah hasn't allowed that ViroBactiZap 5000 or whatever-you-call-it sterilizer machine to be used since the accident.

"At first it seemed to make him happy, drinking so much of the Spurrt, and as it seemed to be helping him through his convalescence, I encouraged it. He was up and around, underfoot all the time. 'Frisky' is the word that comes to mind, although I would not want you to get the wrong idea, not at our age."

"Of course not," I agreed.

"Then, for some reason, he went for a week or so without drinking any of it," she said. "He went back to his regular diet. He was tired all the time although he never felt bad."

"Then what happened?"

"Then he went back to drinking from that batch of Spurrt. He was happier again. When that batch got down to the last bottle after about three months, he put that bottle into his wall safe for some reason. It is still there, and he and I, and now you of course, are the only ones who know about it."

"Not even Elliot?" I asked.

"Oh yes, Elliot knew too."

"Of course, the fellows sent over a new batch of Spurrt after that, but it did not seem to make him as happy. In less than a month he had declined to the state in which you see him here. Listless. Tired. But I cannot get him to stop drinking the Spurrt."

I paused in my explanation to Emily and drained my glass of Cheerwine.

"I'm having some more of this," I said. "You?"

"No, thanks. Besides, we need to get going or we'll be late."

I had indeed lost track of the time. We put our dishes in the dishwasher, made our last minute trips to the bathroom, and headed out the door. The Third United Methodist Church, where the Neighborhood Watch meeting was to be held, was only a few blocks away, and we were going to walk, as we did on most Sundays since it is also the church we attend.

"So what do you think?" I asked her as we strolled along the sidewalk. "Was she telling me all that stuff about her husband just to bring me up to date? Was she trying to explain a situation she found embarrassing? Or was she subtly beseeching me to help her figure out something?"

"What else did she tell you?"

"She mentioned that during what you might call his 'manic' period Mr. Z wanted to see his elder son, Elliot, all the time. She had the impression he wanted to talk about the business, but his speech is unintelligible so neither she nor the son could ever figure out what he wanted. He tried writing notes to Elliot, too, but nobody could read them. Not even Agnes Smith, and she's been his secretary for years. Mrs. Spurr suspected he might have thought he was dying and was trying to pass on some last words of business wisdom to Elliot, but the doctors all claim his physical health is excellent for a man his age."

"Did she show you any of the notes?" Emily asked.

"Yeah, and I brought Xerox copies of some of them home with me, but they're back in my briefcase. I sure couldn't read them either. Except for one."

"What do you mean?"

"Well, it's kind of weird," I said. "It was the last complete note he ever wrote, according to Mrs. Spurr. Right up until Elliot died she occasionally found scribbles on the legal pad Mr. Z keeps on his desk, as if he has tried to write another note, but he never completed one after he … after he lost his energy, is the best way I know how to put it. And since their son died, it looks like he hasn't even tried to write anymore.

"But this last note—I'll show it to you later. It's as if he mustered up every ounce of strength he had in him to get it right, and even then you can barely make out only a couple of words right at the end."

Three cars passed us going in the same direction. They honked. We waved. Neighbors all going to the same meeting.

"Well?" said Emily.

"Well, what?" I said.

"What does the note say, dummy? You do this to me all the time!"

"Oh, sorry. It looks like it says, 'Don't sell.'"

Chapter 6

This, the first meeting of our new Neighborhood Watch Committee, was the meeting to get it organized. About 100 people showed up, which was a pretty good turnout, I thought.

I congratulated Emily, who had been in charge of calling everyone. Soft drinks, coffee and donuts were set up in the church fellowship hall. Great dessert on top of pizza. Krispy Kremes.

We milled around, eating, sipping and making small talk. Emily seemed to know most people there. I knew three or four. As I looked at this sea of mostly strangers I couldn't say our neighborhood represented the great melting pot that was supposed to be America, except as far as mixed European ancestry still might be considered a kind of diversity. Mostly white. A few blacks. No Hispanics. A couple of young oriental-looking men off by themselves, not talking to anybody.

There are some Japanese companies in Greensboro, and the usual plethora of Chinese restaurants. Actually, many of those restaurants are owned by people of Greek descent, and their employees are often of Mexican. One never thinks to ask where the Japanese and Chinese people live. Evidently some of them lived in our neighborhood. I pointed them out to Emily. She didn't recognize them. Which surprised me since she had been the one to call everyone to invite them to the meeting. But she doesn't know everyone either and was just calling from a list. Maybe these two didn't have oriental-sounding last names.

"They look a little rough around the edges," I whispered. And indeed they did, to me anyway. Overweight, dark clothing, needing haircuts and generally a little unkempt.

"I'm sure they're perfectly nice once you get to know them."

"I'd hate to meet those two in a dark alley," I said. "At least until I got to know them."

In my limited experience in civic activities as part of my duties at companies where I have worked, I have found the Japanese don't get involved in community affairs very much. Apparently it's not something they are used to doing in Japan. I resolved to go and introduce myself to the two gentlemen. Of course, I didn't know if they were Japanese. Or Chinese, or Vietnamese, or Filipinos, or Laotians, or what. And where were their wives?

Before I could do it, however, we were called to order by the committee chairman, Don Bledsole, a chiropractor who also happened to be running for City Council. We took our seats, near the front because of Emily's involvement, even though I prefer sitting in the back on such occasions. Bledsole welcomed everyone with a campaign-style greeting, and then he introduced a Greensboro Police sergeant named Ed Truesdale. As Truesdale launched into his well-rehearsed pep talk about how important the Neighborhood Watch movement is and how our activities would mesh with those of the Police Department, I got as comfortable as I could on my little folding chair.

We moved slowly through the agenda. How to patrol the neighborhood, limits to our legal authority, warnings about this and that, especially about not carrying weapons, and so on. My attention wandered. A chiropractor as Head Vigilante? Not my first choice for "Taking a bite out of Crime," and all that. Maybe "Breaking the Back of Crime"? But hey, maybe I should be running the show here. After all, I had just signed up to be a private eye, hadn't I? What was going on at Spurr Nutritionals? Was *anything* going on at Spurr Nutritionals? I wonder what's so special about that "last bottle" of Spurrt Zachariah Spurr was keeping. Why would the Spurrs, or anybody, name their second son Adam? Why is somebody in here wearing too much cologne? How will I feel about all this when I wake up tomorrow, in the bright reality of a new day? Why is somebody poking me in the ribs? Call the vigilantes!

"Mark!"

"What?"

"What are you doing? You've slept through most of the meeting!" Emily looked embarrassed.

"Well, I guess it just wasn't very arresting," I tried.

"Very funny, but anyway I'm glad you got a nap," she said. "We volunteered to take the first shift this evening."

"We did? What you mean 'we,' white woman?"

"Shhh, stop it! I think it will be fun."

"Do I get a gun?"

"Absolutely not. But we do get to carry a CB walkie-talkie."

"Great! We can warn all the truckers to stay away from our dangerous neighborhood."

"You weren't listening at all, were you? If we see anything suspicious we report it to the police who are monitoring channel 9, the emergency frequency. Then we stay out of the way while they investigate."

"Okay," I sighed. "How long is our shift?"

"It's three hours. And since so many people signed up, we only have to do it once a month."

"Terrific."

"I think so. Now let's sign out for the walkie-talkie and get started. We have to go home and get the car."

"Perfect. So glad we walked here."

I looked around for the two oriental guys, but they had

gone. Too bad. We said our good-byes, receiving good luck wishes from the inevitable wags who remained to finish up the donuts, and walked home. On the way, we listened to several different channels on the CB radio. I didn't understand a word of what we heard. Except "Good Buddy" once in a while. And "10-4" and "What's your 20?" We didn't transmit anything.

I was thinking one way to redeem the evening, if we had to sit in the car for three hours, was to find a nice secluded place to park. Unfortunately, I don't recall there being a lover's lane kind of place in our neighborhood. So when we got to the house, I said to Emily, "Since we're going to be in the car for three hours, let me run inside and get my briefcase first. I want you to look at those notes from Zachariah Spurr."

"That's my Mark; always thinking about business," she laughed.

We entered the house by the front door, and I went back to my bedroom-slash-office. My briefcase was not upright on the floor by my desk where I had left it, or thought I had left it. It was on my desk. Puzzled, I opened it. Zachariah Spurr's notes weren't there.

"Emily!" I called. "Looks like we get to be the first to test the vigilante system!"

It took a while for the police to come. After I convinced Emily we had been burglarized, we tried to use the CB walkie-talkie, but couldn't get anyone to answer us. I got disgusted and called 911 on the telephone while Emily, not realizing I was doing that, ran outside where the CB might work better without whatever interference it might be encountering in our house. It did.

Evidently, the 911 phone calls come in to a different place from the CB calls, and so the police had to spend some time comparing notes and trying to figure out jurisdiction or something. Then, when they finally did show up, they had it in their minds that it was a domestic violence situation because the calls had come from Emily and me separately.

By the time we got all that straightened out, the true irony of the situation began to dawn. Here we were, handling the very first shift of the very first Neighborhood Watch program in our neighborhood, and almost before the shift had started something suspicious had happened, on our watch, to us.

The two police officers who responded had some difficulty trying to hide their own suspicions about what was really suspicious, but they were professional about it. By that I mean they weren't too obvious about getting close enough to me from time to time during their visit to try to smell my breath. Less professional was Don Bledsole, the head vigilante himself, who was monitoring the whole thing on his police scanner at home and just had to come over to see if he could "help out."

The problem was we couldn't find any signs of forced entry. Nothing else was out of place. There were no fingerprints. No clues at all. We went over the short list of everybody who has keys to our house. Aside from Allan Whitbread, our next door neighbor who is an Episcopal priest and therefore presumably above suspicion, the list consists of our children, Lisa, Judy and William, all three of whose colleges are at least 60 miles away. No help there.

While they didn't say it in so many words, I'm sure the police officers convinced themselves I was simply mistaken and hadn't actually brought the missing papers home with me at all. Emily did stick up for me, though. Otherwise, I might have started doubting me myself. Finally, the officers finished asking all their questions, searched the house for lurking intruders, deftly ushered Don Bledsole out with them, and departed.

The worst part was our shift still wasn't over, as Bledsole only too happily reminded us on his way out the door. Emily and I locked the house again, got in the car, backed it out of the garage and started down the driveway.

"Are you thinking what I'm thinking?" she asked me.

"Let's see if I am," I said, stopping the car at the end of the drive, dousing the headlights and turning off the engine.

Evidently, I was.

"Are you wearing a new cologne?" she asked.

"I don't wear cologne."

"Oh. Right. Must be my imagination."

We stayed right there, listening to classical music and CB static, diligently watching our house and what little of the neighborhood we could see from where we sat, until our shift ended.

About midnight, after we had been back in the house a short time catching the tail end of a British mystery on PBS to unwind before going to bed, the telephone rang.

"Sorry to call so late, but I saw your lights on and thought you'd probably still be up." It was Allan Whitbread, our neighborhood Episcopal priest. I remembered I hadn't seen him at the vigilante meeting. Conscientious objector maybe.

"I thought you'd like to know," he went on, "two men came to your house while you were out earlier, around seven or eight. I was checking my mailbox and saw them, so I told them you were out. They said they would come back some other time. Very polite, I must say. I hope that was okay."

"No problem," I said, not sure if I meant it. "Did they leave their names?"

"Uh, no. I guess I forgot to ask."

"Well, what did they look like?"

It was probably too late in the evening for them to have been Jehovah's Witnesses, so a description would have been nice.

"Now that you ask, I have to say it was a little odd," said Allan. "They looked oriental and had odd accents."

Chapter 7

In the old British TV series, "The Prisoner," starring Patrick McGoohan, the closing scene each week was a white balloon floating up from beneath the ocean to bob around on the surface after the program credits had scrolled by.

In Hakone, a resort area not far from Tokyo, there is an elite private *ryokan,* an inn reserved for the top executives of the giant Kashimoto Foods Company. On the grounds of the *ryokan* is a luxurious *onsen*, or spa, situated so as to afford its guests a spectacular view of the magnificent Mt. Fuji. I am imagining what it might have been like to be a Westerner observing the events in that *onsen* on a particular day. It is the day after I was hired by Fanny Spurr to write the history of Spurr Nutritionals and, in so doing, to "find out what is going on."

As he approaches the *onsen*, viewing it with Western eyes, the observer is perhaps reminded of the balloon scene from "The Prisoner." Indeed, any such foreign person, or *gai-jin*, might think he is seeing several balloons bobbing in the water as he peers with growing curiosity through the mist rising from the rippling surface of the bath.

Moving closer, careful not to let bare feet slip on the wet tile floor, he might begin to recognize features on the balloons, and then differences which would at first appear subtle, but become more obvious. Noses, ears, eyes, hair. Heads!

Slipping off his light *yukata*, a casual summer kimono, with trepidation, not wanting to intrude, the *gai-jin* quietly showers from head to foot with soap and brush beside the pool before easing himself into the water for a closer look. A burning sensation in the lower extremities, growing to a crescendo of excruciating pain as his private parts submerge, momentarily takes his mind off the bobbing heads. The bobbing heads of naked middle-aged Japanese men, floating in exceedingly hot water.

The heads are talking. His discomfort subsiding, he listens.

"*Wakarimashita, Kashimoto-shachō, demo hoka no kaiketsu wa sukoshi muzukashi desu-ka?*" (Yes, President Kashimoto, but isn't the other solution a bit more difficult?)

"*So desho. Demo oboeteokuyoni, wareware niwa chikaraga arimasu. Warawara wa oki desu. Teki o kowasukotoga dekimasu!*" (Maybe so, but remember, we are strong. We are big. We can destroy our enemies!)

"Yes, Kashimoto-*shachō*"

"What do you think, Yamada-san?"

"It is up to you, of course, Kashimoto-*shachō*. You are the boss."

"I know that. Nevertheless, I believe it is important we observe the traditional *nemawashi.* That is, I want to hear what all of you have to say before I tell you that you are wrong."

"That is wise."

"Yes, very wise."

Heads bob affirmatively.

"In that case," says Yamada, "I must say I think whatever action we take must be taken very soon."

Nishida-san speaks up. "But I would like to return to your earlier observation, Kashimoto-*shachō*, if I may. Who, exactly, is our enemy?"

A head disappears for a moment, reappears. Hands and forearms appear. They squeegee water from the hair and rub it out of the eyes. They place a small, yellow washcloth on the forehead, which tilts back so that the mouth is well out of the water. Hands and arms disappear again. It is Kashimoto. He speaks.

"An excellent point, Nishida-san. Our enemy is not our Japanese competitors. They are controlled through the cartel, the *keiretsu*, and the relationships that have been built over generations of trade. No, our true enemy is foreign competition, especially from America. Japanese consumers are strangely enamored of things American. Even I, I must confess, have such a weakness. I sometimes drink Coca-Cola. My golf clubs are Callaways. My second car after the Nissan President is a Jeep Grand Cherokee. But my watch, on the other hand, is merely an imitation Rolex I purchased in Hong Kong."

The other heads gasp in practiced unison.

Rolex is not an American brand, but nobody is about to mention it. Kashimoto continues.

"*So, desu.* It is true. However, the point is that one reason for the popularity of American products is the uncanny ability of the Americans to innovate. Always they have new ideas. New ideas mean rapid change, and we do not like rapid change. Our way is to take someone else's idea and improve upon it, making it better, always a little better, but at a pace we can set. That way, we remain in control of our lives and our economy. The Americans exercise no control. No discipline. Sometimes they stumble upon new ideas and new products without even trying. They call it 'serendipity.' I believe it is a religious term.

"The Americans at Spurr Nutritionals-san may have done this. They may have stumbled upon something entirely new. The question is, do they know they have done it? If so, then it could change everything! They could destroy the current balance of competitive power. This would be unthinkable!

Therefore, they are the enemy, and they must be stopped! Am I right?"

Heads bob affirmatively again.

"Imamura-san."

"*Hai!*"

"Review the situation for us, and bring me up to date, please."

Imamura begins. "To begin with, we have been watching developments at Spurr Nutritionals since the early 1960's, when we first copied the formula for their popular health drink, Spurrt, as best we could. Not perfectly, I must admit. Something to do with changing valences in the chemical makeup resulting from the unique combination of the ingredients. In any case, we modified the formula somewhat for Japanese tastes, making it less sweet and removing the citrus pulp, and we introduced it here under our own brand name, *Burrsato Ju-su*. It has been quite successful."

Kashimoto interrupts. "Is there anyone here who does not already know all this?"

Heads shake. Everyone knows.

"Imamura-san, you did not have to start from so far back, *ne*?"

"I apologize, Kashimoto-*shachō*."

"*Dozo*. Please go on."

While fast-forwarding his brain, Imamura bows from the waist to his boss from ingrained habit. He gets water up his nose. Kashimoto looks heavenward to avoid showing he has seen Imamura's embarrassment. No one loses face. Imamura again plunges ahead.

"You mentioned the possibility of the Americans having stumbled upon something, Kashimoto-*shachō*," he begins. "May I presume you are speaking of the strange events reported by Tanaka, our man in America, beginning with the accident suffered by Mr. Zachariah Spurr-*kaichō*?"

"That is so."

"Ah, well then," continues Imamura, now comfortable he has found the right place in the story, "we know that Spurr-*kaichō* at first seemed to recover very quickly from the accident, especially considering his advanced years ..."

"Be careful now," admonishes Kashimoto, who must be at least 70 himself, although looking no more than about 55.

"I apologize again, *sempai*," this time stifling the bow. "Anyway, we tend to attribute this to his having consumed, in the space of three months, most if not all of the batch of Spurrt that was made at the time of the accident. Now, however, Spurr-*kaichō* is reported to stay in his room all day, seeing practically no one except his wife, and, most inexplicably, to be unable to communicate verbally or in writing. We do not know if this condition resulted from the accident or from consuming the large quantity of Spurrt, which may have been altered during the accident."

"May I interrupt?" It is Ohbora, speaking for the first time. "We in the Technical Research Division can assure you that in all of our testing of Spurrt, including subjecting it to every imaginable alteration it might encounter from production accidents, as well as those of our own invention, we have never witnessed the side effect of rendering any of our subjects unable to communicate, except momentarily, of course."

"Is that so, Ohbora-san?" asks Nishida. "But what do you mean, 'momentarily'?"

"Well, understandably, the consumption of large quantities of Spurrt in a short period of time can result in the occasional episode of acute indigestion or an over-active intestinal tract, or even a voluminous, extended belch, during the height of which one's normal communication skills may be noticeably diminished, momentarily."

The heads bob again, to a chorus of "*So, so, so, so ...*" All the heads but one.

"Kashimoto-*shachō*, you do not agree?" asks Imamura.

There is no answer. The motionless head slips beneath the surface, leaving the yellow washcloth tenuously afloat.

"My god, he's fallen asleep!"

"Quickly, get his head up!"

Those nearest to Kashimoto prod him back to consciousness before he has swallowed much water, then quickly retreat, everyone acting as if nothing has happened. They have done this before. No one loses face.

Sensing he had better accelerate his pace, Imamura resumes. "Whatever it is, *something* related to the accident appears to have happened to Mr. Spurr. This was apparently noticed also by his son, Elliot Spurr-*shachō*. Tanaka reports that Elliot Spurr spent many late evening hours working at the company's research laboratory, sometimes even sleeping there. This began soon after the accident, and it was as if he were trying to solve a mystery. He never told anyone what he was looking for or, indeed, whether he had found anything, right up until the night he was killed in an explosion and fire in the lab."

"But there is no way even the most highly contaminated Spurrt could be responsible for such an occurrence, according to our tests," puts in Ohbora, "unless one mixes it with a great deal of alcohol."

"Tanaka has in fact reported that many students at the university use such a 'Spurrt cocktail' as a hangover cure," contributes Nishida, "but no explosions have been linked to the practice."

"Exactly," says Imamura, "and the incident was ruled accidental by the authorities. In any case, we do not know for certain what, if anything, the people at Spurr Nutritionals have found out about the apparently contaminated batch of Spurrt."

"But whatever it is, they may find out at any time!" says Yamada, alarmed. "And what could it be? Do we know?

Kashimoto-*shachō*, you have been quiet for some time now. What can you tell us?"

Kashimoto dismisses the question with a subtle wave of his yellow washcloth. Subdued, Yamada ducks under the water as if he had been planning to do so all along and was simply waiting for the right moment.

"Does that bring us up to date, Imamura-san?" asks Kashimoto just as Yamada resurfaces with no small amount of splashing.

Imamura hesitates, to make sure he has understood the question above the splashing noise, then answers. "Yes, except for one thing. Fanny Spurr-*kaichō fujin*, wife of Zachariah-*kaichō*, has hired a private detective."

All attention on Imamura.

"But why?" stammers Yamada. "Surely she cannot suspect Zachariah-*kaichō* of any … you know. I mean, not at his age," glancing at Kashimoto, "and, uh, condition!"

"*Bakamono!* Of course not, you idiot," answers Kashimoto. "Now, Imamura-san, what is this all about?"

"His name is Mark Fairley. He lives in Greensboro, a city not far from Spurrville, and until recently he was an executive with a large company there. He is not really a private detective, and ostensibly he is only supposed to write a history of Spurr Nutritionals for public relations purposes," continues Imamura, "but we suspect there is more to it than that. Spurr-*fujin* has let it be known among those close to her that she is not satisfied with the investigation into her son's accidental death, and we also feel she may finally be giving serious consideration to selling the company, as there are now no younger family members to run it. We think Fairley has been given a secret agenda. It is possible she wants him to continue the work of Elliot Spurr-*shachō* under the 'cover' of his history-writing assignment."

"Well, shouldn't he be neutralized then?" asks a chastened, but indomitable Yamada.

Ignoring Yamada again, Kashimoto gnaws on his washcloth for a moment, his brow wrinkled as well as sweaty. Finally, apparently satisfied with that operation, he rinses the cloth, wrings it out and returns it to his forehead. "No ..." he says slowly. "Perhaps he can be of use to us."

"My report is concluded, Kashimoto-*shachō*," says Imamura.

"Thank you, Imamura-san. Now, does anyone have any other questions or comments?"

Everyone knows this means no one should have any other questions or comments. At long last, it is Kashimoto's turn again.

"Come closer," he whispers, "and I will tell you the secret of the Spurrt. It is a secret we have known for many years as the result of our policy of ceaseless experimentation on all competitors' products, including the work now under Ohbora-san's most capable direction."

A small nod from Ohbora, acknowledging the compliment.

"That is, all come closer except for you, Yamada-san," says Kashimoto. "I want you to go over there and splash around a lot so no one will overhear."

A reluctant "*Hai*" from Yamada, who paddles away, losing face, but only a little.

"It is a secret," continues Kashimoto conspiratorially, "that, if known, would at least revolutionize, but more probably destroy, the health drink industry, not only in Japan, but worldwide. It is a discovery so monumental that ..." And as he speaks and the group gathers more tightly around him, he drops his voice to a level that could no longer be understood by the *gai-jin* observer, even without the dutiful splashing of Yamada.

Presently the heads emerge from their impromptu huddle, the faces registering astonishment, concern, even fear. Except for Kashimoto. There, determination.

"Here is what we must do," he says. "Nishida-san!"

"*Hai!*"

"Tell our friends at Kuroibishi-Whitestone I must meet with them first thing in the morning! We must ask them to prepare something very special for Mrs. Fanny Spurr," he says in a sinister tone. "We must protect the secret at any cost!"

"Hai! Wakarimashita!"

"Imamura-san!"

"*Hai!*"

"Tanaka has done well. But now you must ask him to redouble his efforts to stay on top of the situation. Tell him to increase the frequency of his reports to you. Tell him also to expect a visit from the Kuroibishi-Whitestone people. They will brief him on our plans. Finally, tell him he must get to know this Mark Fairley."

"*Hai!* At once!"

Yamada paddles back to the group. "A question, *sempai?*" he asks.

"Perhaps I shall have someone tell you about it later, Yamada-san," answers Kashimoto.

"Not that question, *sempai.*"

"What, then?"

"Why are we speaking English?"

"For the benefit of that lobster-red *gai-jin* observer over there, Yamada-san. Besides, we always need the practice. Now, let's go have dinner."

"Shall we invite the *gai-jin*?"

"No. He wouldn't like it."

Chapter 8

The morning after the break-in I did call the police to report what Allan Whitbread had said. A Detective Marshall Blue came out and interviewed Allan, Emily and me, but there wasn't much to go on with no fingerprints and no sign of forced entry. At least my credibility was enhanced somewhat now that there was some evidence I hadn't simply let the glamour of being a Neighborhood Watchperson go to my head.

One thing I couldn't figure out was why the burglars only took those particular papers. Why not take my whole briefcase, plus a few valuables, just to make it look like a regular burglary? Why make it so obvious the break-in was connected with Spurr Nutritionals? And of what value were the papers? They were photocopies, after all. Surely the thieves must know I had already looked at them, or that at least I could easily get more copies. Or were they looking for something else? Maybe some evidence I knew something they wanted to know, or they wanted to know whether I knew. Or maybe it was not a burglary, *per se*, but rather a warning of some kind.

And how did they get into the house without leaving a trace? I understood why there would be no fingerprints if the thieves were wearing gloves, but what magic had they used to open a door or window and bypass our alarm system? Had we remembered to arm the system in our haste to get to the Neighborhood Watch meeting? Maybe not. And Detective Blue said thieves can often get into a house these days by simply using a credit card to throw the door latch.

61

I checked out the "Boycott Spurrt" page on Facebook that Mrs. Spurr mentioned, and it was everything she said about it and worse. The cover picture was a shot of the front of the Spurr Nutritionals plant with a large American flag flying upside down at half-mast. Obviously doctored, but somebody had done a good job of it. The page was rife with posts containing all sorts of insulting reports about the plant, working conditions, bad consumer experiences with Spurrt products, and calls to action (boycott the product, dump it in the street, call your Congressman, call your supermarket and tell them to stop carrying Spurrt, etc.), along with photos of rat-infested storerooms, moldy ingredients, leaking oil drums, and "employees" covering their faces, presumably in shame. Snarky comments accompanied most of the posts. The pictures could have come from anywhere; there was no way to associate them definitely with the company. Emily was as shocked as I was.

I noticed none of the posts was recent, however; they seemed to have stopped about three weeks ago. Maybe the perpetrators of this charade had gotten tired of the game.

Still, what had I gotten myself into?

On a whim, and since I was still online, I Googled "Who killed Elliot Spurr?" Google didn't have a clue.

The weekend passed uneventfully. On Saturday I scanned a week's worth of want ads in the *Wall Street Journal*, found nothing of interest, and ran a few errands. Sunday we went to church, followed by a trip to Costco where we bought twice as much as we planned, as usual, a carryover habit from when our kids were still at home and eating through the whole pantry every week. But the free food samples helped us assuage our guilt. I spent some time in the afternoon making a rough topic outline of what a history of Spurr Nutritionals might look like.

Early Monday morning I drove down to Spurrville, remembering to go very slowly past the speed trap, which turned out to be unmanned, and now I was in the Spurr Nutritionals offices about to meet Jim Sullivan, the CFO. Although I had worn a suit and tie and spiffy black wingtip shoes for my meeting with Fanny Spurr, today I was dressed "business casual," which meant light charcoal wool trousers with a nice crease, a light blue oxford button down dress shirt, and a dark green corduroy blazer with an American flag lapel pin. No tie. I had on my old and somewhat worn but still presentable Bally loafers. If I was going on tours of the offices and the manufacturing plant, plus who knew what else, I might as well wear comfortable shoes. I have sneakers, but that's a little too casual.

I had left the main road, from which the huge Spurr Nutritionals, Inc., sign on top of the main building was clearly visible, and found my way to the main entrance to the grounds where I stopped at the gatehouse and introduced myself to the guard on duty, a pleasant looking man whose nametag read "Lonnie."

"My name is Mark Fairley, and I have an appointment with Mr. Sullivan," I told him.

"You're not from around here, are you, Mr. Fairley?"

"I'm from Greensboro," I said with suppressed annoyance.

"I mean before that."

What is it with these people?

What the heck. "You got me; I'm from Up North. But I come in peace."

Fortunately, Lonnie thought that was pretty funny. I think.

"Well, Mr. Sullivan didn't tell me to expect you, but I guess you can go right on in. Just put this Visitor pass on your dashboard, and follow the signs to the visitors' parking lot in front of the main building."

I did and parked in the last space available, not counting the always-empty "Handicap" slots. The design of the building was typical of manufacturing plants in rural areas throughout the South. It was a rectangular monolith of red brick, two stories high, with no windows, squatting on flat land. On my right facing the building from the highway was a large employee parking lot, and in the back was an equally large area for loading and additional parking. On the left was a large, treeless, grassy area obviously available for expansion, although with the main building covering about four acres under one roof, it was hard to imagine the need. But nobody ever said Mr. Zachariah Spurr II wasn't a man of vision and ambition.

Breaking the windowless monotony of the main building's front was an attached modern-looking one-story structure of concrete and glass that housed the executive offices.

In front of this was a modest, well-manicured, lawn with some decorative plantings around a small plaza featuring three flagpoles and a couple of picnic tables. Between the lawn and the building was the small visitors' lot. From the center flagpole Old Glory proudly waved, neither upside down nor at half-mast, flanked by the flag of North Carolina with its venerable motto, *"Esse quam videre"* ("To be, rather than to seem"), and the flag of Spurr Nutritionals, a stylized, energetic-looking red "S" on a kudzu-green field.

I got out of the car and entered a small lobby fitted out with typical waiting room furniture—spartan side chairs, end tables, ficus trees and neat stacks of magazines including *Food Magazine*, *New Food Magazine*, *Modern Restaurant World*, *Processed Food Industry*, *Food Business News* and *Nutrition Today*, all of which looked pristine, in addition to more dog-eared copies of the obligatory *Sports Illustrated*, *Golf*, *Time*, *Reader's Digest* (large print edition), *Ladies' Home Journal*,

Cosmopolitan, Southern Living, Smithsonian and *Guideposts*. Probably complimentary subscriptions since Spurrt ran ads in most of them, except maybe *Smithsonian* and *Guideposts*. And several takeout restaurant menus.

A portrait of Zachariah Spurr I, the founder, adorned one wall, and seascape prints featuring well-known North Carolina lighthouses decorated two others.

I had time to make such a detailed inventory of the reading material because there was no one behind the counter with the sliding glass partition to greet me, and there was no little front desk bell to ding. I waited. For twenty minutes. And looked at the magazines. And wondered why I was the only one in the lobby, given the practically full visitors' parking lot. I knew I wasn't early, nor was I late. I was right on time. Unless Lester County had gone off Daylight Savings Time since my last visit, in which case I was an hour early, but I knew the rest of North Carolina hadn't. So where was everybody?

"Eyes on the rake," said a female voice from behind the glass partition. Or at least I thought that's what she said, since the partition was closed. I looked up quizzically.

"Oh, sorry," she spoke again, sliding the glass open. "I was on break. May I help you?"

"Probably, if you have some pull around here."

"I'm only a receptionist," she said pleasantly. Everybody around here seemed pleasant.

"I'm a Methodist myself," I offered, "but some of my best friends are Receptionists."

"Why, I swanee, I never heard that joke before! It was a joke, wasn't it?"

Actually, that conversation never happened, but I've been dying to use that line somewhere, and now I have.

"Good morning. I'm Mark Fairley, here to see Jim Sullivan," is what I actually said.

"Well, I'm Connie the receptionist, and I'll be glad to show you to his office," is what she actually said, motioning me to a door and activating a buzzer that allowed me to open it and step through.

Connie the receptionist, who in fact was and is a pleasant woman, handed me a Visitor's ID badge on a lanyard which I slipped around my neck, accompanied me to Sullivan's office without further comment and left me with his secretary, to whom I didn't actually speak more than "hello" until I was on my way out and who took me in to Sullivan's office where he rose from behind his desk to greet me with an outstretched hand.

I had decided it would be important to take the initiative in this our first meeting. "Before you say anything," I said, "I have to tell you I'm not from around here."

He looked at me strangely for the briefest of instants before breaking into a big grin. "Oh! Well, neither am I, as a matter of fact."

"As people never tire of reminding you, I bet."

"I think I've finally gotten used to it. It takes a while."

"I'm guessing the New York area."

"Pretty close. New Jersey. Nutley. You?"

"Washington, DC. Grew up in Alexandria."

"Let's hear it for the I-95 Corridor."

"So, you've been here for some time, I take it?" I offered.

"About six years. Didn't want to relocate here at first. I mean, who wants to leave New York for North Carolina? No offense."

"None taken."

"I'd had some success with turnaround situations in my previous life, and Mr. Z found me through a charity board he and one of my old bosses are both on and convinced me I could help the company get through a rough patch. Sugar prices were going through the roof, and we needed some creative financing as well as some more economical manufacturing practices. And by that I mean modernization for greater productivity, not cutting corners on quality. Seemed like an interesting enough challenge, and it has been.

"But I thought Spurrville was going to be some one stoplight town halfway between Narrow Bridge and Falling Rock, not far from Dip and Bump, and that I'd stay a year at most, commuting on weekends."

"Well, it *is* a one stoplight town," I said.

"Yes, and here I am six years later. With my family. We love it here. And I think the company's in pretty good shape too, considering the shocks of the past few months."

After that and an offer of coffee or Spurrt, which I declined, we got down to business pretty quickly. But even though it seemed to me we'd gotten off on the right foot, Sullivan turned out not to be as cooperative as I'd hoped.

"I know Fanny Spurr sent you here and everything," Sullivan said, "but I can't be giving out our financial information to just anybody. We're a privately owned company, not publicly traded, so all this is confidential information."

"I was hoping you wouldn't think of me as 'just anybody.'"

All I wanted at this stage was basic sales and profit figures going back a few years so I could get a feel for how big the company was and what the trends were. Up? Down? Staying about the same? Weakening recently, as Mrs. Spurr had said? How much debt did the company actually have? Was it able to finance itself pretty well day-to-day with maybe only modest working capital loans to stay on good terms with the local bank? How big were its cash reserves?

Because it was a privately held company, I didn't expect to find any financial information on the company website and not much more by Googling it, and I was right. Mostly that turned up PR releases from Heidi Wilton and a few articles from the local newspaper, *The Daily Spurrvillian*, the Raleigh and Durham papers and some food trade magazines like the ones I found in the office lobby, all of which were puff pieces as would be expected. There were a couple of well-balanced articles in *The Wall Street Journal*, *Fortune* and *Barron's*, and a puff piece in *Business North Carolina*, but the reporters didn't have many hard facts to go on. I looked it up on Wikipedia, and the information there too was incomplete. Maybe that was because Sullivan was the one who put it there, I didn't know, although I'd have expected it to be Miss Wilton under instructions from her boss Wash Booker, the sales and marketing VP, since he'd be the one more interested in getting publicity for the company wherever he could.

I'm no expert on how to value a business, but as I recall from merger talks I occasionally got involved in at my previous companies, a figure of ten times earnings is often a benchmark for starting negotiations for a price to buy one out. So I wanted to get a rough idea what that might be in order to see if the stakes were high enough for murder. Of course, I couldn't tell Sullivan that.

"Look," I tried again, "I'm supposed to be writing a company history, and Mrs. Spurr says you're working on a prospectus as part of her plan to put the company up for sale. She said I could get some helpful background information from you and maybe I could help a little with the prospectus, the company history part anyway, since I'm a pretty decent writer—but only if you want my help; I don't want to presume—and I've never had to write a prospectus myself. Anyway, a company history should be self-serving and would be pretty weak if it didn't at least have some sales figures to crow about and some statements about whether the company was growing and profitable. So we have the same objectives. Can we work together on this?"

Sullivan was probably going to Google me and check me out on Facebook and LinkedIn before going much further with me. Hey, why not? I've got nothing to hide, and my Facebook friends and LinkedIn contacts are mostly reputable, although a few might be considered squirrelly by some. Frank Sheldon, Esq., was possibly among them, but since he was also the Spurrs' lawyer, at least he was *our* squirrel.

"Besides," I continued as Sullivan looked at me with a face devoid of expression, although I could see he was thinking about what I'd said, "shouldn't we Yankees stick together?"

"Are you kidding?" he said, finally breaking into a grin, "Everybody knows Yankees can't be trusted!"

"Can I take that as a yes?"

"I guess I can show you some stuff—see what you do with it."

"Thank you. You're an enigma, you know that?"

"Works for me, but don't say that around Wash Booker."

"Why?"

"You'll see."

In the end, after Sullivan made me sign a nondisclosure agreement, he did show me the basic information I wanted to see but only under the condition I couldn't take any of it off the premises. I had to look at it right there in an empty cubicle he let me use. Which meant I had to take copious notes and stuff them into my briefcase, which I didn't bother asking permission to do, but I also didn't think Lonnie the guard would search me on the way out.

Sullivan promised to give me more details later on a "need to know" basis, whatever that meant, if I would ask for them.

Like I said, I'm no expert, and analyzing financial statements is not my strong suit, but I learned a lot. The company was drowning in debt. It was even worse than Fanny Spurr had said. Gross margins—the difference between sales revenue and cost of goods sold—were healthy, however, presumably owing to the investments in efficient production and systems. Operating expenses looked like they'd been kept well under control and were not an unusually high percentage of revenue, but annual sales were on a slight downward trend, and basic operational profitability was mediocre and also declining. Interest on the debt was killing the bottom line.

In effect, Spurr Nutritionals, Inc., was hanging by a thread and would be bankrupt soon if Sullivan and Booker couldn't turn things around or refinance the debt somehow. The information Sullivan gave me didn't show how much the upcoming balloon payment was or the date it was due, but it was obvious it wouldn't take a very big one to shove the company under. There were practically no reserves. I imagined the only reason the banks hadn't foreclosed already was that Spurr Nutritionals was such a big customer and the largest employer in Lester County. Too big to fail? Maybe for a while, but not forever. Spurr Nutritional needed a miracle.

I wondered if Fanny Spurr was fully aware of exactly how serious the situation was and had just been sugar coating it a little for me. And what about Mr. Z, for that matter? Presumably, Elliot had been fully aware.

Fleetingly I also wondered if there would be enough money to pay my fees and expenses. But then I felt guilty. Fleetingly. Still, it sort of put a premium on my getting the assignment completed and billed as quickly as I could.

But then I looked at EBIT, or earnings before interest and taxes, which measures the true underlying profitability of a company from an operating standpoint. It's what financial people look at when evaluating a company for buyout. When I took the average EBIT of the last five years and multiplied it by ten according to standard practice, I got a figure that was definitely big enough to kill for.

Chapter 9

Time for a late lunch before heading home for the day. I still needed to meet Agnes Smith, the walking history book and faithful secretary. And I definitely wanted to meet Heidi Wilton in the Marketing Department and watch the video of Mr. Z's accident, but protocol dictated I should clear it with Wash Booker first, to whom she reported and whom I had not yet met. And I wanted to tour the bottling plant and visit the scene of the accident. Also see the burned out lab where Elliot died. That was a lot, and I knew it was just for starters. An orientation. There was clearly more going on here than met the eye, but what it was wasn't yet clear at all. I had no real idea what to do after the orientation was done.

But I was hungry. I wasn't ready for the company cafeteria, and Sullivan hadn't invited me, so this would be an opportunity to take in some "local color" as they say, which might help make my history write-up a bit more interesting.

From the car I phoned Mrs. Spurr to thank her for setting me up with Jim Sullivan, sugar coated how our meeting went (but not too much or she'd probably see right through me, or it would get back to him. After all, I did get what I'd come for and felt like we'd parted on reasonably good terms), asked after Mr. Z (no change), and told her I'd be in touch.

I eased out of the visitors' lot and stopped by the gatehouse, having locked my briefcase with its contraband notes in the trunk, out of sight.

"Where's a good place to get lunch around here?" I asked

Lonnie, who was finishing off a burger in a Hardee's wrapper, a large cup of Spurrt propped on the ledge in front of him. "I hope there's something besides fast-food. Not that I have anything against it, of course, just in the mood for something a step above, you know."

Why was I explaining myself to Lonnie? Foot going in deeper with every word. Guilt, no doubt. Waiting for him to say, "'Fraid I'll have to ask you to open up your trunk, Mr. Fairley." I thought I was hearing him say it, in fact, but he wasn't.

"'Fraid I'll have to tell you there's only one place I could recommend, Mr. Fairley. You try the Set-A-Spell down on Main Street. Great barbecue. With slaw and hush puppies. And banana pudding. Tell 'em I sent you."

The Set-A-Spell Family Restaurant and Nite Club (That's how it was spelled: "Nite Club.") was at the corner of Main and First Streets, the intersection with the one and only stop light in town. A Wells Fargo bank was cater-cornered across from it, and the other two corners were occupied by the First Baptist Church and the First United Methodist Church. I imagined whatever church the Receptionists attended was over on Second or maybe Third Street, if there was a Third Street. I'd have a look later. Next door on Main was Lester Bros. Hardware ("Since 1895"), and around the corner on First was Lester Bros. Dry Goods ("Since 1894"). Could there be a Lester Bros. Wet Goods nearby?

I could see the town square a block farther down Main, where I imagined the Town Hall would be, and probably the Sheriff's office too, since Mrs. Spurr had said there was no Spurrville police force. And the jail.

The Set-A-Spell had a sign saying "Parking in Rear," but the alley looked to be partially blocked by a dumpster, and although I could have gotten my car past it I easily found a spot in front. All the motorists in what must have been a normally bustling downtown had apparently decided to park in the Spurr Nutritionals visitors' lot today.

I fished around in my pocket for a quarter and put it in the parking meter. Fifteen minutes. A bargain. Two more quarters, two dimes and a nickel went in. Happy to contribute to the Lester County treasury since, at least indirectly, it was financing my living expenses for the next few months while I worked for Mrs. Spurr.

The hand-lettered sign just inside the door said "Please Seat Yourself." I did, choosing a table that faced the intersection so I could keep track of the phases of the changing stoplight in case I got bored with my meal. Red and green are my favorite colors. Yellow not so much.

The décor was typical what I'd call "family restaurant classic": Brown tile flooring, sturdy wooden tables and chairs, no tablecloths, and cheap stainless steel silverware wrapped in rolled paper napkins with a self-sealing paper band. Each table was adorned with a paper napkin dispenser and a wicker condiment caddy displaying miniature plastic Corona-Lite-beer-bottle salt and pepper shakers, sugar, an assortment of little artificial sweetener packets, little plastic cups of non-dairy creamer (only a tad smaller than Fanny Spurr's demitasse teacups), ketchup, barbecue sauce, vinegar and Texas Pete. On the brown paneled walls were black and white photographs of Spurrville scenes from what looked like the 1940s and 50s, fanciful cartoon pigs to reinforce the barbecue theme, a few replicas of antique Coca-Cola and Spurrt advertisements (no Pepsi or Cheerwine?) and an Uncle Sam "I want You for US Army" poster which may have been authentic. A small stage in the far corner held an electronic keyboard and a mic.

Overall, it was kind of dark in the Set-A-Spell, but enough

sunlight came through the front windows to keep it from being dreary. Overhead fans kept the air moving.

Barely had I gotten settled when a menu appeared in front of me attached to the hand of a pleasant-looking middle-aged woman whose name, according to her nametag, was Clara.

"You're not from around here, are you?" she said.

"Uh …"

"If you were, you'd have said 'Hello' when you came in. Everybody at least says 'Hello.'"

"Hello."

I hadn't seen anybody to say hello to, and I told her that.

"Don't matter; we can hear you from the back."

"Well, please excuse the faux pas, uh, Clara. I hope this doesn't mean I can't get some lunch."

"'Course you can, hon. Lunch from 11:00 to 3:30, dinner from 4:30 to midnight, and breakfast all day except we're closed for mopping up from 3:30 to 4:30. Entertainment starts at 8:00 on most Fridays and Saturdays if the crowd's big enough. Five-dollar cover charge, no minimum. It's only 2:00 right now, so you're good. And what's a 'fo pa'?"

"Just an expression. Do you have a lunch special?"

"Barbecue's darn good today. That's special."

"I've heard about it. With hush puppies and slaw, I'll bet. And banana pudding."

"You do seem to know your way around, for a stranger," she said.

"I've been talking to Lonnie over at the Spurrt plant," I admitted. "He's an expert on Spurrville stuff, apparently."

"That he is. And any friend of Lonnie's is a friend of mine. I'm Clara Fritts," she announced, dropping the menu on the table and offering her hand, which I shook. "You can call me Clara."

"As opposed to 'Mrs. Fritts'?"

"No, because it's what my friends call me. Anyway, it's *Ms.* Fritts. I'm not married at the moment, but I'm no Missy."

"Of course." Feminism at work in the heartland. "I'm Mark Fairley, and you can call me Mark."

"Well that's a lot better than calling you 'Visitor,'" she said.

I had forgotten to take off my ID badge. I did it then and stuffed it into a pocket.

I looked across the empty room. "Where is everybody?"

"It was pretty busy in here around noon, but nobody tells me where they're going after lunch, and I don't ask."

"Of course."

"So, what can I getcha, Mark?"

"Well, ahem, the barbecue sounds good."

"You want it all the way?"

Whatever that meant.

"I guess so," I said. "Why not?"

"What to drink?"

"Uh, I guess just iced tea, please, with lemon."

As I'd told Emily many times, in my experience iced tea served in barbecue restaurants in the South comes in two varieties only: unsweet and too sweet.

"Can I get it sort of medium-sweet?" I asked.

Another faux pas, but not a big one this time.

"I'll get you some unsweet and you can put the sugar in yourself, hon. Less complaints that way."

And Ms. Clara Fritts was off, presumably to the kitchen.

It was indeed a good meal, in spite of Clara hanging around my table making conversation throughout. Obviously, I was some sort of novelty, or she was simply a lonely woman in spite of her outgoing nature. Maybe because of it.

"We don't get many strangers around here," she said. "Last ones I remember were a couple of Chinese-looking guys who dropped by last week. They didn't order anything, just asked if they could leave some takeout menus for their restaurant in Raleigh. Can you imagine? I tossed them right in the dumpster."

That was interesting.

And I learned a few other things. First, as I might have guessed, Sheriff Belton ate there often. Clara was impressed I knew him.

"Cecil's a good man," she said. "Likes a lot of Texas Pete. You know that comes from over in Winston-Salem, don't you?"

I did.

Had she mentioned the Chinese guys to the sheriff? Yes.

In all her nine years at the Set-A-Spell she'd only seen one accident at the intersection, a four-car pileup during a thunderstorm that had knocked out the power all over town so the stop light wasn't working and the "cars just came a-barrelin' on through all at the same time and crashed into one another. It was a mess. Glass and car parts all over the place, but everybody was okay."

I asked about the statue of a man on horseback I thought I could see in the town square.

"That's old Earnest K. Lester," she said. "He was in the Civil War, and his family founded Spurrville before that."

"Why don't they call it Lesterville then?" I asked.

"They did. Well, actually it was Lestertown, but then the Spurrs got so well-known and successful, the Chamber of Commerce convinced the City Council to change the name back in about 1955, and the state approved it. Thought it would be good for local business. You know, put us on the map since everybody knew about Spurrt."

"Did it work?"

"Didn't hurt any, I guess, but it sure caused a big falling out between the Lesters and the Spurrs, I can tell you, even though it's still Lester County. Billy Lester owns the dry good store and the hardware store, and he and Mr. Z aren't on speaking terms to this day."

Then she asked the inevitable "What brings you to Spurrville?"

I told her I was working on writing the history of Spurr Nutritionals for Mrs. Spurr. That got her a little excited.

"There's some other things I could tell you, Mark, believe me. I hear things. And so do my friends over at Hardee's and at the Walmart. Some good and some bad. Come back when you have more time to, you know, set a spell."

I said I would. Then I took a chance.

"Do you think those menus you threw away might still be in the dumpster?" I asked.

"Well, let's see, the trash pickup is on a Wednesday morning and I threw them away, um, Wednesday afternoon if I recall right, and this is Monday, isn't it? So maybe."

"Mind if I have a look?"

"Knock yourself out."

Pregnant pause. I waited for it.

"But why on earth do you want to do a thing like that? What's it they call it? Dumpster-diving or something?"

"Believe it or not, I get to Raleigh from time to time, and I'm curious what restaurant thinks it's so good people would come all the way from Spurrville to eat there."

She nodded thoughtfully. I paid for my lunch, tipping generously, and then I went dumpster-diving in the alley. I could hardly believe it. Do real private detectives do this? Fortunately, although the menus were on the bottom, all the other garbage had been neatly bagged so they were loose and easy to retrieve, and not too dirty. I'd dodged a bullet this time. I unlocked my trunk and put them in my briefcase. Which I locked. There were seven minutes left on the meter.

Come to think of it, historians *are* sort of detectives too.

On my way out of town I slowed way down to wave at Sheriff Belton. He waved back. In fact, I went so slowly we could have played a hand of poker between the speed trap and the county line. In a way, maybe we were. I hadn't yet mailed in the fine from our first encounter, and I had forgotten to ask Mrs. Spurr if she could "fix" it.

Chapter 10

A History of Health: The Spurr Nutritionals Story
By Mark L. Fairley
With Agnes Smith, Archivist

(Excerpt)

Birth of a Nation's Deliverance

In 1937, the popular drink we now know as Spurr's Restorative did not exist.

Times were hard. The Great Depression had been going on for eight years. People lucky enough to have jobs worked long hours. Not all had good food on the table. The world seemed on the verge of war in Europe. Amelia Earhart disappeared. A pall hung over America, an anxiety, a fatigue, an ennui. There was no way to get a "pick-me-up" that also offered a balanced nutritional supplement.

Quick energy and healthy nutrition from food or drink were separate concepts delivered by separate products that were hardly ever thought of in the same breath. There was coffee. There was tea. There were vitamin and mineral tonics and elixirs of every description, some beneficial and some downright dangerous. And there were the cola drinks, some of which originally contained cocaine, an addictive narcotic that is now a controlled substance. But there was no Spurr's Restorative.

It was a harsh world.

But a young soda jerk at Dull Bros. Rexall in Siler City,

North Carolina, began experimenting with carefully measured mixtures of fruit juices, barley and kudzu extracts, vitamins, minerals, herbs, cod liver oil, sugar and caffeine in carbonated water. He tried them out on some of his customers. Slowly, over the course of many months, he perfected an "energy drink" many of his customers liked. Keeping the recipe a secret, he quit his job at the drug store and set up a makeshift factory in an empty barn on farmland owned by his family 10 miles from town. Employing a few members of the family, he started production. He went slowly at first, making small quantities to sell at drug stores in the area, but already he was calling the product Spurr's Restorative.

That young man was Zachariah Spurr.

Young Zachariah had a dream, as many young men do. But Zachariah acted on his dream. He dreamed of being somebody—not just somebody important, or somebody rich and famous, although all of these things did come about. No, young Zachariah dreamed of doing something to benefit mankind. What better benefit than offering one's fellow man the opportunity to feel good, to feel healthy and re-charged, to have dietary peace of mind? And all for only the price of an occasional bottle of a good tasting nonalcoholic drink that could be shared with friends and family. Using the limited means at his disposal, applying hard work and smart thinking, and, yes, a little luck, Zachariah shaped and molded his dream. The result was Spurr's Restorative. It was affordable to everyone, even in those difficult pre-War years.

The world changed.

Chapter 11

General Tso's Golden Chicken Pagoda is located in the Airedale Shopping Center in Raleigh. The Airedale is a strip mall, anchored at one end by a large independent drug store and at the other by an Exxon station that has seen better days. The pay phone still works and even has an intact phone book attached on a chain, and the original driveway dinger hose still rings the bell, so that's something. It's hard to tell if these anchor stores are providing stability to the shopping center or simply weighing it down. Other tenants include a used furniture store, a pizzeria, a barber shop, a florist, a chiropractor, a bar and grill, a day spa, a music store, a shoe repair shop, and a law office.

General Tso's is basically a hole-in-the wall tucked between the Game On Video Game and Comic Shop and the Great Skinnections Tattoo Parlor ("Tattoos While You Wait"). In front, three parking spaces are marked off, each guarded by a small sign saying "15 Minute Parking for General Tso's Only. Others Will Be Towed at Owner's Expense." That's a lot to put on a small sign, and it's unclear whether the towing expense will be paid by the miscreant car owner or General Tso.

Inside, it's six steps from the door to the chest-high counter where you order takeout or take a right turn to sit at one of three small tables where you can eat the takeout if you are too hungry to wait until you get home or back to your office and must eat immediately. A too-large beverage cooler and a trash receptacle partially block a straight-line walk from door to counter, and a long wooden bench sits just under the plate glass window that lets some daylight in past the signs and small posters taped on it for viewing from outside. Posters advertising circuses, folk music gatherings, meetings of the Chinese Student Club, Chinese cooking classes, Raleigh Symphony Orchestra performances, and March Madness ACC and NCAA college basketball tournament schedules. From the bench it's an easy reach to the wire stand that holds various free shopping newspapers like *Thrifty Nickel* and *Pennysavers*, real estate brochures and various well-thumbed magazines, including *Modern Chinese Restaurant World,* to peruse as wait-time or take home reading.

At the southeast end of the counter is a small aquarium holding a half dozen koi. General Tso's owner, Nikos "Nick" Papadopoulos, was not above giving a nod to the feng shui traditions he imagined some of his customers might appreciate or even practice themselves. He had read in *Modern Chinese Restaurant World* that "Placing feng shui aquarium in you (sic) home and office is powerful way to draw auspicious chi of prosperity and good luck into a space." Furthermore, "The koi fish has powerful life force, demonstrated by ability to swim against current and even travel upstream. Characteristics associated with koi are: Ambition, Courage, Perseverance, Good Fortune, Success, Prosperity, and Longevity." Of course, Papadopoulos didn't believe a word of such nonsense and thought of koi, a fancy word for carp, as nothing more than overgrown goldfish. The description of what demonstrated their "powerful life force" could just as easily apply to spawning salmon, he thought. But PetSmart didn't stock salmon, and they would probably be too big for the aquarium anyway.

Opened in 1992, General Tso's Golden Chicken Pagoda was Nick's first restaurant, and because of that it was his favorite.

Since then, he had parlayed his Ambition, Courage, Perseverance, and Good Fortune into substantial Success and Prosperity in the restaurant business. Longevity was still to be proven, but so far the outlook was good. He now owned eight restaurants in the Raleigh area, including General Tso's: three Mexican, two Italian, one Indian and a Hardee's. None of them was Greek, although much olive oil and yoghurt could be found in the recipes used in all but the Hardee's and General Tso's.

Nick had also read in *Modern Chinese Restaurant World* that the number eight was lucky in Chinese culture. "People with the lucky number 8 have big intuition and insight, so they have potential to explore undiscovered thing. They are bestowed with special gift of being inborn businessman, and can achieve all his plans step by step." Obviously, Nick now had no more need for feng shui personally, if indeed he ever did, but nevertheless he kept the aquarium for appearances sake.

Just now, Nick was surveying the scene in General Tso's from the kitchen, looking out from far behind the order counter and observing two of his employees who were currently on break and in an apparently intense conversation at one of the three tables in front with a well-dressed man who was a frequent visitor to the takeout restaurant, although, come to think of it, he never ordered anything to take out. Or to eat there, for that matter. Aside from those three, José Hernandez the Mexican cook, and Nick himself, the place was empty, although the lunch hour had been busy.

Nick liked Tom Ake and Jerry Bono, both of whom had been with him for three years, ever since they dropped out of Durham Tech. Even so, if asked by anyone doing background checks on his employees, Nick would have described Tom as "dumb as a post" and Jerry as "dumber." Had they worked in one of his Mexican restaurants he might have characterized them as "one taco short of a combination plate" or in Hardee's as "a few fries short of a Happy Meal" (in a grudging nod to McDonald's). And one of them, he wasn't sure which, wore far too much cologne. Tom maybe. But they showed up on time, their work was adequate and they were loyal, qualities he admired in his employees. More-than-adequate work would have been better, but loyalty trumped the missing comparative. His only complaint was they were over-diligent in their efforts to distribute General Tso's takeout menus all over the place, for which he paid them extra based on how many they distributed each week and how much new business they generated. Each menu offered a 20% discount for first-time customers. His printing bills had tripled since he'd brought the young men aboard, but business was up too, so he guessed it more than evened things out.

Most of Nick's employees in his eight restaurants were legal Mexicans, or Mexican-Americans as he had to keep reminding himself (why nobody called Nick a Greek-American escaped him), even in the Italian, the Indian and the Hardee's. No one seemed to mind or even to notice. However, Ake and Bono were of Polynesian descent, their grandparents having emigrated to the US mainland from Hawaii after the Korean War. In a Chinese takeout restaurant, they fit right in, looking as Chinese as anyone could expect. Yet if they appeared elsewhere, even in such a place as rural Lester County, and spoke a few words to someone who was not looking at them, that person was not likely to say, "You're not from around here, are you?" That was because they were born and raised in the Raleigh area and consequently sounded as Southern as anyone else.

But when they were on duty in General Tso's, Nick made them wear little paper chef hats and speak with fake Chinese accents. Authenticity sells egg rolls. Never mind that egg foo young and chop suey, staples of the General Tso's menu, are not dishes that originated in China. Even the provenance of the popular dish called General Tso's chicken itself was iffy. So fake authenticity was a consistent theme and seemed to work, although rarely had Nick seen any real Chinese people in the place. Which may have been just as well since such customers might have preferred to speak Chinese when they ordered and to assume Tom and Jerry could respond in kind.

Although he wasn't purposely eavesdropping at first, Nick couldn't help hearing bits and pieces of the hushed conversation between the middle-aged mustachioed stranger and the two young men. Unconsciously, he edged closer to the back of the order counter so he could hear better. He began wiping the counter with Lysol spray disinfectant and a paper towel, a menial task usually reserved for Tom or Jerry, but which Nick was not above doing if need be in spite of his Ambition, Courage, Perseverance, Good Fortune, Success, Prosperity, and potential Longevity.

"I just need you to go out one more time," the stranger was saying. "Actually, maybe two more times, I'm not sure. It depends on what you find."

"But why?" asked Tom, the less dumb. "We're tired of it, nothing seems to come of it, you won't tell us what we're supposed to be looking for, and you're hardly ever happy with what we find, if anything—although we do like the money, and we're happy to leave the takeout menus—but it's getting too risky."

"Yeah," said Jerry.

They were not using their fake Chinese accents.

"Just don't take unnecessary risks. Now first, I want you to put a scare into that new guy from Greensboro. Stealing those copies of my father's … I mean old Mr. Spurr's notes from his briefcase was good, but you know I never asked you to do that."

85

Nick thought the stranger was smart not to encourage those two to act on their own initiative. They probably had no idea how to distinguish between a necessary and an unnecessary risk.

"However, they're mostly illegible," the stranger continued, "and by now he knows something's up. I don't care how you do it, but make him go away."

"You mean …?" said Jerry.

The stranger looked at him. "No, I don't mean … I mean just scare him enough to quit playing private eye. But don't hurt him. Jeez, don't kill him!"

"That'll cost more, of course."

The stranger sighed. "All right, how about $35?"

"Forty," said Tom.

"Done."

"Great!" said Jerry. "We know what we're doing is probably wrong, but like my daddy always said, 'Sin is only a three-letter word, so how bad could it be?'"

Nick had never before thought of Jerry as having a father. He thought maybe he'd crawled out from under a rock.

"One other thing," said the stranger. "In the future if you ever do run across any papers or documents again that look like they might be important, take pictures of them with your smartphones. Don't steal them."

"Hey, why didn't we think of that?" said Jerry.

The stranger let that pass.

"Okay, scare the Greensboro guy. What else?" Tom again.

By now, the stranger had noticed Nick's proximity. He hunched forward and began to whisper. "I'm still not sure what it is exactly, but look for anything that can help explain why a big Japanese company wants to buy Spurr Nutritionals. Whatever it is, if it was in the research lab, it's not there now, so it might be in the office area. Documents, reports, photographs. Anything you can pick up. I don't mean literally pick up, but take pictures of, like I said. It might have been in the lab, but the Sheriff's men and the insurance company scoured the place after it blew up, and they didn't find anything. Of course, they weren't looking for anything specific, but anyway I'm pretty sure it wasn't there or it would have been in the news."

"Wait, the lab blew up?" Tom.

"A natural gas leak, apparently."

"Cool!" said Jerry.

"Not cool," said the stranger. "Someone … very close to me … was killed. You didn't hear about it? It was in all the papers and on the news for days."

"Must have missed it," said Jerry, happy that at least he wouldn't ever have to go sneaking around *there* again in the dead of night. It was too scary. But he hoped the menus had survived.

The stranger kept talking, but Nick couldn't make out any of it after the man had started whispering. Too bad. Sounded interesting. Maybe he'd ask Tom and Jerry about it later.

Eventually, the stranger straightened up and resumed speaking in a normal voice. What Nick heard was, "Remember, I still want you guys to wear gloves and keep using your fake Japanese accents out there."

Chapter 12

I didn't look at the limp menus until I got home. Emily had picked up some sushi at Harris Teeter, and it looked like we were going to have it for dinner with some beer for me and ginger ale for her. No dishes to wash, which was how she tried to plan things on Mondays before going to her circle meeting at the church. However, therefore, no beer for Emily.

"They're from General Tso's Golden Chicken Pagoda," I said.

"What's from General whose-it's Chicken what?" said Emily.

"These menus. I fished them out of a dumpster where I had lunch."

"You had lunch in a dumpster?"

"No, I mean a dumpster next to where I had lunch."

"Why on earth would you do that?"

"What, have lunch, or fish menus out of a dumpster?"

"Cut it out! Just tell me about it."

I did. Emily thought things over.

"That Sullivan character doesn't seem so nice," she said finally.

"Yeah, but I think he's okay. He's under a lot of pressure, and I guess he's just doing his job. Trouble is, financial guys sometimes aren't very creative about how to grow a company. They're better suited to cost-cutting than investing in marketing, although I will give him credit for the investments in state-of-the art equipment and systems even though it turns out the company got overextended. And I can see why Sheriff

Belton likes the barbecue at the Set-A-Spell so much. It was pretty good."

The banana pudding had been very good too—so good I ordered a takeout portion to bring home to Emily. But banana pudding doesn't go well with sushi, so she put it in the fridge for later.

Emily went off to her church meeting, and I went to my little bedroom office to make a few notes. My briefcase is outfitted with a built-in combination lock, but until the break-in I had never bothered to use it. It calls for turning little brass wheels so certain pre-chosen numbers line up, kind of like on a slot machine, allowing you to pop the latches. I don't like it because the wheels are hard to turn, especially if your fingers aren't completely dry, but I'd forced myself to get into the habit of doing it since the break-in. It hadn't been locked that night, and since the police had found no unusual fingerprints on the briefcase or anywhere else in the house, the whole thing was still an uncomfortable mystery. Emily and I weren't losing any sleep over it, but we now keep the porch and deck lights on all night, and we had a light sensor installed on the pole lamp that illuminates our front walk so it would come on automatically at dusk. These measures were among those recommended by Officer Ed Truesdale at the inaugural Neighborhood Watch meeting. We make extra sure to activate the alarm system whenever both of us are going to be out of the house. And now I lock my briefcase. New habits.

I unlocked the briefcase and started to work, but the beer had made me sleepy so I didn't work long, and eventually I watched some TV in the den. Mostly channel surfing.

I must have been dozing when Emily got home around 9:00 p.m. because she startled me.

"Look at these, Mark!"

"Huh? Look at what?" I was disoriented.

"These!!"

Emily was holding up four large sheets of paper. They looked like menus. They looked familiar.

"Why did you take those to your meeting?"

"I didn't, of course! They were there. In the church fellowship hall. Pastor Bob said he found them after the Neighborhood Watch meeting last week and he didn't know what to do with them."

So now I had four more takeout menus from General Tso's Golden Chicken Pagoda in Raleigh in addition to those I had retrieved from the Set-A-Spell dumpster. Remembering the two out-of-place Asian-looking men we had seen at the meeting who disappeared before it was over, I decided to show all the menus to Detective Blue. I assumed the police still had an open case on the break-in and remembered what Allan Whitbread had reported about the strangers at our door that night. Maybe the menus were clues. Maybe there would be useful fingerprints.

Emily shared some of her banana pudding with me before we went to bed. The vanilla wafers had gotten soggy, but it was still very good.

Chapter 13

Americans and their love of nicknames, thought Tadashi "Tad" Tanaka as he drove to the Raleigh-Durham airport to pick up the two Kuroibishi-Whitestone investment banking people who were flying in from New York this morning.

It would be his first meeting with these two, although in a manner of speaking he had been on the Kashimoto Foods' payroll for two years and knew of the longstanding Kuroibishi-Whitestone efforts to help Kashimoto Foods acquire Spurr Nutritionals. Tanaka was their "man on the ground" who provided information about goings on at Spurr Nutritionals and within the family as best he could. It was part of the quid pro quo in exchange for Kashimoto paying for his tuition, books and lodging at UNC-Chapel Hill and the expenses of a leased Honda Civic. A red one. He'd managed to befriend Trey Spurr, son of Elliot Spurr, the late president of the company and a fellow student at UNC. He leveraged this friendship to get information. Some of it was of interest and some of it worthless, but since he was in no position to tell the difference, he just passed on whatever he could and let the people in Tokyo figure it out. That attitude helped him cope with increasingly frequent twinges of conscience over being disloyal to Trey—an orphan after all and whom he genuinely liked— and what probably amounted to industrial espionage. But, hey, a scholarship is a scholarship. Hard to turn down a "full ride," as the Americans called it.

Yes, Americans gave nicknames to everyone and everything,

it seemed to him. James was Jim, or Jimmy. William was Bill. Barbara was Barb. Margaret became, inexplicably, Peggy. Mary was Mare, which he'd been taught in English class meant a female horse. And the practice didn't seem to be governed by gender, race, religion, socio-economic status, celebrity, geography, political leaning, sexual preference or anything else. Jennifer Lopez was J. Lo. It wasn't enough to shorten the Alexander in New York Yankees baseball player Alexander Rodriguez' name to Alex. No, it had to be A-Rod.

"Trey" wasn't short for a longer name; it was short for a concept. Trey's real name was Zachariah Spurr III, or "the third." Substituting "Trey" for the name of a third son or third in a family of men who had been named after each other did seem to be mostly a regional practice, he had to concede. Tanaka knew "trey" was a three in playing cards, dice, or dominoes and went with the terms "ace" for one and "deuce" for two. It came from the Old French *treis* or Latin *tres*, meaning three, as in modern Spanish. It was far less universal than calling a same-name son "Junior." To make matters even more confusing, however, often "Junior" was also used by fathers to refer to or call for their sons who were *not* named after them, or it might be used merely to refer to someone younger than the speaker or to demean someone. Tanaka had never heard of a same-named son being called Deuce or a first-born being called Ace, although he had once or twice heard "Ace" used as a semi-derogatory salutation, similar to "Pal," "Buddy" or "Sport," which were also nicknames but he didn't know for what.

Over at Spurr Nutritionals they did not call Zachariah Spurr II, the retired chairman, "Deuce." When they weren't calling him Mr. Spurr, they called him Mr. Z, or sometimes among his friends at the Lester County Country Club simply "Z," according to Trey. One letter. Sort of the ultimate nickname, he thought.

Tanaka had a British friend named Pamela, also a student at Carolina. "Everyone here insists on calling me Pam. I hate it!" she wailed one day over tea in the Student Center after a chemistry class. Earl Grey for her, green for him. "I'm not a stupid cooking spray, for heaven's sake!" He understood her frustration only too well.

Growing up in a suburb of Tokyo, Tanaka was steeped in the Japanese tradition of using honorifics with names for men and women alike and sometimes even for objects and buildings that have special significance, like *Fuji-san* for Mt. Fuji, the iconic volcano that symbolized Japan. At home, Tanaka was accustomed to being called Tanaka-*san*. Colleagues might call him Tadashi-san, using his first name, but only on close friends was bestowed the privilege of using the first name alone without the honorific "*san*," and even then only in private encounters, never in public. Individuals who have achieved some rank or status above the crowd might be given loftier honorifics. For example, Watanabe-*sensei* in the case of a teacher, or Kashimoto-*shachō* for the president of a company, or Yoshida-*honcho* for a manager or group leader, the word picked up by US servicemen during WWII and incorporated into English, as in "Okay, who's the head honcho here?"

So, even though Tanaka had studied American English in school and spoke it well and without much of an accent, and even though he knew Americans were hopelessly informal, still he was not prepared for his first day on the UNC campus during which everyone he met said, "Tadashi, eh? Do you mind if I call you Tad?"

Tad!!?

He'd looked it up. It meant "a small amount," "a little bit" or "somewhat." That was a difficult come-down, especially since he was at least an inch taller and weighed more than the average Japanese man his age, the result of frequenting Tokyo's versions of McDonald's and Dunkin' Donuts while growing up. Why couldn't it at least be "Ted"? Or even "Teddy"? Teddy Roosevelt was apparently well thought of in America as a rough and ready guy, and his name seemed to carry a lot more weight, and—let's be honest—masculinity than "Tad" with its connotations of diminution. As in "tadpole."

The only "Tad" he knew of in American history was Abraham Lincoln's little son, Thomas, nicknamed Tad because as a baby, according to his father, he "wriggled like a tadpole." A small boy! Which was in fact yet another of the official Merriam-Webster definitions of the word. Little Tad's biggest claim to fame besides his father's renown was initiating in 1863 the practice of "pardoning" Presidential turkeys on Thanksgiving. The turkey's name was Jack.

Tanaka had thought of preempting the situation by adopting an American nickname of his own choosing. Like "Jack," a good, solid male name no longer associated with turkeys, apparently. It was a nickname for "John." Though not any shorter than John, it was still a popular nickname for reasons that escaped him. *What were the rules?* But he knew the conversation would go something like this:

"Hello, I'm Tadashi Tanaka, but you can call me Jack."

"Why?"

So "Tad" is what he was stuck with. At least his college instructors called him Mr. Tanaka, if sometimes dismissively it seemed to him. But he was a good student so there was no reason for them to disrespect him for anything other than his unfortunate nickname.

He expected that the two executives from New York would call him Mr. Tanaka too. Maybe even Tanaka-san. Although American, and Caucasian, they would know the traditions of Japan because their paychecks depended largely on staying in Kashimoto's good graces. They would be respectful.

He left the Civic with the motor running at the pick-up curb just outside the baggage claim area and took up a position between the entry doors and the carousel that had not yet started dumping bags from the flight his visitors had come in on. He held up a hand-lettered sign: Kuroibishi-Whitestone. Presently, he was approached from the restroom area by two middle-aged men wearing suits and pulling small rolling suitcases. The shorter of the two seemed to be walking unsteadily.

"Tadashi Tanaka?" the taller one said, hand extended.

"Yes."

"I'm Jack Johnson, and this is Bill Wright. With Kuroibishi-Whitestone."

"Nice to meet you both," answered Tanaka. (Ah, he thought, a man named Jack.)

They shook hands all around. "Good flight?"

"Not bad if you like pretzels and tomato juice," said Wright. "I don't. A little vodka and Tabasco makes it all right again though. Nothing like it for getting rid of white knuckles."

"Bill doesn't like to fly," said Johnson. "Has to prepare himself."

"Ah. Well, the car is right out here."

The two men pointed themselves toward the door and began following Tanaka with their luggage.

"Say, Tadashi," said Johnson, "do you mind if we call you Tad?"

"Oh, come on, Jack," protested Wright. "Show some respect. I think we should call him Tad-san."

Chapter 14

I spent Tuesday running errands. Got Emily's car inspected so we could renew the registration. In North Carolina you pay property tax on your car when you apply for renewed license registration. But you can't get the license renewed unless the car has passed inspection. They've got you coming and going. But the process is pretty smooth and can be done conveniently online, except for the actual inspection, of course. Maybe someday they'll even figure out how to do that.

Emily and I made a run to the Salvation Army to drop off some unneeded winter clothes for which we could get a tax deduction. Went to Lowe's for bird seed, potting soil and tomato plants. Then to Food Lion for a few items Costco only stocks in regimental-size containers.

None of this took my mind off the history assignment, however, so it wasn't as if I were taking the day off from work. Why did I feel I had to justify myself? It wasn't that Fanny Spurr, my boss, was keeping tabs on me as far as I knew. My guilty feelings were probably just a habit from when I had a real job and was expected to appear during certain hours and look busy.

Wednesday was pretty much like Tuesday except I did make some more notes for the history, and I phoned to set up Thursday appointments with Wendell Cox, Agnes Smith and Wash Booker at the plant. All were available.

My musings over the goings-on in Spurrville late that afternoon were interrupted by a call from Detective Blue. The fingerprints on the takeout menus were Pastor Bob's, Emily's and mine. Not much help there. But since the menus were from a Chinese restaurant and we saw two maybe-Chinese strangers at the Neighborhood Watch meeting, and Allan Whitbread thought our nocturnal visitors were "oriental," the police did suspect the events might be connected. Blue thought it would be worth a call to one of his counterparts in the Raleigh Police Department to ask him to drop by General Tso's one day and eye the employees to see if any matched the descriptions the three of us had given him. And to see if the food was any good, presumably. And whether he (or she) might get a courtesy discount beyond the 20% promised on the menus.

Chapter 15

A History of Health: The Spurr Nutritionals Story
By Mark L. Fairley
With Agnes Smith, Archivist

(Working notes)
Possible titles for this section:
Zachariah Spurr, the Dreamer
The Long Spurrt to Vim and Vigor

<u>The Dream Takes Flight (early growth and development—
Spurrt and Zachariah I)</u>

Slowly at first, and then more rapidly, Spurr's Restorative catches on, and distribution expands to the whole state of North Carolina and the southern counties of Virginia.

In 1939, borrowing money from the local bank, Zachariah Spurr then builds a real bottling plant in nearby Lestertown, engages wholesalers and does some advertising on the *Grand Ole Opry* radio show and in the *Saturday Evening Post to build brand awareness beyond the local region*. Spurr's Restorative, or Spurr-juice, as it comes to be called by the locals, then grows over the next five years from a regional success to national renown.

Zachariah marries the former Esmeralda Darlington of Lestertown, his high school sweetheart. Zachariah Spurr II is born.

Spurr-juice goes to war in 1942. Helping our troops, exemption from sugar rationing for the product, stories from the front, etc.

Change of product name from Spurr's Restorative to Spurrt.

By the end of WWII, Spurr Nutritionals, still family-owned, has become a multi-million-dollar business producing original Spurrt as well as several spin-off products. It employs over 300 people and is the economic mainstay of the community.

Introduction of other products:

Spurrt Lyte*

Spurrt Cookies

Spurrt Chips

Spurrt Chewing Gum

Spurrt Toothpaste

The eventual discontinuance of all but original Spurrt and Spurrt Lyte.

Competition: In addition to soft drinks such as Coca Cola* and Pepsi*, dozens of elixirs, tonics and patent remedies compete with Spurrt, but Spurrt tastes better than the medicinal concoctions. This is revolutionary, running counter to the prevailing wisdom that the worse such a product tastes, the more efficacious it must be. (Think of the old Listerine® germ-fighting mouth wash.)

The current plant opens in April 1950, just in time to supply our Korean War troops with a quick, nutritious pick-me-up.

Because of the importance of Spurr Nutritionals, Inc., to the area, locals begin referring to Lestertown as "Spurrville." In 1955, Lestertown is officially renamed Spurrville, county seat of Lester County. The Lester family is not happy.

In 1959 Zachariah Spurr II, having worked in the Spurr Nutritionals mail room and plant during summers while in high school and college, graduates from North Carolina State University with a degree in business management and begins working in the Sales Department, travelling the Southeast to call on supermarkets and pharmacies.

Spurrt tries to distance itself from Geritol', a popular vitamin and iron supplement of the day, marketed as a remedy for "iron-poor tired blood" and shrouded in controversy over possible harmful side effects. Spurrt is different because while it does contain vitamins and minerals, there are also fruit juices, caffeine, carbonation, much less iron and no alcohol. It provides the user with all the body's daily requirements of vitamins and minerals, and, because of the caffeine and sugar content, it does indeed have the effect of a quick "pick-me-up," especially when consumed between meals. (Maybe develop a separate section on the whole industry—history, growth, size and competition.)

Zachariah II is promoted to president, but his father stays on as chairman. Zachariah II marries Fanny Spainhour, his high school sweetheart, and they have two children, Elliot and Adam.

(Mention unsuccessful attempts to expand internationally, especially Japan.)

Chapter 16

Adam Spainhour Spurr, BS, MS, Ph.D., hated himself. He hated his father and his late brother Elliot too, but mostly he hated himself. For hating his father and his brother, even if his hate was justified many times over. It was just that now with his father sick and Elliot gone, these objects of his hate were beyond his ability to make them feel it. Or to make things right with them, if he ever came around to wanting to do that. His options were limited. How had he come to this?

By being named Adam, for a start. Elliot was the first-born, so if anybody should be named Adam it was Elliot. But no. Everybody naturally assumed Adam was the first-born, the elder son. He didn't try to correct them, but it hurt. Those same people also assumed Adam should be running Spurr Nutritionals instead of Elliot, and they wondered, often aloud and as often behind Adam's back, why he wasn't. It was only natural, wasn't it—the first-born carrying on the family business? If that were so, he thought, why didn't they name Elliot Zachariah III instead of letting the name skip a generation and fall on Elliot's son, Trey? That way they could have at least avoided this whole Alphonse and Gaston routine.

And his initials, a constant source of pain, especially throughout his childhood.

A.S.S. What were they thinking??

Growing up, brother Elliot was first to get to try everything. He got the first bicycle. Elliot got a job at the company ahead of Adam. Even though it was only a summer job in the mailroom, it looked heavenly to Adam. Adam eventually worked there too for a while, but he didn't get as much joy out of it as Elliot seemed to. Elliot graduated from UNC-Chapel Hill with a BA in business and no distinguishing honors. They threw a big party for him and after a summer at the beach house, an extended party in itself, they sent him off to Wake Forest to get an MBA. Adam had more of a scientific bent and graduated *summa cum laude* from Duke with a degree in chemistry. There was only a much smaller party for Adam, at which Elliot had too much to drink and spilled the beans in public about the family's attitude toward Adam. "No head for business," he said.

So, while Elliot came back from Winston-Salem, married his high school sweetheart, Lucy, and began rising through the ranks at Spurr Nutritionals as his father's protégé, Adam was still at Duke, a Ph.D. now and Distinguished Professor of Chemistry to be sure, but not considered a "core" member of the family. No head for business.

Would all this have been different somehow if only Adam had been named Elliot and Elliot had been named Adam? Who could know? Would a different name, by itself, have given Adam a "head for business" or made Elliot love chemistry the way Adam did? Probably not, he had to admit. But still it was unfair. Unfair.

Adam Spurr didn't hate his mother, Fanny, of course. The nurturer, the sympathizer, the encourager, the protector, married to an arrogant, domineering man and shown no sympathy or support by her self-absorbed elder son. She loved his and Elliot's early crayon drawings and construction paper Valentine cards and hung them on the refrigerator with little magnets. When he or Elliot needed help with their homework, Fanny was there. Zachariah was not. When schoolyard bullies acted out, it was Fanny who called their parents and set things straight in no uncertain terms. She came to their soccer matches after school. Zachariah did not. She was in the audience for the school play. Not Zachariah. When they needed a push to get their college applications in on time, it was Fanny who gave it, who read their "personal statement" essays and suggested improvements, and who followed up with the admissions departments to make sure her boys were receiving the proper attention until they got accepted.

Why Fanny hadn't protected the boys from their father's capricious naming scheme he didn't know. He did hold that against her, but it didn't outweigh the positives. Yet he felt even Fanny was slightly disappointed in him.

So here he was, the bachelor professor in the ivory-towered halls of academe.

The trouble with being a bachelor these days, he had observed, is people assume you are gay. Adam wasn't gay, just unlucky in love. He'd been engaged once, to a girl he met while an undergraduate. Trouble is, *she* turned out to be gay. He lost track of her after graduation when she broke off the engagement and moved back Up North somewhere. She had been using him as a decoy because in those days it wasn't "cool" to "come out of the closet."

The experience soured him on women, and he never made much of an effort to form new relationships after that, throwing himself instead into his graduate studies and massaging his passion for chemistry.

Women didn't come knocking on his door unless they were students angling for a better grade or people from the campus LGBT community inviting him to their various meetings and protest rallies. They wouldn't leave him alone, convinced he had to be one of them and acting betrayed, even angry, when he refused their entreaties. And it seemed like they were always protesting something, all the time. It was a constant bother. He didn't have time for it. These days you're some kind of a pariah if you *don't* come out of the closet. In fact, he suspected it was getting so that even people who weren't gay pretended to be in order to fit in with the "progressive" crowd.

But that wasn't what was really troubling Adam.

For reasons he couldn't put his finger on, Adam was distressed about his father's accident and failure to recover the ability to communicate, and he was truly saddened by Elliot's death, maybe because they were brothers after all and had gotten along well as children, and probably because he knew Zachariah and Fanny were taking it so hard. And because his nephew Trey Spurr was now an orphan.

But something else was going on in Spurrville. He could feel it. Something had shifted.

Adam knew of his father's behavior changes immediately after the accident as Zachariah drank his way through the cases of Spurrt that passed through the ViroBactiZap 5000 machine with him, which Adam thought, in his chemistry Ph.D. wisdom, could possibly have been tainted somehow during that process. Then his father's curious reversion to a near-sedentary state once the spurious Spurrt was gone. He knew the overtures from rival companies, and especially that Japanese one, Kashimoto Foods, had become more frequent and intense since the accident, and logic told him his mother might now be thinking seriously of giving in to their appeals and selling the company since she was in no position at her age and with his father incapacitated and Elliot gone to run it herself.

Shouldn't he, Adam Spurr, the only surviving son of the only son of the founder, and a major stockholder, have some say in the company's future? Wasn't he by rights after all now the only legitimate heir to the presidency of Spurr Nutritionals? Why should that self-important carpetbagger, Jim Sullivan, ascend to the throne?

He knew of Elliot's recent obsession with spending nights in the lab doing no one knew what. Elliot was no chemist. But if it was a chemistry related quest he was on, maybe something to do with how any characteristics of Spurrt might have changed as a result of exposure to the ViroBactiZap 5000 machine, for example, why didn't he swallow his obvious pride and ask for Adam's help, which Adam would have been happy to provide in spite of his disdain for his older brother? Adam still had some loyalty to family. But no. Shut out again.

Adam sensed there was opportunity here. He didn't know what it was, but maybe, just maybe, it was something that might offer a path to winning the respect he so craved from Zachariah and Fanny and the other Spurrvillians who must be laughing at him behind his back. Or, failing that, to get back at them somehow. Big time. There had to be something he could do.

He resolved to find out what was going on. But he couldn't do it in the open. He didn't want to appear too curious. And if anything went wrong he wanted fingers of suspicion to point away from himself. Ideally toward the Kashimoto company, whom he sensed were his rivals in whatever undertaking this might lead to. He needed help.

That was why he had hired Tom Ake and Jerry Bono whom he first met when they had delivered takeout from General Tso's Golden Chicken Pagoda to a colleague's retirement party in Durham some months before. They fit his criteria for clandestine operations perfectly. They looked Japanese, like Ninjas in street clothes. They looked intimidating, some might say even thuggish. Since there weren't any real Japanese thugs available for hire in central North Carolina, these two would do nicely. Nobody around here would be able to tell the difference. And they were morons.

They turned out to be dependable morons, however, and

he had few complaints. If they were spotted doing anything suspicious, people close to Spurr Nutritionals would assume they were Japanese thugs probably hired by Kashimoto. Their unauthorized theft of copies of his father's mostly illegible notes from that Greensboro guy, Mark Fairley, had proved to be a major breakthrough. When he read the only note that was readable, the one that said "Don't sell," he knew something was definitely up, and with it might rise Adam's star as well.

No head for business! It was time to show them. To show everyone.

Chapter 17

A funny thing happened on my way to the plant on Thursday. Actually, it was a scary thing, and I didn't know what to make of it at the time.

Looking back on it, I sort of remember noticing a strange car parked across the street from my house when I pulled out of the driveway. Ordinarily, I wouldn't have thought anything of it, since my neighbors often have company or relatives coming to visit, and sometimes it's more convenient for them to park their cars at the curb in order to leave the driveways free for use by their hosts. What was odd about this car, though, was it wasn't parked directly in front of a house. It was parked between houses, so it looked out of place. As I said, I paid no attention at the time. Besides, it was raining, and I was thinking about the drive to Spurrville and hoping I wouldn't get behind too many tractor-trailers spewing up torrents of water and reducing my visibility to near zero.

Fortunately, the rain had stopped by the time I got to Siler City. As I crossed US 64 and stayed on US 421 heading south toward the Spurrville turnoff, I thought I noticed someone following me. You know the uncanny feeling you get when something just doesn't seem right. Why did I think the red car was following me? The way it pulled up close behind me and then dropped back, repeatedly? That it never passed me even though I slowed below the speed limit a couple of times to see what would happen? There wasn't much other traffic on the road, and 421 is two lanes in both directions on that stretch, almost like an Interstate, so passing involved no risk, and all the other cars passed me easily. But the red one never did.

When I turned off for Spurrville, there it was, still behind me. I know I'm not the only person who drives from Siler City to Spurrville every day, but this wasn't that. And now it was following me even closer than before, not dropping back, even tailgating me from time to time. Things had now gone from curious to frightening, even though at that stage I couldn't imagine I was in any real danger. How we talk ourselves into, or in this case out of, things!

What was I going to do? Did I need to do anything? Should I pull over and wait to see if it stopped too or just passed? What if it did stop? What kind of a conversation would we have had? What if I had unknowingly cut him off back there somewhere, way before I even noticed him, and this was a case of road rage? What if he had a gun?

Suddenly, a plan came to me. In hindsight not a very good plan, but it was what came to me in the moment, and it seemed brilliant at the time.

I would not slow down at the Lester County speed trap. Maybe the sheriff would stop us both and then we could sort things out.

I sped through the speed trap, the red car right behind me. Sure enough, Sheriff Belton's jellybean cruiser emerged from the bushes, antennas swaying and blue lights flashing, and pulled over … the other guy, but not me. Not what I was hoping for, but okay. Let Belton deal with whatever and whoever it was. I could always ask him about it later.

I slowed down and made it to my first appointment at the plant with time to spare.

Chapter 18

By noon I had toured the plant with Wendell Cox, visited the bottling line with the ViroBactiZap 5000 machine, now silent and cordoned off with yellow Caution tape, watched the video of Mr. Z's accident several times including in slow motion under the watchful eye of Heidi Wilton, the pleasant young marketing trainee, and had a lengthy chat with Agnes Smith, the walking history book.

Lonnie the gatehouse guard had issued me a Permanent Visitor's Pass for my dashboard, and Connie the receptionist had given me a Permanent Visitor ID badge with my name on it and a much nicer lanyard than the temporary one, which I turned in. The concept of a Permanent Visitor was straining my brain, which worried me because I expected to need all my mental faculties for the rest of the day's activities. I wondered if Permanent meant I could never leave. Like in "Hotel California" by the Eagles. In the end I decided it was better than Perennial Visitor, which implied somebody who showed up regularly and probably wore out his or her welcome, or Repeat Visitor, which had criminally recidivistic connotations. Or they could say Frequent Visitor and give me award points each time I showed up.

Agnes looked 110 years old but still had a spring in her step that would have made a 70-year old jealous. Seriously, she didn't look that old at all, but since Fanny Spurr, herself pushing 80, had described Agnes as "a nice old lady," I guess I saw what I had led myself to expect. Even so, and aside from

113

her ebullience, if you'd seen Agnes sitting in a chair in a nursing home she wouldn't have looked out of place: Thin face and figure, thinning gray hair, white cashmere cardigan sweater with blue cornflower patterns on the pockets and buttoned all the way up, dark skirt, support stockings and sensible shoes. I wonder what insensible shoes look like.

Others in the office told me later she was never without that sweater, or another like it, and constantly complained about being cold. She would turn up the office thermostat when no one was looking, which drove everybody crazy, especially in the summer. Nevertheless, she was loved by all. I personally found her pleasant and helpful.

Agnes had never married. Spurr Nutritionals was her career and her life, and I supposed Mr. Z and then Elliot had more or less become like surrogate husbands. In spite of the nursing home image in my head, I never once saw Agnes sitting in a chair. During our first meeting, she sat on the edge of her desk, explaining what was in various folders and files she wanted to share with me as resources for my history project.

"May I call you Agnes?"

"Of course."

"I understand you are considered the company historian if ever there was one, so I'm hoping my presence on the scene, especially as an ignorant newcomer, isn't too upsetting. The last thing I want to do is step on anybody's toes, especially yours."

"That's very sweet, Mark, but it's not a problem. In fact, I was somewhat relieved to hear from Mrs. Spurr that she had retained you. Don't tell anybody, but I am starting to feel my age. Just a little bit, mind you, but still. And I miss Elliot terribly. We all do. And the truth is, it's one thing to be the repository and custodian of all this memorabilia and other historical material when people have questions or need to know things for speeches and the annual report and whatnot, but it would be quite another to actually have to write it up as a coherent history. I'm not sure I'd be up to that."

"Thank you for pulling all this together for me. I want you to know your name will be on whatever I write."

"That's not necessary, but you're welcome, and if you have any questions just let me know."

"Oh, and I want to thank you for one more thing."

"Yes?"

"Thank you for not saying, 'You're not from around here, are you?' when we met."

"Oh, it was obvious."

The plant tour started at the Employee Entrance, fittingly enough. Agnes accompanied Cox and me, proudly pointing out what seemed to her to be important features and stops along the way that she felt the casual observer might overlook. I had the impression they didn't get many visitors, so this was a rare treat for them—an excuse to show off their company. I couldn't blame them. Spurr Nutritionals was a real red-blooded American success story.

Among the last stops was a large display case in the main entrance hall of the massive plant. Trophies, memorabilia and artifacts from the history of the company filled it almost to overflowing. Agnes acted like it was her personal treasure trove, but Cox was more modest, at least on the surface.

Here were athletic trophies, team pictures, food industry awards, a progression of examples of Spurrt bottle designs from early to present-day, one particular bottle that won The International Design Excellence Award 30 years ago and again 25 years ago, and in a smaller display case within the big display case, the 1 Millionth Bottle of Spurrt. In another the 5 Millionth Bottle. In still another the 10 Millionth Bottle. Then the 100 Millionth Bottle. Getting cocky now.

Cox noticed the 100 Millionth Bottle looked like it had been jostled slightly out of place, maybe by vibrations from plant machinery or trucks going by, so he unlocked the big display case and the smaller one and carefully, almost lovingly, replaced the special bottle as Agnes looked on.

"How many people have a key to the display case?" I asked. I don't know why I asked. Maybe it seemed like a good detective-type question. I was starting to get into the role, apparently.

"Just about anybody who wants one," Cox answered to my mild surprise. "Me, Agnes here, the custodial staff, the security guys, Heidi Wilton from Marketing, all the officers including Wash Booker, Mr. Z, Elliot. Maybe Mrs. Z. Probably others. Why?"

"No reason. But I guess now I'm wondering what's the point of keeping it locked."

"Well, if we have a group of school kids touring the plant, for example, we don't want anybody tempted to mischief," he said.

"Do you have school kids touring the plant very often?"

"Never."

"But now that you've brought it up," said Agnes, "it sounds like it might be a good public relations idea. I think I'll mention it to Heidi."

Unfortunately, I probably couldn't get away with charging Fanny Spurr extra for my idea.

I saw portraits of the two Zachariahs looking very paternal, photos of Outstanding Employee Award winners from throughout the years, a small meteorite that landed in the employee parking lot in 1957 (along with a certificate of its authenticity signed by an astronomy professor from NC State), and photos of the five-foot meteorite crater taken from various angles in two of which stood Mr. Z the First holding a shovel.

Fortunately, no one had been hurt. Also on display was the original 48-star American flag that flew over the company's original bottling plant in 1939, the American flag that was flying over the plant on the infamous December 7, 1941, the original 49-star American flag that flew over the current plant from January 1959 with the admission of Alaska to statehood until the admission of Hawaii in August 1959, the first 50-star American flag to fly over the plant, an American flag that had flown over the Capitol Building in Washington, DC, on the 50th anniversary of the groundbreaking for the current plant, donated by a Congressman, photos of the groundbreaking for the current plant in two of which stood both Zachariahs holding shovels, photos of the groundbreaking ceremony for the research laboratory in two of which stood Mr. Z the Second and Elliot Spurr holding shovels, and so on.

Stuff like that. There were no takeout menus.

When the tour ended back at the office area, I thanked both of my guides and said I looked forward to spending more time with them as my project unfolded.

Then I had lunch in the company cafeteria, by invitation this time, with Wash Booker, the sales and marketing VP.

Lunch with Wash Booker was more pleasant than my first encounter with Jim Sullivan. It was interesting too, if not very revealing about what might be going on behind the scenes. He didn't seem to know much about that, but he could have simply been putting on a good poker face, especially since I was still a stranger and an outsider. But he was cordial, and I felt we would get on well. Trouble was, we didn't get to finish our conversation that day.

One of the tightropes you walk in a job like this is winning the confidence of the people you have to rely on for the information needed to get your work done while allaying their fears that you are a spy for the big boss, who in this case was

Fanny Spurr. They were used to working for Mr. Z, and more recently Elliot, but they weren't yet used to reporting to Jim Sullivan, and they'd never known Fanny very well, much less me, so there was an opportunity for double or maybe even triple jeopardy as far as they were concerned. I didn't blame them for being, shall we say, circumspect.

I tried to confine my probing to areas that would seem to fit with my official historian assignment. Mostly.

"You're not from around here, are you?" I opened when Wash Booker and I had settled into our seats in a private corner of the cafeteria. I had chosen a Jell-O fruit salad, chicken and dumplings, a slice of lemon meringue pie and, of course, sweet tea with lemon. Booker had spaghetti, garlic bread and unsweetened tea.

"You've got me there," he said with a grin. "Not many of us here are from Up North, which is pretty obvious. Just Jim Sullivan and me, I think. And now you, of course."

"Jim told me how he got here, but what's your story?" Hoping he would talk so I could dive into my Jell-O salad.

"It all started in a log cabin out behind the manor house on a plantation in Mississippi," he began.

I stared at him.

"Not buying that, are you?" he said.

"No, but I like it. Can I use it in the company history?"

"Better not. Truth is, I'm from Philadelphia, went to Exeter, then Harvard and then back to Philadelphia to get an MBA at Wharton. After Wharton and the Army, I paid my dues in the product management ranks of Procter and Gamble in Cincinnati and then decided to try my wings somewhere else. I spent some time in Atlanta at Coca-Cola. Then, since I do have some roots in the Carolinas, I applied for a sales job here at Spurr five years ago, moved with my family, and worked myself into this position. They didn't have a proper Marketing

Department back then, so I built one. A pretty good one, if I do say so."

"And you do say so."

"Yes, I do. But it's not all peaches and cream." The food reference seemed to remind him he hadn't started on his spaghetti, which he then did.

"I can imagine."

"No, you probably can't. See, I'm not the only black person working here, as you've probably noticed, but I'm by far the most senior."

"That must give you some satisfaction."

"Of course, I'm proud of my accomplishments and grateful to those who've helped me along the way, but it's no bed of roses, believe me."

"I don't understand."

"It's true some of the other black employees look at me as some sort of role model, which is fine if only I can keep living up to it. But others think I've sold out to The Man. To them, I'm not black enough. Most of the white folks don't seem to notice or care one way or the other, but a few don't really know what to make of me. So, it's like Kermit the Frog once said, 'It's not easy being green,' or in my case black. I'm kind of an enigma."

"I was warned not to use that word around you."

"That's why I used it first. Get it out of the way, you know."

"Ever thought about being named president of the company whenever they decide to replace Elliot?"

"Ha! You know I'm probably *too* black for that!"

"I'll withhold judgement on that if you don't mind."

"Fair enough."

"Switching from beds of roses and peaches and cream, if it's okay, tell me about the marketing business."

"Some people don't really understand what Spurrt is all about. They think it's an ordinary soft drink, like Coke or

Cheerwine. But it's much more than a refreshing jolt of sugar and caffeine. It has other ingredients. Nutritional ingredients, as the name 'Spurr Nutritionals' implies. And that's our edge if we can get people to see the benefits. It's got some actual fruit and vegetable juices in it, and it provides all the body's daily requirements of most key vitamins and minerals. Plus, because of the sugar and caffeine, it can indeed have the effect of a quick "pick me up" if you drink it between meals. In fact, it was originally called Spurr's Restorative."

"Agnes told me."

"Right. So, category-wise it blurs the line between soft drink and energy drink, which sometimes confuses the trade— meaning the retailers, the stores that sell our products. Energy drinks are becoming a bigger and bigger business in this country, and we want Spurrt to be in both camps."

A few more bites of his spaghetti and a big sip of tea.

"Of course it still has to be fizzy and taste good with no unpleasant aftertaste," Booker continued, "so we work on that very hard. Old Mr. Z the First got it pretty much right with his original mix, but over the years we've tweaked the formulas here and there to keep up with modern tastes. Sometimes we tell people we've tweaked it—you know, 'New and Improved!' —and sometimes it's too subtle for that so we just roll it out quietly and don't say anything."

"You said formulas, with an 's,'" I said. Which was hard because I had a mouthful of dumpling and had to take care not to spit any of it out with my sibilants.

"You want me to say 'formulae,' like in Latin? Maybe I went to Harvard, but we don't do Latin here."

"Ha ha. No, I meant you used the plural, so what different formulas do you have?"

I knew about regular Spurrt and Spurrt Lyte, but I hadn't paid much attention to any other varieties yet.

"Sad to say, right now we only have regular Spurrt and Spurrt Lyte. Mr. Z the Second always thought that was enough. Fortunately, I was able to convince Elliot we need more than that, and last year he finally gave us the go-ahead to beef up the Research and Development department, which reports to Wendell Cox, and start working on some new products. Not only more varieties of Spurrt, but also other nutritional products in keeping with our core values and brand image."

"Such as …?"

"Can't divulge that just yet, I'm afraid. It's not yet part of the company history, so you, my friend, don't need to know." Booker said it with a wink, but I got the point.

"That's when we built the research lab and moved R&D out of the plant and into their own place, properly equipped," Booker continued. "Per Jim Sullivan's wishes we skimped on the cost of the building and went with a pre-fab metal thing, but the equipment was state of the art for food companies."

"I guess the explosion was quite a setback," I said.

"Well, yes, but we'll recover."

"What about international expansion?" I ventured.

"That's a different story," Booker said. "It's been tough. You're basically shipping water, which is heavy and expensive to ship, so once you've exported it you have to charge high prices for it, which puts you at a disadvantage against local brands."

"But what if you build plants in other countries and source the raw materials there?"

"Now you're talking like a businessman instead of a writer."

"I was, once."

"Well, I meant it's a good idea. I'd like us to do that, but Sullivan … I mean Jim … says we can't afford to make the investment. We could start in Mexico, for Pete's sake. It wouldn't be that difficult, and it wouldn't take a whole lot of capital.

Licensing somebody already in the business there might work too and wouldn't call for a big investment, but then we'd have to divulge our *formulae*, and we don't ever want to do that."

"I see." A sip of my iced tea.

"Or we could ship it as a dehydrated syrup, like Coca-Cola does, and license bottlers to reconstitute it and distribute it. Sort of a compromise, but the issue there is the formula is much more complex than Coke's, and quality control would be a major headache.

"But we'll figure it out, and Jim will eventually come around. Now what I'd really love to do is get us into Japan. The market for energy drinks is crazy big there and growing. Problem is, the *keiretsu*, or cartels, keep out foreign competition. The best way to get in is to acquire one of their companies, but none of them is about to sell out to an American company. Another way is to let one of them buy us out, and Mr. Z and Mrs. Spurr are having none of that, and I kind of agree with them. Have you heard of Kashimoto Foods?"

"No, I haven't." Mrs. Spurr had told me a Japanese company had made numerous overtures, but she never mentioned Kashimoto by name, which I now thought was odd.

"Giant company in Japan. They've been pestering us for years to let them acquire us, but we've always said no. Lately, they've been even more insistent, especially since Mr. Z's accident for some reason, and now Elliot's death. They probably think we're more vulnerable now, and frankly I'm concerned they might finally make Mrs. Spurr an offer she can't refuse."

Booker was closer to being right than he realized. I had the impression he wasn't fully aware of the company's dire financial condition. It wasn't my job to tell him.

Just then we both noticed a commotion over by the cash registers near the cafeteria entrance. A man in a tailored tan uniform was standing there, and the cashiers were pointing in our direction. The man strode over to our table. It was Sheriff Belton.

"Afternoon, Mr. Booker. Mr. Fairley," he said.

"Sheriff." Booker.

"Sheriff." Me.

"Thought I might find you here," Belton said, now looking only at me, "especially since when I asked at the office they told me you'd be having lunch."

"It's a pleasure to see you, as always," I ventured. I assumed this visit had something to do with this morning's incident at the speed trap, which I had almost forgotten about. "I gather you and Mr. Booker already know each other."

"We got acquainted a few months ago down at the, uh, traffic stop," said Booker. "Naturally, I think he was profiling me."

"You got that right," retorted Belton. "Looked like the perfect profile of a speeder to me. Besides, my little radar gun is 'no respecter of persons,' as it says in the Bible."

"He's right," said Booker, turning to me with a grin, "I *was* speeding. But I learned my lesson, and I've been an honest man since then."

That settled, Belton turned to me. "I'm guessing you probably know why I'm here," he said.

Wash Booker got up as if to leave.

"Looks like you two have things to discuss," Booker said. "I've got another meeting, so I'll take my leave if you don't mind."

"Of course," I said. "Thanks for our conversation; it was very helpful."

"Anytime." He left. I hadn't even started on my pie.

Belton dropped into Booker's seat.

"Who was that fellow in the little red car you were travelling with this morning?"

123

"I'll assume that's a rhetorical question since I saw you stop him. And I was not 'travelling with him.'"

"No need to take offense. Yeah, I stopped him all right. Turned out to be another stranger. Japanese this time. Claimed he didn't know you."

"Maybe not, and I definitely don't know him! But he was following me. Suspiciously, I thought."

I described my highway encounter with the stranger, but Belton didn't seem impressed.

"Who is he anyway" I finally asked.

Belton took a small notebook out of his shirt pocket. "Name's Tadashi Tanaka. From Japan, like I said. License and registration were in order. And his student ID from UNC-Chapel Hill and his passport. Couldn't hold him."

"What do you mean, 'couldn't hold him'? You didn't give him a ticket?"

"Well, turns out he's a friend of Trey Spurr. You know, Elliot Spurr's son who's also a student over there?"

"So?"

"I called young Mr. Spurr from the spee- I mean the traffic stop, and he confirmed it. Plus, Mr. Tanaka apologized real nicely and said he still wasn't used to driving on the right side of the road. Seems in his country they drive on the left, although how they can manage that is beyond me."

"Couldn't you *see* he was following me? Very closely?"

"Mr. Fairley, what I saw was two speeders, one behind the other. Just me by my lonesome there so I couldn't stop the both of you safely now could I? And, as everyone knows, the cops' golden rule about speeders is we always stop the red cars first."

A little sheriff humor?

"Besides, I knew it was you in the first car, and I knew where I could probably find you later so we could have a conversation. And now I have."

He looked pleased with himself. I was seething.

"You didn't let *me* off when I told you I had an appointment with Mrs. Spurr."

"Well, you weren't a friend of hers, not then anyway. And you're not from around here."

"And a Japanese guy is?"

"He's a friend of the family, like I said, and an honest-to-goodness foreigner too, not just somebody from Up North. Besides, I suppose young Mr. Spurr could use all the friends he can get, being an orphan and all."

"Especially a Japanese friend?"

"Widens his horizons, don't you think? Anyway, it seems neighborly to cut foreigners some slack."

Slack is right, I thought to myself.

"Like why you've never questioned the two Chinese-looking men you've seen around town? Was this guy one of them?"

"No, I'd never seen him before."

"Have you seen those other two around lately?"

"Not for a while now, no. But I am thinking I might just strike up a conversation if I do see them again."

"Maybe they're all working together," I ventured.

"Maybe, but what at?" said Belton.

That was a tough one. All I could think to say was, "Well, uh, skulking and speeding, for one thing. Or two things." But it didn't sound like the stuff of conspiracy to me and probably wouldn't to the sheriff either, so I didn't say it.

"Well, what about the other two, the Americans you said were obviously from out of state?"

"Haven't seen them lately either, but Clara over at the Set-A-Spell says two strangers came in for lunch yesterday. Not the first time. Told her to call me if they show up again. She remembers you too. Liked you. Can't quite see why."

More sheriff talk. I didn't take it personally.

"Said two Chinese guys were in there too, about a week ago, and you fished out some menus they left after she tossed them in the dumpster. Why would you do that, Mr. Fairley?"

I told Belton what I'd told Clara Fritts: "Believe it or not, I get to Raleigh from time to time, and I'm curious what restaurant thinks it's so good people would come all the way from Spurrville to eat there."

"Mr. Fairley, I'm not buying that. I think there's something up and you're right in the middle of it. If there's something up in my county, and especially if it has to do with the Spurr family, which this seems to, I need to know about it."

Then he just looked at me. It was my turn to talk. He wasn't going anywhere. Offering him my pie wasn't going to make him leave either.

Sheriff Belton might have his limitations, and his world view was parochial, but he was a loyal man, and I believed he was honest and trustworthy, especially since Fanny Spurr had vouched for him on that score, so I decided to trust him. I didn't know what was going on either, and maybe he could help somehow. I already had two police departments involved in this, so why not a third? And what choice did I have anyway?

"Sheriff Belton, do you have time for a story?"

"I love stories."

He sat back in his chair and eyed my pie, which I shoved over to him with a clean fork and napkin while I told him about the oriental-looking strangers at the Neighborhood Watch meeting, the break-in at my house, the missing copies of Mr. Z's notes, the General Tso's Golden Chicken Pagoda takeout menus found at the church and the Set-A-Spell with no helpful fingerprints, this morning being followed by a new Japanese guy, and so on. All of it except my ulterior assignment for Mrs. Spurr and the "Don't sell" message on one of Mr. Z's notes.

126

"I don't know what it is, but I agree something's not right here," is what I ended with.

"Mr. Fairley, I know you're a writer and all, but I think you're letting your imagination run away with you here. Besides, don't you think you might be harboring just a little racism?"

"Harboring" was not a word I would have expected from Belton, but I let it pass. Racism? I couldn't counter with "Of course not; some of my best friends are Chinese" since I didn't actually know any.

"You're right. I'm probably just imagining things. You did say you'd speak to the four strangers if you see them again, so I'll leave the conspiracy investigation in your capable hands."

"No need for sarcasm, sir." He napkined some of my meringue from his mustache. But not all of it, unfortunately.

"None intended. I appreciate your letting me know about Mr. Tanaka. And thanks again for not stopping me this morning."

"Oh, I am giving you another ticket though. Here it is. You can just mail it in, like before."

I hadn't yet.

"And thanks for the pie."

Chapter 19

By 2:00 p.m. I was at the door, or what was left of it, of the research laboratory where Elliot Spurr had met his unfortunate end not many weeks ago. For some reason they had not yet started on clean up and repairs, but there was a selection of garden rakes, brooms and other cleaning tools nearby. I assumed insurance would pay for rebuilding, but I made a mental note to ask Sullivan about it.

I was accompanied once again by the manufacturing VP, Wendell Cox. Poor Agnes Smith was understandably still too overwrought to visit the lab just yet, so history-writing-wise it was up to me. Cox didn't seem too keen to show me around either, maybe out of respect for Elliot or maybe because the place had a dismal feel to it, but I needed to see for myself if I could deduce anything from the state of the ruins. I have no idea why I thought I could do that, nor did I have any idea what I was looking for, but a detective has to start somewhere and be willing to get his hands dirty, and this seemed a likely place.

Hands-dirty-wise I had dodged a bullet at the Set-A-Spell dumpster, but with all the soot here in the lab it didn't look like I would get off so easy this time.

"I realize this can't be left out of the company history you're working on," said Cox before we went in, "but I hope you'll be discreet."

I assured him I would be.

Cox was a rugged-looking man, heavy-set without being

fat. He was a no nonsense type guy who'd been a master sergeant in the Marine Corps and served tours in Iraq and Afghanistan before going to NC State on the Post 9-11 GI Bill and starting at Spurr as a machinist in the packaging department. It hadn't taken him long to become plant manager owing to his self-confidence, work ethic, problem-solving skills and ability to learn quickly. He still had his military bearing, and people skills weren't his strong suit, but he was apparently admired, respected and trusted. He was pleasant to me, but there was no question who was in charge as we worked together. When later I asked him about his work philosophy as plant manager, he answered quickly: "It's very simple. Wash Booker comes up with the sales forecast, Jim Sullivan approves it and tells me what to make and how much, and that's what we do."

The laboratory was housed in a small, free-standing outbuilding behind the main plant and alongside one edge of the employee parking lot. A construction-size dumpster sat in one of the parking spaces, presumably awaiting the cleanup. The lab was out of sight from the road but easy enough to get to. As Wash Booker said, it was a steel prefab thing that looked like it was built from a kit and almost meant to disintegrate if there were an explosion, the way NASCAR cars are designed, supposedly for safety reasons, to fly apart in collisions, much to the delight of fans who have paid good money and waited hours through beer-soaked tailgate parties to get into the stands hoping to see just that. It didn't engender confidence in the company's commitment to new product research, which I guess is what Wash Booker was complaining about, but the equipment was state of the art, and at least the building was built even if it did stretch the already thin finances. And disintegrate it did.

Though I was only wearing my old Bally loafers that had

seen better days, Cox had on a nice pair of wingtips, so we donned blue paper booties to protect our shoes and gingerly stepped across the threshold into what looked to have been a tiny reception area, and that's where I got my first surprise. There were a half dozen partially charred General Tso's Golden Chicken Pagoda takeout menus lying on what was left of a coffee table. I asked Cox if I could take them. He eyed me suspiciously for a second before saying, "Sure, why not?" as if I were from outer space. I would pick them up on the way out, dust them off, put them in my briefcase, currently locked and secured in the trunk of my car, and then give them to Detective Blue as soon as I got back to Greensboro. I didn't tell Cox any of that.

The more serious damage could be seen as soon as we entered the lab itself. Not much was recognizable because of the fire that followed the gas explosion. Charred, splintered furniture and scientific apparatus were strewn around like a king-size game of pick-up sticks gone haywire. I saw what looked to be the remains of a couple of cases of Spurrt and at least one case of Spurrt Lyte, but it was impossible to tell what Elliot might have been doing with them, if anything, or with anything else. Although a steel building is theoretically fireproof even if it does fly apart at the seams when provoked, its contents are not, and what with all the flammable furnishings and equipment, not to mention who knows what kind of chemicals might have been stored there, it was a disaster waiting to happen and did. It looked like about the only thing that survived was a large, red Kidde fire extinguisher lying impotently intact in what used to be a corner.

"Should we be wearing face masks in here?" I asked.

"No, sir, the volunteer firemen hosed the place down pretty well so there shouldn't be too much dust and soot in the air. Unless we stir it up. We're not going to do that."

"No, we're not. Sorry, but I have to ask, how exactly did Elliot Spurr die?"

"Overpressure from the gas explosion," said Cox. "We first thought it might have been smoke inhalation or that he burned to death, but the medical examiner said it was the force of the blast itself, before the fire got going. From his body position they think he was thrown from that cot over there so they're pretty sure he was asleep when it happened. It was three in the morning, and it woke everybody up as far away as town. It was loud. The ME said he died instantly, so he didn't suffer, thank God."

I couldn't make out anything that still resembled a cot, but I didn't say anything as Cox went on.

"The fire marshal said it looked like the gas had built up for a long time and was ignited by a spark from an egg timer. Mr. Spurr might have had it set to wake him up at a certain time, like maybe at some point during an experiment. We have no idea what the experiment might have been."

"And the egg timer?"

"What about it?"

"Where is it?"

"Insurance company took it. I guess they needed something to go on, but they and the fire marshal and Sheriff Belton never did figure out what caused the gas leak in the first place. No way to blame it on somebody or something. Negligence somewhere though, if you ask me."

I agreed. It didn't make sense.

"What kind of security system did this place have?" I asked.

"No surveillance cameras, if that's what you mean. They were installed, but they weren't working yet. Some kind of software problem, and we were waiting on the manufacturer to send somebody around to fix it. So it was just a night watchman who was somewhere else on his rounds when this happened, as verified by our old watchclock system. Otherwise, just smoke detectors that didn't help because there was no smoke until the explosion occurred, and an intruder alarm system like you probably have at home, which would have been turned off while Elliot was in the building. That'll probably change now."

"Mind if I poke around a little?" Time to get my hands dirty, and something on the ground had attracted my attention. I was about to get my second surprise.

"I guess so. Just, you know, don't stir things up too much."

I bent down for a closer look. It was almost totally buried under the rubble, but I could tell it was metal, and it looked like it had once been shiny. I picked it up. It had some heft to it. Solid construction, whatever it was. It resembled a small faucet. If it had once been attached to something, it had clearly been blown off in the explosion.

"Do you know what this is?" I asked Cox.

He studied it.

"Looks like a faucet or spigot to me," he said.

It was looking more and more like a nozzle of some kind to me, not so much a faucet, and it was serrated and had a handle with a blue plastic button of some kind on top, like it might have been labeled "hot" or "cold"—probably "cold" since it was blue.

"No, wait," said Cox. "It's a gas jet—I should know since I supervised installing all the equipment in here. You know, like from chemistry class? You probably used one with a Bunsen burner when you were in school."

"Whoa! Let's see."

I rubbed the blue button clean with my thumb. Sure enough, it said "GAS."

"Do you think this one is turned on or off?" I said.

"Let me see."

He took it and cleaned the rest of it off as best he could with a handkerchief.

"Well?"

"You know what?" said Cox, "I think it's in the 'on' position. See, the handle is in line with the nozzle, which usually means 'on.' 'Off' would be the handle at a 90-degree angle to the nozzle."

"Can you be sure?"

"I think so. I hate to do this, but if I blow through the nozzle with the handle lined up like it is, air should go right through to the back end, which would normally connect to the input from the gas line."

He screwed up his nose, placed the nozzle between his lips, and blew gently. Soot came flying out the back end. Then he turned the handle perpendicular to the nozzle and blew again. Nothing.

"It was open," he said, looking at me with growing concern. "What do you think it means?"

"I'm not sure yet," I said, even though I was indeed pretty sure. "Let's see if we can find any more of these."

Cox went outside and came back with a couple of rakes and two pairs of work gloves, which we put on. We raised some dust as we worked, but it was unavoidable, and when we finished we had turned up five more gas jets identical to the first one and all in the "on" position.

"I'm not sure what we should do now," I said, even though I was dead certain, but I was hoping Cox would take the initiative since this was his territory.

"Well I sure do," he said, pulling out his smartphone. "I'm calling Sheriff Belton."

It took Belton only six minutes to get there—I timed it—and he did it without the blue light and siren. I had to give him credit. Why alarm the whole plant?

He strode into the ruins without bothering to put on booties, gave me a perfunctory nod, and listened to what Wendell Cox had to say while I nodded in appropriate places.

Belton put the gas jets into individual plastic evidence bags, labeling each one with a felt marker.

"Might be fingerprints on these," he said authoritatively. "Besides yours, I mean."

"Now what, Sheriff?" said Cox.

"Now I call in the SBI."

Pulling out his own smartphone, that's what he did. SBI stands for State Bureau of Investigation, North Carolina's version of the FBI. These are the big guys in North Carolina law enforcement and forensic investigations, and again I had to hand it to Belton. No petty territorialism with him.

Finally, he turned his full attention to me for the first time since arriving.

"You can't just wander around in here anymore, Mr. Fairley," he said. "As of now this is a crime scene."

Never mind a "Thanks so much for coming up with this critical evidence the rest of us missed the first time around in our hurry to bring closure to the case."

Probably a knee jerk reaction and a mistake on my part, and maybe even unlawful, but I didn't mention the takeout menus to Belton, and he didn't see me grab them on my way out. Cox stayed behind with Belton awaiting the arrival of the SBI, and I hoped he had forgotten about them. I went home. Still wearing my blue paper booties.

Chapter 20

Now I *really* wanted to know what on earth had I gotten myself into. Strange Japanese or Chinese, or whatever they were, men skulking about, a landscape littered with takeout menus from a Raleigh restaurant with a ridiculous name, disagreements over the marketing strategy of a big company whose bankruptcy seemed imminent, and now not one but two speeding tickets. A strange phone call from an apparently retro gas station. These were on a level of risk and intrigue I could handle.

Having my house broken into and papers stolen from my briefcase, being followed dangerously closely by a nut in a red car who may or may not have been staking out my house too, and especially discovering Elliot Spurr may have been murdered put things into a whole different category. Was I in danger from people who wished me harm or just in danger of being an innocent bystander to mayhem? And if I, then what about Emily? Or even our children?

Who else was in danger? Fanny Spurr? Jim Sullivan, ostensibly next in line to be president of Spurr Nutritionals? And who was perpetrating the mayhem, and why? Wash Booker, jealous over not being considered for promotion? Kashimoto Foods, frustrated in their desire to buy Spurr Nutritionals? Or somebody else lurking out there, perpetrating mischief with who knows what motive?

Emily was not happy.

Should I get a gun? I could probably get a handgun permit

in about three weeks that would let me buy a pistol I could keep at home or take to a firing range. But that would only cover us if somebody broke in while Emily and I were in the house—a possibility. Or attacked me at the firing range—less likely, but still … But it wouldn't provide protection for me on the road. For that, I would need a concealed carry permit, an option with much more flexibility but which would take months to get. North Carolina requires you to qualify on a range, take an all-day class and fill out an application that starts your county sheriff on a 90-day background check process *after* you appear at the sheriff's office by appointment to get your application notarized. I looked into it, and in Guilford county where I live the classes were booked up two months out, and appointments with the sheriff were another two months out, so altogether it would have taken me over half a year to get a gun. And it wouldn't make Emily feel any better. Maybe worse. By then I figured this assignment would be over with anyway, one way or another. Getting a gun illegally by some sort of shortcut was out of the question.

Friday morning, with Emily's reluctant approval, I drove back to Spurrville hoping to spend some quiet time in the little office Agnes Smith provided for me where I could actually begin writing the company history with Jim Sullivan's financial information and Agnes' notes and scrapbooks in hand.

It proved impossible. Talk in the office was only about the SBI visit and the rumor they had discovered Elliot Spurr was murdered, although no one actually knew exactly what the SBI might have uncovered that would lead them to that conclusion. Wendell Cox wasn't talking, having been sworn to secrecy by the sheriff. Belton wasn't talking to anybody but the SBI and Fanny Spurr. Certainly not to the media, although he and "unnamed sources close to Sheriff Cecil Belton" were "quoted" frequently in the feverish wall-to-wall coverage that was on every TV channel. I hadn't been sworn to secrecy, but I wasn't about to talk either, and since nobody knew I'd been at the lab yesterday except Emily, Belton, Cox and maybe Agnes, who was distraught but discreet, nobody asked me anything. I think I'd mentioned my afternoon plans to Wash Booker too, before we were interrupted by Sheriff Belton, but he was equally discreet, which I appreciated.

No work was getting done. None. Nobody in the office could talk of anything else. Phones went unanswered. The plant shut down for the day. No deliveries were accepted. Little groups gathered around the water coolers and in the break areas. Many people simply went home after a few hours. Even Lonnie the gatehouse guard left his post, which was unprecedented. I decided to drive around town, see some areas I'd not toured before and maybe have lunch at the Set-A-Spell to find out if Clara Fritts had any genuine wisdom to shed on the situation. It turned out she didn't, but I saw and heard a lot anyway.

One of the strangest sights, which had nothing to do with possible murder in the research lab, was a sign in the yard of a private home in a small neighborhood not far from downtown. "Deputy P.D. Rivers for Sheriff," it said simply. I'd definitely have to ask Sheriff Belton about that.

The town of Spurrville was in an uproar. In fact, the whole county was, and the Raleigh media were feasting on it, so at least some people were happy. There had not been a murder in Spurrville since … well, since ever. It was unheard of. Nobody knew what to think. If you looked a certain way at the statue of old Earnest K. Lester, the town's founder and Civil War hero on his high horse in the town square, you could imagine him either girded for revenge or saddened beyond tears. Or both in turns. But revenge against whom? Nobody knew yet. There was only speculation.

"Are they sure it was murder? Not suicide?"

True, there hadn't been a suicide in Lester County since forever either, and "Elliot Spurr had so much to live for," including taking care of his son, Trey, off at college, so taking his own life didn't seem likely. It was back to murder.

"But who would do such a thing?"

"Somebody from Up North, probably. Somebody just passing through."

"Blow up a building in the middle of the night just to kill somebody you don't know? And there was nothing missing, according to the news, so it wasn't robbery."

"Maybe it was somebody he did know. From his past."

"He'd never been anywhere besides the beach, Chapel Hill and Winston-Salem except when he took Lucy on that cruise to … where was it again? Alaska?"

"The Bahamas."

"No, it was Bermuda."

"Who cares? He surely didn't pick up any enemies on the cruise."

"How can you know that?"

"Oh, shut up!"

"Don't you tell me to shut up! You got any better ideas?"

And so the prevailing theory by in-the-know wannabes was that Elliot had been murdered by an old enemy from a cruise ship, passing through Spurrville in the night, who happened to find him asleep in the lab and finished him off, leaving no trace. The media ran with it.

If nothing else, it took the spotlight off crime in Durham for a while. I'm sure the criminals cut back on their nefarious activities when they realized they weren't getting their usual media coverage.

The weekend was ahead, and I decided I should go back home and avoid the Spurrville circus for a few days, so I called

Mrs. Spurr, expressed my condolences as best I could, and told her I didn't want to add to the confusion by coming back there right away and that I'd continue working on the case from other angles. Besides, it was time to plan a trip to Chapel Hill and Durham to meet Trey and Adam if they were available. And maybe a side trip to Raleigh to have a look at General Tso's myself, although I didn't tell Emily that.

Mrs. Spurr understood and was gracious as always. I was ready to give her a brief summary of my work and findings so far—though they didn't add up to a whole lot other than the obvious discovery at the lab—but I sensed she wasn't up to it just then. I could only imagine the strain she was under now and what must be Mr. Z's mounting frustration at being unable to communicate his thoughts about these new developments. We could schedule another Florida room meeting at her convenience later.

She did mention one other development, however. Two men had shown up at her door that day claiming to represent Kashimoto Foods, the Japanese company Wash Booker told me had been trying to acquire Spurr Nutritionals for years. It was the first time she had mentioned the Japanese company by name to me.

"Were they Japanese?" I asked.

"No, they were definitely Americans. New Yorkers from their accents. I had never seen these two before. A Mr. Wright and a Mr. Johnson, if I remember correctly. They said they were authorized to make an offer for the company that was far better than anything Kashimoto had offered before. It made me angry, Mark. How insensitive! Today of all days. I am afraid I was rather rude to them and told them if they did not leave immediately I would call Sheriff Belton."

"Did they leave?"

"Yes, they did, but they looked confused, bless their hearts, almost as if they were surprised by my reaction."

"Well, it's possible they really didn't know what was going on here today."

"Perhaps. Do you think I was too harsh?"

"No, ma'am, I don't. Good riddance to them," I said.

It seemed to me the worst that could happen, assuming these guys or Kashimoto weren't behind Elliot Spurr's apparent murder (but who could be sure?), was they'd come back later with an even better offer. I didn't say that to Mrs. Spurr.

After that, I called Emily to let her know I was coming home early so she could warn her boyfriend not to be there when I arrived (our little joke). She told me Detective Blue had called and was especially interested in the partially charred menus and my story of what I found in the ruins of the lab. He would run these new menus for fingerprints. No word had come yet from the Raleigh detective sent to check out General Tso's.

Because I had the time, there was one other stop I wanted to make on my way out of town. The speed trap. As a guest this time, not a customer.

In my travels around Spurrville and vicinity, I had noticed several signs and billboards saying, "Buckle Up and Re-elect Sheriff C.D. 'Seedy' Belton. He's got no time for crime." It wasn't an election year.

The sheriff was dutifully manning his position, radar gun in hand, when I pulled up behind the old Caprice. Its antennas were swaying only a little due to a slight breeze. A colorful "News 16" van with a big satellite dish on top was just pulling away as I got out of my car and walked over to his.

"Well now, Mr. Fairley, to what do I owe the pleasure of your interfering with police business?"

I presumed he was joking again.

"I just want to get better acquainted, seeing as how you're a figure of major importance in these parts and might be an important figure in my own investigations. For the company history and all, you know."

"No sense trying that TV folksy stuff with me, unless you're kidding of course. I can take a joke now and then, you know. But I warn you, I'm tired. Spent the rest of yesterday and most of this morning with the SBI people. Draining."

I had to hand it to him yet again. He seemed to be the only person in town who wasn't apoplectic over the murder rumors. Above the madding crowd for sure.

"I can imagine. I guess you know the whole county is in an uproar."

I like that word a lot. Uproar.

"Let 'em enjoy themselves. Keeps them out of my hair. Except the reporters, of course, but I know how to discourage them."

"Does that mean you just gave that van a ticket?"

"Yep. Now what is it you need? I can give you a little time since you're now a friend of Mrs. Spurr's."

"Just a few questions, if you don't mind," I said. "Let me start with an easy one. Why do they call you 'Seedy'?"

"Most folks think it comes from my initials, C.D., for Cecil Dwayne. But really it's a nickname from school days. Kids started calling me 'Seat,' like for 'seat belt on,' get it? Belton, belt-on?"

"I get it."

"You know how kids can be. Mean sometimes. Eventually, it went to 'Seaty' and then turned into 'Seedy,' and that's what stuck. A few of those kids went home with bloody noses at first, but then I sort of got used to it. Maybe even a little proud of it. Until I found out what 'seedy' means. Still, it's served me well, especially at election time. Good for name recognition and all. And if people think it comes from 'C.D.,' well that's okay too."

"But it's not election time and there's nobody running against you. Never has been, according to what I've heard."

"Could happen someday. You never know. And if you get caught in my speed trap without your seat *belt on*, you're in double trouble!"

"I take it those campaign signs I've seen all over are permanent."

"Yep."

"Wait, I take back what I just said about you running unopposed. I did see one sign for somebody else. 'P.D. Rivers for Sheriff'?"

"Oh, that's just little PeeDee, one of my deputies. He thinks I don't know about the sign. That's his own front yard that it's in. He's not *really* running against me. Not enough backbone, that man, though he's competent enough as a deputy. I think he's testing it out to see what it feels like. He's not an official candidate for anything, according to the County Board of Elections, which is mainly Clara Fritts and a few of her friends.

"Seems like things are pretty tight-knit around here," I said.

"And going to stay that way too, friend. We're a very small county, Mr. Fairley. Small budget too. I've only got two deputies, including ol' PeeDee there, and they're part-time on call and only come in when I need them. Plus, I do have a dispatcher who works days at the office and another one who works nights from home. The day girl doubles as a secretary and filing clerk, and she handles all the background checks for gun permits. Of course, that part doesn't keep her too busy since most everybody in Lester County already has a gun."

"Is the small budget why you're still driving around in this old Caprice?"

"Nooo, I love this car. Old Betsy. She's seen me through thick and thin. When the bad guys see Seedy Belton driving Old Betsy with the blue lights on, they *know*, you know?

144

People think twice before they cross the line in Lester County."

I didn't want to remind him one could certainly take that literally.

"My deputies have a new Dodge Charger with all the latest fancy cop stuff," he went on, "but they have to share it or use their personal cars because of the budget. Why am I explaining all this to you, anyway?"

"Because you are a courteous and considerate man, Sheriff. But why 'Betsy'?"

"Short for Elizabeth."

"Right. So?"

"So I just like the name, that's all. And when I hear Mrs. Spurr say 'Heavens to Betsy,' which she does a lot, it's sort of like she's giving me and my car a blessing, you know?"

Chapter 21

DURHAM, N.C. (UP)—Duke University officials say student protesters are occupying a reception area near the school president's office for a fourth day.

School spokesperson Randall McCrae said the protesters were still sitting in near President Arthur Willoughby's office in the iconic Allen Building which houses the school's administrative functions and which is closed for a third day. Officials say ten students are involved in the sit-in. The students want the school to abandon its traditional "Duke blue" school color for something "less offensive," or alternatively they want at least two other colors added in order to promote "diversity and inclusiveness," and they want three administrators fired for "disrespecting" a petition to that effect signed by six other students out of the school's total population of approximately 15,000.

Sophomore Miranda Melenkampf, a spokesperson for the protesters, told reporters at a hastily-called press conference, "We object to blue because one color all by itself is not inclusive, and that might offend someone, especially anyone who doesn't like blue. Also, blue is traditionally associated with sadness, and we don't want anybody to feel sad or 'less than' because of it being forced upon them against their will. On that score, we are pro-choice. Although many people think blue is a soothing color, it represents bad luck, pain and mourning in China and India, and we don't want to offend any of our Chinese or Indian brothers and sisters. Also, blue, albeit a different shade, is the color used by UNC-Chapel Hill, and we hate them. Furthermore, we think 'Blue Suede Shoes' by Elvis Presley is a stupid song."

During the press conference, the protesters displayed signs with slogans such as: "No More Blue!" "Blue? BOO!" "Ditch Blue or We Sue!" "When God Made the Rainbow She Didn't Stop with Blue!" "Other Colors Matter!" "Outrage 'R' Us" and "We Demand Inclusiveness" "And Diversity!" the latter slogan requiring two signs held side by side, one of which was briefly displayed upside down before being called to the student's attention by a reporter.

Asked what other colors might be added if blue is retained, Ms. Melenkampf said the protesters will solicit recommendations from the whole student body and then hold a vote. "It should be determined by a fair and democratic process. But we favor magenta and lime green at this time, and maybe off-white, for reasons we will make clear as soon as we reach agreement on them among ourselves. Personally, I like magenta, and I'm the leader."

"Also," said Ms. Melenkampf, "we demand that during Exam Week the university supply all students, free of charge, with sugary, caffeine-laden soft drinks like Coca-Cola, Pepsi and Mountain Dew so we can pull all-nighters and be fresh and ready to take tests the next day. But not Cheerwine or Spurrt because those are local North Carolina products and therefore presumed to be not inclusive enough."

In addition, they want a $15 minimum wage for all student protesters.

The students say their sit-in will continue until their demands are met. "The reason we're being listened to is because we're loud, we're visible and we're here," sophomore Algernon Wu told the assembled protestors and reporters. "In other words, obnoxious. We're going to stay that way."

Talks between the sit-in participants—who have spent three nights sleeping in Allen or in tents erected near the front door—and administrators were conducted throughout the weekend and will resume tomorrow morning at 11 a.m., giving the protesters time to sleep in, another of their demands. Once that meeting has been held, Duke officials say they'll continue to negotiate with students only after they leave voluntarily.

"They don't scare me," said junior Rhoada Beatwix, one of the students in the building, earlier Sunday. "They're going to have to come in and physically arrest me."

"Or we could just expel each and every one of the little punks and then go clean house in the Admissions Department," said President Willoughby, who asked not to be quoted.

Chapter 22

Monday came soon enough. It was time to get acquainted with the two family members I hadn't met: (1) Trey Spurr, son of the late Elliot and a student at UNC, from whom I might learn something about his errant Japanese friend Tanaka if nothing else, and (2) Dr. Adam Spurr, Elliot's younger brother now teaching chemistry at Duke and, according to his mother, having no interest in the Spurr Nutritionals business. Or "no calling for the business"—isn't that how Fanny Spurr had put it? Something like that. I'd have to check my notes from our meeting in her Florida room, a place that was so far turning out to be literally the only bright spot in this whole case. (I'd gotten used to calling it a case by now.) Assuming those notes too hadn't been stolen from my briefcase while I was having lunch somewhere.

The Chemistry Department at Duke University is in the French Family Science Center (FFSC), which according to the university's website is a relatively new 275,000 sq. ft. state of the art research facility that was partially funded by a $30 million gift from the Bill and Melinda Gates Foundation. It's on the so-called West Campus and is within sight of and an easy walk to the famous and iconic Duke University Chapel and Bell Tower. Cameron Indoor Stadium (home of the Duke Blue Devils and "the crown jewel of college basketball's classic venues," per the website) and the Duke Basketball Museum and Sports Hall of Fame are also on the West Campus but some distance away, so I didn't have any expectation of spotting legendary Coach Mike Krzyzewski during my short visit to see Adam Spurr.

The equally iconic Allen Building, housing the administrative offices and the site of almost non-stop student protests over one thing or another, is only a few steps beyond the Chapel and was currently inaccessible owing to an impromptu tent city sit-in and barricades of sofas and end tables hauled from dorm rooms and lounges by rival dissident student groups elbowing one another for positions around the building from which to publicize their various causes. Adam Spurr later told me there was a sign-up sheet in the Allen Building where student protesters could reserve positions and times for their demonstrations, but the students weren't presently allowing each other access to it.

Fortunately for me, Adam's office was in the French Center with most of the other Chemistry professors. There were several Visitor parking spaces open in front of French, so I didn't have to spend the morning driving around the campus looking for one that didn't require some kind of permit sticker, as is the case at so many colleges.

There wasn't time to notice whether there were any takeout menus lying around in the lobby before Adam, an average-size, pleasant-looking man with slightly graying hair, a mustache and a small goatee, greeted me warmly and walked me to the faculty lounge.

"We can get some coffee in here first, and maybe a Danish if the TAs haven't already cleaned them out," he said.

I noticed a slight family resemblance, except for the facial hair of course, but there seemed to be a bit of an edge to him that Fanny Spurr hadn't displayed, at least not in my presence. He was cordial, but somewhat reserved and tentative, almost as if he were anticipating something he wasn't looking forward to.

When I called him over the weekend to set up our meeting,

he seemed surprisingly receptive. I hoped his attitude hadn't changed.

There were several takeout menus in the faculty lounge, but I didn't see any from General Tso's.

"I'm not sure what to call you," I began as we found chairs in his cramped office, books and papers stacked here and there like so much academic cordwood. Magazines too. *Chemistry Spectrum*, *Chemistry World*, *Journal of Analytical Chemistry*, *Chemistry Today* (Is there a *Chemistry Yesterday*? If so, Adam probably had it. *Chemistry Tomorrow*?) Also, strangely I thought at the time, *Modern Chinese Restaurant World*. I guess there is a lot of chemistry involved in cooking.

"I don't know very many Ph.Ds."

Instead of taking a seat behind his desk, he took one of the side chairs like the one I chose. The classic "I'm just an ordinary guy" gesture, but I appreciated it.

"I mean, is it 'Dr. Spurr'? 'Professor'? 'Adam'? Which do you prefer?"

"Actually, I prefer 'Your Holiness,' but I don't get that kind of respect anymore."

I loved that, and it was a whole lot better than "You're not from around here, are you?"

"Then I take it 'Adam' is okay."

"Certainly, if I can call you Mark," he said.

I do have an MBA, but the idea of someone calling me Master Fairley was not appealing.

"Of course." Preliminaries out of the way, I relaxed a little.

"You're not from around here, are you?" he said.

"Greensboro," I said. Sheesh!

"Sorry. I knew that. It's just a reflex, I guess."

A reflex that was giving me acid reflux.

"So," Adam continued, "My mother tells me you are writing a history of Spurr Nutritionals."

I nodded.

"I would have thought Agnes Smith was more the candidate for that sort of thing since she's been there a long time and has been collecting material for years."

"I agree, and she is a true living treasure trove of information, but when I met her the other day she seemed, well, tired. I wonder if recent events have knocked some wind out of her. I presume Elliot was the object of her loyalty for the past few years, and now that he's gone maybe she's thinking of retiring. She didn't say that, but she seemed almost relieved when I arrived on the scene. I know she's going to be very helpful."

"I'm sure she will be."

"Sorry I brought up Elliot so abruptly," I said. "I was going to ease into it more deftly than that."

"Thanks, but no problem. He's dead, and that's that. Terrible way to go though. I hear he was in that lab building at all hours practically every day since my father had his relapse. What do you think he was doing there?"

"I was hoping you could tell me." Did Adam know what we'd found in the lab on Thursday? "Have you talked to your mother lately?"

"Not since last week when she called to tell me about you."

So he didn't know. This would be interesting. And tricky.

"Do you like chemistry, Mark?"

"Who doesn't like chemistry?" I said, somewhat warily. "Although I have to admit I took it in high school mainly to avoid biology where I'd have to dissect a frog."

"Most people tell me that, and it used to bother me that chemistry was somehow relegated to the status of a substitute elective. But, chemistry … well it's the stuff of life, as we all know."

"'Better Living through Chemistry,' wasn't that the slogan a few years ago?" I offered.

"Actually, it was 'Better Things for Better Living ... Through Chemistry.' DuPont had it right. Unfortunately, they dropped the 'Through Chemistry' part 15 or 20 years ago, and now their slogan is 'The Miracles of Science.' A waste of words, if you ask me. Almost as bad as the one BASF is using: 'We Create Chemistry.' What arrogant nonsense! Who 'creates chemistry'?"

"God seems to have done a pretty good job," I ventured.

"Exactly! But I should be careful since BASF is one of my biggest clients. I've taken quite a bit of their money over the years in speaking and consulting fees."

"I won't mention it in the company history," I promised.

Our conversation went on in this vein for several more minutes, Adam expounding on the virtues of chemistry and those who love it, including himself, bragging about how much money he'd made from speaking engagements, consulting and publications, his most famous being "Valence, Your Unseen Bondage Friend," a treatise *Time Magazine* picked up and turned into a video that somehow went viral, further increasing Adam's demand as a visiting speaker and consultant ("I don't think I've had time to actually teach a real student in a classroom for the past six or seven years now," he enthused. "They keep me on at Duke because I make them look good."), and me trying to figure out how to steer things back to what I'd come to see him about. I was beginning to forget what that was.

"I don't have quite as much money as Bill Gates," he continued, "but if I did, and if I used some of it to build this fancy state-of-the art chemistry building, I'd definitely not put my wife's maiden name on it like he did. Well, maybe if I had a wife. Which I don't. But how does 'The Adam Spurr Chemistry Is Everything Center' sound to you?"

I stared at him.

"Just kidding, of course. A little professorial hubris."

"I won't put that in the company history either," I said.

"It's just I think names are important. And chemistry."

"Of course, I'm just getting started on the company history," I began again, "and I don't know all the family members very well yet, but there is one question that leaps to mind."

"You mean, 'Why isn't Adam part of the family business?'"

"Well, yeah, since you put it that way."

"And especially since my name is Adam and people assume I'm the elder son, in line to take over from my father."

"That too, I guess."

Truthfully, it was hard for me to relate on an emotional level to Adam's plight, although intellectually it was pretty clear. I am also, like Adam, the second son. I have an older brother named Matthew. My father, Peter, was a devout Methodist and believed in giving his children Bible names. According to him, if he and Mom had had two more sons, which they never did, they would have named them Luke and John in that order. When telling this to me and my brother, which he did frequently as we were growing up, Dad always finished the story with, "And that's the Gospel truth!" I don't think that meant he thought our names were a joke, mostly because Dad didn't have a well-developed sense of humor, although every time he said it, my mother, Evelyn, would say, "Oh, Peter, now stop it!" So we were named in an order that at least had some rationale to it, and I always knew where I stood. A solid number two. I don't know what they'd have done if they'd had daughters.

Emily and I have two daughters and a son. We thought about several different naming schemes before we knew how many children we would have and what their genders would be. Larry, Moe and Curly. Manny, Moe and Jack. Shadrach, Meshach and Abednego—good biblical names there. Dad would have approved. Chico, Harpo, Groucho, Gummo and

Zeppo. Magda, Zsa Zsa and Eva. In the end we went with Lisa, Judy and William simply because we liked those names.

"I don't know why I should be telling you all this," Adam went on, "but I doubt my mother would have hired you if she didn't think you'd be discreet."

I nodded.

"Elliot had all the breaks, you know. Smart, aggressive, 'Mama's boy,' and all that. And maybe he deserved them. After all he is, or was, my brother. In any case, I always liked science. As a boy Elliot got the Daisy Red Ryder BB gun while I got the chemistry set. But you couldn't tear me away from it. It's like I was obsessed. I never went so far as to blow up a toilet with dry ice, but you know what I mean."

I nodded again.

"It's not that I had no interest in the business. In fact, I thought a chemistry background would be an asset to a food company and maybe I could rise to some kind of senior staff position as a chemist or researcher or something even if I never got into top management. I would have been happy with that. But then I kept hearing my mother and Elliot telling everyone, 'Adam doesn't have a head for business.' It discouraged me, but it also made me determined to excel in some field or other so I could say, 'Hey, look at me now!' and I guess I have. I'm not head of the department here because I don't much care for the administrative side of things. Which, come to think of it, is consistent with not having a head for business, I suppose. But I'm happy. And I think I'm making a worthwhile contribution.

"And I've made a lot of money that I've invested wisely, so on that score I don't see how anybody can say I have no head for business. And if the family ever asked for help I'd gladly give it. But they never did, and they never do. To them, I'm just their boy who teaches chemistry over at Duke."

Adam was working himself up again. I was torn between letting him continue in hopes he would say something even more revealing versus slowing him down so he wouldn't succumb to an internal chemical reaction of some sort in his agitated state. I opted for the latter.

"Do you like Chinese food?" I asked.

"Not very much. Too many chemicals. MSG and so on. Why?"

"I'd have guessed you would like it for that very reason."

"Are you mocking me?"

"Maybe a little."

"It's okay; I'm used to it by now. And it was a worthy attempt," he conceded.

"Actually, it's because I'm curious why you would have *Modern Chinese Restaurant World* in your magazine pile."

"Really?" he said, glancing, I thought somewhat furtively, at the pile. "I hadn't realized. Can't think where I might have picked that up."

"Adam, sorry to get so personal again, but with all the recent changes at the company, do you still think there's no place for you? Or have you completely given up hopes of that, no matter what?"

"There might be something there for me," he replied slowly. "I can't say I haven't been thinking about it. I know Wash Booker wants to develop some new products, and I think I could help. But I don't have much clout there, at least not for the time being. And I know Mother says the big Japanese company has been coming around again, and she's thinking of selling. She said that's why she hired you to write up the history before that happened. But I don't think my father really wants to sell."

How would he know about Mr. Z's wishes? Only Mrs. Spurr and I – and Emily – had read Mr. Z's scribbled note to that effect, as far as I knew.

"Why would you say that?"

"Oh, I don't know. It would seem too out of character for him to be willing to give it all up. And to a foreign company at that."

"You mean to people who aren't from around here."

"You know what I mean."

I didn't, but I was beginning to suspect I did. Detective's intuition? Maybe. But then I thought (don't ask me why), What kind of a detective name is "Mark" anyway? Too wimpy. Adam, maybe. Not Mark. How about something like Dirk? That sounds good and solid. Someone with a penetrating intellect. Dirk Fairley.

I glanced at my watch, remembering I had two more stops to make before day's end. Like it or not, it was time to drop the bomb.

"You say you haven't talked to your mother since last week."

Adam nodded.

"Then you don't know the latest developments in Spurrville."

"Apparently not. What?"

"The town is in an uproar because when Wendell Cox took me into the ruins of the research lab I discovered the gas jets had been tampered with."

"You're not serious!"

"I am. The explosion doesn't look like it was an accident anymore, Adam. It looks like your brother may have been murdered."

At that, Adam went white as a sheet.

He was silent as I gave him a few more details, and then he said, "Thank you for telling me. You have to leave now. I must call Mother."

Chapter 23

The drive from the Duke University campus to the Carolina Coffee Shop on Chapel Hill's East Franklin Street, directly across from the UNC campus, is only 10 miles, but it took me a good 45 minutes to get there because of the lunchtime traffic on US 15/501, the main route between them. On top of that, I had to drive around for another 15 minutes looking for a place to park.

Trey Spurr had agreed to meet me at the coffee shop in lieu of his dorm room in Mangum Hall. He said I wouldn't like the dorm because it smelled like stale beer. It was just as well because it looked like there was a group of student protesters blocking any traffic trying to enter the campus itself. Trey later told me it was members of the Carolina Nihilist Society, a relatively new group of mostly sophomores that declared itself into existence and then out of existence fairly regularly. It was hard to keep up with them as they sprang in and out of existence like Schrödinger's cat depending on whether anyone was paying attention to them or not. They didn't seem to have any demands, and their motto seemed to be "Leave us alone and we'll leave you alone except for our demonstrations that tie up traffic and are generally annoying." This week the Society was in existence and waving signs with slogans like "Less!" "More!" "Enough!" "Whatever!" and "Matter is Nothing and Nothing Matters!"

Far from being just a coffee shop, the CCS is a full service restaurant and bar. Founded in 1922, it is reputedly the oldest in North Carolina, although that seems to ignore the Salem Tavern in Winston-Salem, which George Washington supposedly visited. Although it serves beer, its aromas were mouth-watering and had nothing stale about them. The brick walls would give the impression of eating outdoors were it not for the framed pictures and built-in bookcases that adorned them. That, and the white dropped ceiling, of course.

I walked in and immediately spotted someone who might be Trey. It wasn't, but from a booth halfway back Trey spotted someone who might be me. It was. Trey came forward and introduced himself. It was obvious he'd heard about the murder investigation, probably from his grandmother. A pleasant-looking young man with neatly trimmed four-day facial hair, as is the custom among many young men these days apparently, he was all gestures and questions, telling me he was anxious to get to Spurrville as soon as possible and had only kept our appointment because he'd heard I was the one who had found the damning evidence. He wanted to pick my brain first.

No sooner had we sat down in his booth than an equally pleasant-looking young woman appeared with an order pad, a dozen or so white straws sticking out of her apron pocket.

"Hi! I'm Shawnisha, and I'll be your server today! Let me tell you about our lunch specials. First …"

Suddenly somebody started playing the French national anthem. Loudly. In my pants.

I'd forgotten I'd recently changed my ringtone from the opening keyboard riff from The Who's "Baba O'Riley" (sometimes erroneously called "Teenage Wasteland") to "La Marseillaise" because Emily thought the riff was "monotonous." It was Emily calling.

"I'd better take this," I said to Trey's mild consternation as Shawnisha wandered away, not to be seen again for a long time. "Be right back."

I rose and went out the front door and into the alley running next to the restaurant so as to be somewhat shielded from street noise.

"Detective Blue wanted me to tell you they didn't find any fingerprints on the menus you picked up in the lab rubble," said Emily once we had established contact.

"Nothing, huh?"

"No, but he said the SBI did find some DNA on three of the gas jets you picked up, which surprised him."

"Surprises me too, but at least it's something, anyway. Could be a break."

"Except the DNA on two of them isn't from anyone in the national DNA database."

"Foreigners maybe?"

"He said maybe, but he doubts it," she said. "Not everyone is in the database yet, since it's still pretty new. You and I probably aren't in it since we haven't volunteered and we've committed no crimes."

Except my two speeding tickets. But Sheriff Belton hadn't asked for a mouth swab.

"What about the third one?" I asked.

"Wendell Cox, according to Detective Blue."

"Well, that figures, since he put one of them in his mouth to verify it was in the 'on' position." Cox probably had DNA on file from his Marine Corps days.

"I assume Blue will pass all that on to the Raleigh detective."

"He said he already has."

"Okay, thanks for letting me know. I'm in Chapel Hill with Trey Spurr right now, but I should be home in time for dinner. How's it going there?"

"Swimmingly. Laundry and then an early lunch at Costco."

"A Polish and a Pepsi?"

"No, silly. The samples. They were great today."

Returning to Trey's booth, I noticed Shawnisha pretending to ignore me, but there were glasses of ice water and menus on our table. And napkins, silverware and two straws. I also noticed a young man who appeared to be Japanese (well, oriental anyway) leaning down to whisper something to Trey. He looked up and saw me. His eyes went wide. Then he turned and ran to the back of the restaurant, practically throwing himself out the exit door.

"Sorry. It was my wife just giving me an update on something," I said nonchalantly (wouldn't want to appear chalant, you know, among strangers).

"No problem," said Trey, looking around, presumably for Shawnisha. "I'd really like to stay and get acquainted, since Grammy says you're doing important work for the company, but like I said, I need to get home now that it looks like there's a killer on the loose. You order what you want, but I'll just have a coffee to go."

That was a switch. First he wanted to stay and talk, and now he couldn't get away fast enough. Kids today. What had the oriental guy said that threw him into such a panic?

I was hungry. My morning with Adam and the drive over here had given me an appetite. When Shawnisha finally reappeared I ordered a French dip sandwich with provolone and pub fries and an iced tea. The subtle irony of my order was lost on Trey. Callow boy. Shawnisha seemed to have recovered her equanimity but appeared a bit disgruntled again after Trey only ordered a coffee to go.

"Will that be all?" she said and sauntered away before we could answer.

I figured by now it was okay to tell Trey everything I knew about the case, which I did quickly because there wasn't much other than about the open gas jets I had found. I wasn't going to speculate on what they meant, other than the obvious possibility, or on who might have been responsible, assuming it wasn't Elliot himself. Nobody thought it was. I'd continue to leave the speculation to the professional speculators, mainly the media and others with too much time on their hands, while the police and SBI did whatever it was they were going to do. I left out the stuff about strangers around town and at our Neighborhood Watch meeting, the theft of papers from my briefcase, the odd business of the takeout menus, and maybe even—I had almost forgotten—Emily's strange phone call from a 1960s gas station, which may or may not have anything to do with anything. I did ask Trey if he'd ever been to General Tso's Golden Chicken Pagoda in Raleigh. He said he'd never heard of it, and why did I ask. I couldn't give him quite the same song and dance I'd given Clara Fritts and Sheriff Belton, so I just said it was a name that had cropped up in conversation somewhere, which satisfied him.

The food came eventually, brought by a waitress who was not Shawnisha. There being no more information I could offer him, Trey appeared all the more anxious to get going. I hadn't gotten to know him at all, but I presumed there would be other opportunities.

"Well, thanks again for stopping by, Mr. Fairley, but I really need to go if you don't mind."

"No, I understand. It's nice to have met you anyway. I'll take care of the coffee."

"Thanks." He rose to leave, coffee in hand.

"Oh, and by the way," I said before he turned away, "who was that guy I saw with you when I came back in? Seemed in a pretty big hurry not to meet me. Which is odd, since I'm not from around here."

"Oh him," said Trey. "Yeah, he did seem to be in a rush all of a sudden. That was my friend Tad Tanaka. I'll have to introduce you next time you're in town."

In a way, we'd already met. I pictured young Tad speeding off in his bright red roadster.

Chapter 24

Nick Papadopoulos was not happy.

Gazing unseen into the customer area of General Tso's Golden Chicken Pagoda from the shadows of the kitchen, far behind the order counter, he could see there were customer-type people in the restaurant. But nobody was ordering anything.

Lunch hour traffic had been good, and Nick had been okay with letting his employees Tom and Jerry, as well as the cook, José, take a break out front when it had slackened off. They had sat quietly eating the free food he provided as one of the perks of employment at General Tso's, which was fine. The food cost him only a little, and the disposable wooden chopsticks were the cheapest he could find in the restaurant supply catalog.

But then the middle-aged mustachioed stranger with the small goatee had shown up again, engaging Tom and Jerry in excited but hushed tones. Not ordering anything.

Then another stranger had come in, flashing a badge. A local Raleigh detective, from the looks of him. Clean shaven, balding, corduroy jacket, and jeans. Cowboy boots. And a holstered gun. Talking to Tom and Jerry and the middle-aged mustachioed stranger, who looked scared out of his wits, although Tom and Jerry didn't seem too upset.

Not ordering anything.

José sat frozen after telling the detective his name and that he was the cook. Tom, Jerry and the detective speaking in normal Southern accents, José using a Mexican accent. The middle-aged mustachioed stranger's accent unidentifiable. The detective peering into the darkness of the kitchen and failing to notice Nick lurking there. The koi in the aquarium appearing unconcerned.

Nick noticed the aquarium glass looked scummy. Not that he cared about the fish, but some customers might be put off. Jerry was supposed to keep it clean. Better reassign that to Tom.

Then yet another stranger came through the door. Also clean shaven, but wearing a suit and tie and expensive-looking but scuffed loafers. Overall, somewhat preppy looking, if Nick understood what the term meant. Younger than the middle-aged guy with the mustache and goatee. No gun that Nick could see.

It looked like the new stranger and the mustachioed middle-aged stranger recognized each other. The new stranger looked stunned.

"Adam! What are you doing here?" the new stranger said.

Before "Adam" could answer, the new stranger's gaze fell upon Tom and Jerry.

"And you two. Haven't I seen you before?" he said, staring at them.

"Don't think so," said Tom, looking down at the remains of his egg foo young as if he wanted to bury his head in it. Jerry said nothing.

"I'm pretty sure of it," the new stranger said. "It's why I came here."

"And who might you be?" said the detective.

"I might ask you the same," said the new stranger. "No, wait, wait, don't tell me. You're the Raleigh detective?"

"Well, I am *a* Raleigh detective, but yeah, you've got it. Jake Keil. And I guess that makes you Mark Fairley."

"Good deduction. Greetings from Marshall Blue. I was beginning to wonder if you really existed."

"Good police work can't be rushed."

The two shook hands. They exchanged business cards.

Maybe one of them would order something. Or both of them. It would be like Christmas.

But no. They kept talking, not even sitting down. Keil said to Fairley, "Are these the two guys you saw?" referring to Tom and Jerry.

"You mean at the Neighborhood Watch meeting?"

"Yeah."

"I think so. It's kind of hard to be absolutely sure with those hats they're wearing."

"Off with the little paper hats, boys," commanded Keil.

The hats came off slowly.

"Yeah," said Fairley, "it definitely could be them, I guess."

"'Definitely could be'? 'I guess'? C'mon, Mr. Fairley, that wouldn't sound very convincing on the witness stand."

"Right!" said Jerry. "And besides, we've never been to Greensboro!"

"Shut up, Jerry!" said Tom.

"Who said anything about Greensboro?" said Keil.

"It's them all right," said Fairley.

Adam hid his face in his hands. José remained frozen in place. The koi remained unconcerned.

Keil made Tom and Jerry show him their drivers' licenses while he wrote their names down on a notepad he produced from a jacket pocket.

"Maybe I should take a picture of them with my phone and show it to my neighbor—see if he thinks they're also the ones he saw skulking around my house later that night," Fairley said.

"Yeah, let's do that, why don't we?"

Keil and Fairley took out their smartphones and snapped

pictures of Tom and Jerry. Keil took a few more shots of the restaurant while he was at it. *I should ask for royalties*, Nick thought.

Then Fairley looked hard at the detective.

"Aren't you going to arrest these two?" he said.

"On what charge? Wearing too much cologne? Which somebody sure is, by the way."

Both Fairley and Keil looked at Tom and Jerry. Jerry looked at Tom. Tom scowled at Jerry.

"We know from the menus that one or both of them had to have been at the lab at some point," Keil went on, "but we can't put them there the night of the explosion yet. Also, there's no proof they're the ones who broke into your house and stole the papers from your briefcase."

"Seems obvious to me."

"Obvious doesn't cut it. Solid evidence does, and so far all we've got is circumstantial."

"Sounds like you're a script consultant for TV cop shows."

"Sounds like you have a problem with authority, Mr. Fairley."

"I meant it in jest."

"Anyway, I am curious about this other guy. 'Adam,' you called him?"

"Adam Spurr. He's the surviving son of Zachary and Fanny Spurr, and he's a professor over at Duke."

"Well, well, a professor no less," said Keil, moving closer to Adam. "I'm sorry for the loss of your brother, Professor Spurr, but maybe you can answer Mr. Fairley's original question. It was something like, What's a respectable academic like yourself doing hanging out with guys like these in a place like this? Isn't this kind of far from Duke to come for a late lunch?"

This was getting to be too much for Nick. He would have to intervene soon.

"That's what I'd like to know," said Fairley.

"That's why I put it that way," said Keil.

Adam visibly gathered himself to respond, but it took a few seconds. The two standing men waited. Tom and Jerry were now as frozen as José.

"Actually, I first met these two gentlemen when they delivered takeout from here to a colleague's retirement party in Durham some months ago. The food was good, and they seemed very professional, so I took an interest in them. I've offered to have them audit some of the courses in my department. Haven't I, boys?"

Tom and Jerry nodded vigorously. José remained frozen.

"And I drop in here from time to time to check on them. See how they're doing, you know."

Nick seethed from the kitchen. *And you've never once, never even once ordered anything.*

"Actually, I live in Raleigh," Adam continued, "not far from here."

"Looks like you haven't ordered anything today, Professor," observed Keil.

Got him! thought Nick.

"No, not today. I already had a big lunch at the faculty club after I met with Mr. Fairley this morning."

"A get-acquainted meeting for a project I'm doing for his mother," Fairley said.

"I see," said Keil.

Fairley again looked hard at the detective.

"What are you looking at *me* for?" said Keil. "I know he's lying, at least partly, but that's not much to go on."

"But why is he lying? That's what I want to know."

"That's the big question, isn't it? Why are you lying, Professor Spurr?"

"I most assuredly am not, of course!" answered Adam.

Keil looked hard at Adam for a few seconds and then said, "Okay, well I think we're almost done here."

Fairley looked frustrated.

"Ah, Mr. Ake, Mr. Bono," continued Keil, "one more thing. Let me help you with your trash there."

With that, Keil picked up the remains of Tom's and Jerry's lunches and took them to the big trash receptacle next to the too-large beverage cooler near the entrance while they looked on with surprise. Nick saw Keil surreptitiously put their chopsticks into separate pockets of his jacket before dumping the rest of the trash. I can't reuse them so it's not stealing, he thought.

Fairley, Keil and then Adam made as if to leave. Finally, it was too much for Nick. He hiked himself up to his full 5' 8" height, the veins on his neck throbbing and his face the color of the koi in the aquarium (still unconcerned), strode out from the shadows behind the order counter, crossed to the door and intercepted them. José darted back into the kitchen.

"Who the crap are you?" demanded Detective Keil.

"I am Nikos Papadopoulos, the owner of 'a place like this,' as you call it! And I have just one question: Are you guys going to order something, or am I going to have to charge you rent!?"

That evening, Mark and Emily Fairley, Detective Jake Keil and his girlfriend Elsie Malone, and bachelor Professor Adam Spurr had Chinese takeout for dinner. So much of it that even a whole hour later they were still not hungry again.

Chapter 25

Duke Students Discover Allen Admin.
Building is Sham

DURHAM, N.C. (UP)— Student protesters at prestigious Duke University in Durham woke up late yesterday morning to a disturbing revelation growing out of their observation that during their still ongoing week of agitating to abandon Duke blue as the school color by conducting a sit-in at the university's Allen Building which ostensibly houses the school's administrative offices, no one on the administrative staff ever showed up for work.

According to the protesters, and reluctantly confirmed yesterday by school spokesperson Randall McCrae, the Allen Building is a sham, a symbolic venue the university erected in 1952 for the sole purpose of giving students a place to hold protest demonstrations. Very little university work goes on there, and it is usually staffed only by a skeleton crew of plainclothes campus police posing as receptionists, clerks and custodians even though there are fully furnished offices with real names and titles on the doors. The real administration offices are in a secret underground location in suburban Durham, and the president and senior administration officers only come to the campus on ceremonial occasions or to meet with student protesters.

"How else would we ever get any real work done?" said

McCrae. "Of course, we want to create and foster an environment where students are encouraged to learn to exercise civic responsibility by practicing this absurd behavior, but it means protests, 'occupations,' 'negotiations' and constant, never-ending disruptions of all sorts. Who could put up with it? It would be enough to drive anyone crazy. This has been our way of dealing with it, and it has worked well for almost 70 years."

"It makes me very sad, kind of blue in fact, that the administration has felt they could get away with this outright fraud. It's not fair, and it just adds to our growing list of stuff to protest," said sophomore Myra Gribble at a hastily-called press conference, flanked by a half-dozen fellow protesters waving signs with slogans like "Come Out Come Out Wherever You Are!" and "You Can Hide but You Can't Run!"

"They don't scare us," she said. "We're going to stay right here, especially since we don't know where else to go. But we'll find out, and then they're going to have to come in and physically arrest us."

"Though we have disagreed about the specifics of their demands and their choice of means, I respect (the protesters') underlying passion for making Duke and the world a better place," Duke President Arthur Willoughby said by telephone from an undisclosed location, possibly the real administrative offices. "Or we could just expel each and every one of the little punks and then go clean house in the Admissions Department," he said further, asking not to be quoted.

Chapter 26

Raleigh Senior Police Detective Jake Keil was no stranger to the ways of getting petty, and often not so petty, criminals to reveal themselves. He had worked his way up from the uniformed ranks and then rotated through several of the centralized detective units, including Fraud and Forgery, Homicide, Drugs and Vice, the Gangs Unit, and his favorite, Criminal Enterprise, where he currently served and which he thought of as a beautiful oxymoron. If criminals applied themselves as much to legitimate enterprises as they did to their unlawful ones, they'd all have good-paying jobs and be model citizens, he thought wryly. Some of them might even be on the police force.

What was so attractive about a life of crime? he often wondered. You're going to get caught, and you're going to serve time. These phrases running through his head, as they frequently did, had a nice ring to them. Almost poetic. He could almost hear them as lyrics in a song. "What's so great about a life of crime? / When I finally getcha, your ass is mine, 'cause / You're gonna get caught, an' you're gonna serve time." Boop-boop-ba-doop.

Would it sound better as a rap song, or maybe blues? Keil played rhythm guitar in a pick-up band of fellow officers on weekends, appearing occasionally at informal department functions, nursing homes, and similar gigs. They'd wanted to call themselves The Police, but that was taken. They had settled for The Cops. Elsie Malone thought it was a cute name.

175

Keil's colleagues liked to call him McGruff the Crime Dog because he was relentless in his pursuit of criminals and was known as a case closer. "Dogged" was their word for him. He pretended to be offended by this, but secretly he thought it was a good thing, especially after he learned the winning name for the Ad Council's famous crime fighting cartoon bloodhound had been submitted in a contest by a New Orleans Police officer. "Take a bite out of crime!" That was Jake Keil.

After the events at General Tso's Golden Chicken Pagoda, Keil had driven back to the unit office, bagged and marked as evidence the sticky chopsticks he'd pocketed from Tom Ake and Jerry Bono's trash, emptied the pockets and neatly folded his corduroy jacket on a side chair where it would remind him to take it to the dry cleaners on the way home, and sent the chopsticks off for DNA testing. The question was, would these samples match anything in the database, and would they match what was found on the open gas jets Mark Fairley had found in the Spurr Nutritionals research lab? Okay, two questions actually.

And you wouldn't expect to find DNA on metal gas jets that had been through an explosion and fire; that was a surprise. Just as surprising was what they found it in—a combination of spittle and snot. Was that significant?

Three questions altogether.

Those two guys, Tom and Jerry, were definitely up to something. He could feel it. He just didn't know what it was yet, except there had to be some connection with the events at Spurr Nutritionals. And that lying professor, Adam, was involved somehow. Had to be. But in the murder of his own brother? Doubtful, but these days you never knew. He would have to look more closely into Adam's affairs.

After dispatching the chopsticks, he called Greensboro

Police Detective Marshall Blue, the SBI, and Sheriff Cecil Belton in quick succession and brought them up to date.

Now except for checking out Adam Spurr, there was nothing to do on this case but wait. But that didn't mean rest for Jake Keil. Other cases, other places. Including an apparent conspiracy to defame Spurr Nutritionals on social media with false claims of poor quality and outright product sabotage. A Criminal Enterprise if ever there was one. Who was behind such a thing? And why? He picked up the phone again and called Spurr Nutritionals' attorney, Frank Sheldon, Esq.

Chapter 27

I got home later than expected but had called ahead to alert Emily and tell her I was bringing Chinese so she wouldn't have to cook anything. At first, she was angry I hadn't told her I planned on stopping at General Tso's after my meeting with Trey Spurr ("You could have gotten hurt!" "Probably not with a Raleigh detective there." "But you didn't know he'd be there!" "I didn't know Adam would be there either." "My point exactly!" "Spur of the moment thing." "Stop making puns!").

Eventually she was mollified, and we both had to admit the food was pretty good for "a place like that." She was ravenous because her lunch of Costco samples had been an early one. We stayed up past our usual bedtime while I told her about my day and listened to hers.

Having gorged on General Tso's chicken, sweet and sour pork, cashew chicken, egg foo young, chicken with broccoli, white rice, fried rice, wonton soup, spring rolls, Chinese donuts and fortune cookies ("You will meet a short, ugly stranger" and of course, "Help, I'm being held prisoner in a Chinese fortune cookie factory!") and put enough leftovers in the fridge to make at least two more meals, I was not particularly hungry for breakfast the next morning. I settled for coffee and a bowl of Cheerios with a few blueberries sprinkled on top. From Costco.

I was also sleepy, so I made the mistake of putting the heaped teaspoon of instant coffee granules into the mug of hot water without putting in the sugar first. By the time I realized my mistake it was of course too late. The water boiled, and the concoction fuzzed up like a vibrating brownish-white hairball. Nothing to do but go ahead and put in the sugar, which lay on top of the fuzz momentarily before slowly penetrating it. I tried to make a fancy heart design on the surface like the baristas do with lattes at coffee shops, using the handle of my spoon, but I made a mess of it. Finally, I got the thing stirred up sufficiently to dissolve the sugar, and although the drink was still fuzzy, it tasted surprisingly good. The texture didn't bother me like it usually would have. Maybe my tastes were changing.

It had been one heck of a day. Five hours of driving. Two encounters with Adam Spurr, both of them weird. A too-short encounter with Trey Spurr, which meant I would have to reschedule. A disturbing scene involving a frightened Adam, the two Japanese-looking guys named Tom and Jerry who definitely had been at our Neighborhood Watch meeting, and the by-the-book Raleigh detective Jake Keil (not a bad name for a detective, by the way. Almost as good as Dirk.). The restaurant owner Papadopoulos jumping out of the shadows and scaring us, or at least me, half to death. And weirdest of all, Tad Tanaka showing up with Trey in Chapel Hill and making a run for it when he spotted me. I knew from Sheriff Belton he was a friend of Trey's, but why run away from me? Especially after trying to drive his car up my tailpipe a few days before. On second thought, maybe because of it.

After breakfast, I checked the Boycott Spurrt page on Facebook again. No changes. I thought of posting a fake comment or two to see if it would get a rise out of someone who might then respond. But I didn't want to identify myself, and that's when I realized I would have to create at least one, and maybe several, fake Facebook accounts to accomplish that, and I didn't want to bother. Let the SBI and police work on that. In fact, it occurred to me they had probably done exactly that already, and some of the snarky comments I had seen might have been merely planted as bait by law enforcement. So I called Frank Sheldon, Esq., instead.

Frank confirmed the posts were fake, but reluctantly.

"I guess Fanny Spurr told you about it," he said. "And the alleged mouse parts in the Spurrt Lyte?"

"Of course."

"The two complainants don't exist, as it turns out, which was a relief to Mrs. Spurr, but somehow they got media coverage. We reported the boycott page to Facebook, and they would have taken it down at our request, but we wanted to leave it up as bait while the police try to work out who is responsible. We sort of suspect the Japanese company, Kashimoto, because who else would have a motive to run Spurr Nutritionals' prospects down and maybe get a better price for it in an acquisition? But Fanny Spurr says they've always been very nice and treated her and Mr. Z with respect. Plus, they keep coming back with better and better offers. Anyway, Facebook needs a court order before they'll help identify the perpetrator, so we'll probably ask for one."

The page had gotten some publicity, and therefore probably a great many hits, because anonymous callers had tipped off the media about it, but for the most part, according to Frank, the media were reporting the company's official position that the page was a malicious prank with no basis in fact. Good for the media. Responsible journalism, sort of.

"You knew about all this when you called to tell me about this job, didn't you?"

"Of course."

"And you didn't say anything."

"Not for me to say anything."

"I thought we were friends."

"Attorney-client privilege. You know, like the sanctity of the confessional. Besides, did I get you the job or didn't I?"

"I admit that, but I'm not sure I'm ready to thank you for it yet. I will say it's been … interesting," I said.

"From what Fanny Spurr and Detective Keil tell me, I'd have to agree," said Frank.

"So you know that's like the Chinese curse, 'May you live in interesting times.' By the way, have you ever been to General Tso's Golden Chicken Pagoda in Raleigh?"

"Can't say I have."

"Food's pretty good, but I feel like there's a curse there somewhere!"

"Listen, congratulations on finding the gas jets anyway. Could be the key to all the stuff that's been going on."

"That you can't talk about."

"Right."

Clearly, I wasn't going to learn anything from Frank Sheldon, Esq., on this occasion, assuming he actually knew anything more at all, and I was therefore not inclined to tell him much more either. But there was one more thing.

"What do you know about Tad Tanaka?" I asked him.

"Nothing. Who is he?"

"Oh, just some college kid I ran into in Chapel Hill. Friend of Trey's and Japanese, so I thought there might be some connection to the case."

"So it's a 'case' now, is it?"

"What would you call it? Listen, I gotta go. Talk to you later, Frank." I hung up.

I had texted my smartphone photos of Tom Ake and Jerry Bono to Emily yesterday afternoon and asked her to run over and show them to Allan Whitbread when he got home from his church, which she did. Allan said he thought they might well be the same men he saw outside our house the night of the Neighborhood Watch meeting, but he couldn't be sure because it was too dark. So that was inconclusive. Emily herself, like me, had no doubt they had been at the meeting, however.

I called Detective Keil and told him what Emily and Whitbread had said. I suggested he send his own photos of Ake and Bono to Sheriff Belton to see if he recognized them and if he would then show them to Clara Fritts at the Set-A-Spell for confirmation from her. I was pretty sure it was redundancy, but I didn't want the Sheriff to think I was withholding evidence.

Keil told me about the chopsticks and promised to let me know if there was a DNA match. He also told me he was going to take a closer look at Adam Spurr. Better Keil than me, I thought. Finally, he said he'd already brought Detective Blue up to date and would let him know about Emily and Allan as soon as he got a chance. Then I told him about Tad Tanaka, which wasn't much, but it seemed to interest him.

That left me with nothing specific to do the rest of the day but look at my company history notes again, maybe start on a first draft and think about the case. Hard. Emily was getting more used to the shenanigans I was encountering and seemed a little more at ease because now not three but four law enforcement agencies were involved, but I knew she had her limits. And I couldn't blame her. We needed some resolution before things escalated even more, which it seemed to me they would sooner or later. Something nefarious, and dangerous, was definitely afoot. So, like Sherlock Holmes, I needed to ponder.

I told Emily I would now retire to my bedroom office, to think. "It is quite a three pipe problem, and I beg that you won't speak to me for fifty minutes," I said to her, quoting from Conan Doyle's "The Red Headed League."

"I shall do better than that, sir," she replied. "I shall grant you all of fifty-one minutes, and then I shall require your services to assist me in removing a number of potted perennials from the portico to yonder verandah. Besides, you don't even have one pipe, let alone three. At least you'd better not. Not in my house."

"Insufferable woman!" I remonstrated, throwing up my hands and stalking off.

Chapter 28

Bill Wright and Jack Johnson, the bewildered Kashimoto Foods ambassadors from Kuroibishi-Whitestone, and a frightened Tadashi Tanaka, their designated driver and undercover college student, waited in Wright's room at the Raleigh-Durham Airport Hampton Inn. Johnson in the desk chair, Tanaka in the uncomfortable easy chair next to one of the double beds and Wright standing. Wright and Johnson were about to check out and return to New York, but Wright needed an adult pick-me-up, not a Spurrt, and had pulled two beers from the room's mini-bar. He was working on the second one, and some pretzels.

"Two for the air!" he said with mock cheerfulness. "Get it? Not 'one for the road' but 'two for the air'?"

Johnson and Tanaka, drinkless, got it but weren't in the mood even for mock cheerfulness. It had been a disastrous week so far, and things didn't look like they were going to get any better.

First, Tanaka had failed in his clumsy attempt to shadow Mark Fairley to find out what he was learning about the secrets at Spurr Nutritionals. In the process, he'd been stopped for speeding, although thankfully his fast talking with the sheriff had saved him from getting a ticket, but he thought it must be obvious to Fairley he was following him. Then, a startling chance encounter with Fairley at the Carolina Coffee Shop, where eye contact was made, causing Tanaka to flee in fear and disgrace, losing face in Trey Spurr's presence. Trey would be confused by this and would start asking questions Tanaka could not, dare not, answer truthfully. Tanaka had been avoiding him since.

For the two men from the prestigious international investment banking firm of Kuroibishi-Whitestone it was worse, although it didn't seem so to Tanaka. First, on the day of their arrival in the area, and unbeknownst to them until too late, evidence was found that led the authorities to believe Elliot Spurr might have had been murdered, completely turning the whole town of Spurrville on its ear, in fact all of Lester County for that matter. Then, when they innocently paid a courtesy call on Mrs. Fanny Spurr to update her on Kashimoto's interest in acquiring Spurr Nutritionals, having no idea of this new circumstance in her life, Johnson and Wright were politely thrown out on their ears. Well, not so politely. They'd tasted the wrath of a steel magnolia (though none of the three had ever heard that term). What that encounter might portend for the future of their relationship with her and their prospects for carrying out Kashimoto's wishes was uncertain at best. Terminal at worst. The solution might not be as simple as sending Fanny Spurr a sympathy card and a dozen roses.

"We'll bounce back from this somehow," ventured Wright, munching a pretzel. "It wasn't our fault. How were we to know?"

This rationalization had been going on all during the ride to the hotel in Tanaka's red Honda Civic, but Johnson had remained silent, having none of it. Now he spoke up, with some irritation.

"But we *should* have known, Bill. It's our job to know. And it's not Tad's fault. His job was to tail Fairley, not give us the latest Spurrville news, although I must say the tailing Fairley part was pretty shabby."

Tanaka sank lower in the uncomfortable easy chair.

"Don't worry, Tad-san," said Wright. "You're just a kid. You'll be fine. Come out smelling like a rose."

Tanaka didn't know what that meant, but it didn't sound all that good. He didn't want to smell like a rose.

As a college student here in America, he might be "just a kid," he mused, and therefore not expected to shoulder much responsibility, but in his culture the importance of a college education could not be overstated. Incredible pressure is put on Japanese students to pass the exams necessary to enter university, and for those who don't get in it's like the end of life. Literally, in many cases, as the suicide rate among students in Japan attests each year. Never mind plenty Japanese without degrees make more money than do many who have them and probably have a lot more freedom. It is the cachet of the university education that is everything. To fail that is to lose face, big time, as the Americans would say. So for Tanaka the question was, would Kashimoto Foods continue to support him at Carolina?

To top that off, all three men were sensitive enough to realize the finger of suspicion in the death of Elliot Spurr might sooner or later point to Kuroibishi-Whitestone and Kashimoto Foods. Who else but the largest and most aggressive corporate suitor would have anything substantial to gain from creating havoc within Spurr Nutritionals? The only saving grace in this for Tanaka was nobody but the Kuroibishi-Whitestone people knew he worked as a spy for Kashimoto. But he looked Japanese. He *was* Japanese. And he remembered Sheriff Belton mentioning two other suspicious characters who'd been seen around town. Oriental-looking, just like him. Japanese? No one knew, but to Americans all Asians look alike.

Johnson and that fool, Wright, would go back to New York,

have dinner at the Trump Tower or somewhere, come up with a clever scheme to right their ship and then laugh it off as a future war story for cocktail parties.

Not so easy for Tanaka. There was only one thing for him. Not *harakiri*. Not in the 21st Century anyway, but almost as dire. Something equally central to Japanese culture.

He would have to apologize.

A lot.

***

A few hours later a telephone rang in the plush executive office suite on the top floor of the headquarters of the Kashimoto Foods conglomerate in the Shinjuku business district of Tokyo.

"Moshi-moshi" (Hello?)

"Tanaka degozaimasu." (This is Tanaka speaking)

"Hai!" (I'm listening.)

"Moshiwake gozaimasen. Shippai shimashita. Mattakumotte ohazukashii. Owabishimasu." (Please excuse me. I have failed. I am a disgrace. I apologize.)

"Mosukoshi kuwashiku hanashite kudasai." (Can you be more specific?)

"Fairley-san no atowotsuketeiruuchi tukamatte shimaimashita. Sonoato Spurr-san to issyoniirutokorowo mirareteshimaimashita. Mondaini narudesyou. Spurr-san no shinyowo ushinaimashita." (I was caught while following Fairley-san. Later, he saw me with Trey Spurr-san. There will be questions. I have lost Spurr-san's trust.)

"Wakarimashita." (Understood.)

"Moshiwakenai. Taihen moshiwakenai. Owabishimasu. Kokorokara." (I am sorry. Very sorry. I apologize. Profusely.)

"Moshiwakenai?" (You are sorry?)

"Hai!" (Yes.)

"Taihen moshiwakenai?" (Very sorry?)

"Hai! Taihen Moshiwakenai. Owabishimasu." (Yes, very sorry. I apologize.)

"Kokorokara?" (Profusely?)

"Kokorokara to moshiagemashita." (I said profusely.)

"Kareraha Spurrt no himitsuwo hakkenshitato omoimasuka?" (Do you think they have discovered the secret of the Spurrt yet?)

"Wakarimasen." (I don't know.)

"Soredewa zannendesu. Taihen zannendesu." (Then you should be sorry. Very sorry.)

"Desukara moshiwakenai to moshiagemashita. Taihen moushiwakenai. Owabishimashita. Kokorokara." (I said I was sorry. Very sorry. I apologized. Profusely.)

"Dai jobu desu." (All right, it's okay)

"Moshiwakenai." (I'm sorry.)

"Mokekko! Mojubun desu!" (Stop! Enough!)

"Sumimasen." (Excuse me.)

"Mokekko. Tsugino shijiwo matsuyoni." (Shut up. Wait for further orders.)

"Wakarimashita. Arigato gozaimasu. Sayonara."

"Hai! Sayonara."

Chapter 29

"Good morning, Mr. Spurr. Are you feeling all right today?"

"No."

"I'm sorry to hear that. But you're no worse than before?"

"No."

"Will it be all right if I ask you some questions about the company?"

"Yes."

"May I call you Mr. Z, sir?"

"Yes."

I was asking the questions, and Mr. Z was responding with head nods. He still couldn't talk or write intelligibly. Fanny Spurr was in the room with me, encouraging her husband and lending credibility to what must have seemed to him an unlikely, even stupid, task on my part. Especially to a previously articulate, robust man who had been used to commanding hundreds of employees and influencing the economic and social life of a whole town. But after Mrs. Spurr had explained my idea to him, he was going along with it, so far.

"I don't know why nobody has thought of doing this before," Mrs. Spurr told me when I arrived earlier that morning after calling her the previous afternoon to set up this meeting. "It seems so simple."

"It was you who gave me the proper perspective," I told her, "by giving me access to everything and the motivation to get to the bottom of whatever is going on here. Before, it was like the story of the blind men trying to describe an elephant."

I was buttering her up, but it was mostly true.

"I don't think I know that story, Mark."

Oops.

"Everybody involved has been looking only at one or two pieces of the puzzle, like blind men feeling maybe only the elephant's trunk, or his tail, or his wrinkly skin. They can't see the whole elephant, only the parts each one can touch, so they're never going to agree on an accurate description of it."

"I see."

I wasn't sure she did but, committed now, I pressed on.

"But you've given me the opportunity to see the whole animal at once, even if I've had to view it from many different angles at first and then try to put all the views together."

"Oh. But you are not saying Spurr Nutritionals resembles an elephant, are you?"

"No, ma'am."

"Because elephants are big and clumsy. And you would not want one to step on you, heavens to Betsy."

"No, but elephants have excellent memories, they can communicate over great distances, they are very social and loyal to their families, and they can get a lot of work done if they're given good direction. Not unlike the spirit of Spurr Nutritionals, it seems to me."

"That is very good."

Whew!

Mrs. Spurr and I had started the morning with my bringing her up to date on my budding relationship with Sheriff Belton, my meetings with Jim Sullivan, Agnes Smith, Wash Booker and Wendell Cox followed by my encounters with Adam and Trey, the surprising events at General Tso's, including the identification of Tom Ake and Jerry Bono as the suspicious-looking oriental men who were suspected of stealing the notes from my briefcase, and what Detective Keil was doing with their chopsticks. She was already aware of most of it but was as surprised and mystified as I about Tad Tanaka's odd behavior on the highway and at the Carolina Coffee Shop ("What did Trey say about it?" "I didn't really get a chance to ask him.") and what the relationship between Adam and the two General Tso's employees might be.

She had little to tell me, mostly because the SBI had not yet reported anything to her since my discovery of the open gas jets. Although I told her of my limited progress on the company history, she was much less interested in that than in the other goings-on.

Now we were in the Florida room with Mr. Z and getting down to the real reason for my visit. Fortunately, it was a partly cloudy day, so I didn't have to squint constantly at my list of questions. The teensy teacups had been collected by a maid, and I was in gentle interrogation mode.

In my three-pipe think session, it occurred to me we all might be missing something right under our noses. During the first months after his accident on the bottling line, and even up to my first visit with him, Mr. Z had been desperately trying to communicate *something*. Something that seemed important, at least to him. He was agitated and active, almost manic, and he wouldn't stop scribbling illegible notes. At the same time, everybody except his wife had been treating him as if he had lost his mental faculties along with his ability to speak and write. Then, inexplicably, he had become much less active. No less active than a normal man of his age, but far less so than right after the accident. More than one doctor had examined him. There was no discernable medical explanation. Had he simply given up out of frustration? Out of grief over the loss of his son, Elliot? Nobody knew.

Add that to the fact that everyone around him was used to deferring to him about almost everything, treating him with great respect and never challenging him, and now was pretty much avoiding contact with him out of fear or because he appeared to be nothing more than a sick, grumpy old man, and what was the point? Therefore, it was no wonder no one had explored the path on which I was now embarking. Maybe it was indeed Mr. Z himself who held the key to the mystery that surrounded us. Were we ignoring a potentially rich wellspring of information who could shed light on this whole baffling situation? It was too big a possibility to ignore.

If Mr. Z could answer "yes" and "no" but we still didn't know what was going on from his perspective, maybe no one had been asking the right questions.

I began to put together a list of questions. It was only a starter list of course, a guide list, since many questions would have to be formulated on the spot depending on his answers. The yes and no approach would be tedious, and no doubt Mr. Z would become fatigued or impatient, or both, before it was done. As would Fanny Spurr and I myself. It was a glorified version of "Twenty Questions," and I didn't know whether the category was animal, vegetable or mineral. I hoped it would be worth it.

From my briefcase I extracted my replacement copy of the one scribbled note of his that we could read. Mrs. Spurr had asked Agnes to scan and e-mail it to me after mine was stolen.

"Do you recognize this note, sir?"

"Yes."

"Does it say, 'Don't sell'?"

"Yes." Emphatic nodding. He took a swig from a bottle of Spurrt Mrs. Spurr had given him in lieu of tea.

"Is there a reason for this that you think no one knows but you?"

"Yes."

"Is it related to your accident at the plant?" I was thinking about the changes in his behavior during his recovery. First full of energy, now more lethargic.

"Yes."

"Does it involve your current disability?"

"No."

"Does that mean you are confident Mrs. Spurr and Mr. Sullivan and the others can continue to run the company successfully?"

"Yes."

At this, Mr. Z's eyes took on a look of pleading, and he began gesturing impatiently as if he wanted me to get back to some area of questioning that was more in line with what was on his mind. I hate to say it, but it reminded me of Lassie the wonder collie trying to tell the grownups little Timmy had fallen down a well or something. Again.

Speaking of which, a phone rang in another part of the house, and then a dog started barking. It was déjà vu all over again. Then silence.

"Does it have anything to do with the ViroBactiZap 5000 machine?"

An emphatic "Yes."

But what? I forged ahead, the sun having come out now, making it harder to read my notes.

"Anything to do with the batch of Spurrt that went through the machine with you?"

"Yes." Emphatic again.

I was putting it indelicately, but my excitement level was growing. From here on I was on my own. I abandoned my notes at this point so the sun was only a minor annoyance.

"Did you drink from that batch?" Of course I knew the answer, but this was for the record.

"Yes."

"Did anyone else ever drink any from this batch?"

"No."

"Because you forbade them?"

"Yes."

"Did you drink all of it?"

"No."

That was interesting.

"I know you saved one bottle from that batch, and Mrs. Spurr tells me it's in your wall safe."

"Yes."

"Are there more of those bottles?"

"Yes."

I wanted to know how many and where they were, but I couldn't think of a quick series of yes or no questions to get at it. As if sensing my dilemma, Mr. Z rose and shuffled over to a closet. The closet was locked, but he pulled a keychain from his pocket, selected a key and opened the door. Inside, on the floor, was a full, pristine case of tainted Spurrt. If pristine and tainted can be used in the same sentence.

"I had no idea," gasped Mrs. Spurr. "Heavens to Betsy, why did you keep this from me, dear?"

Mr. Z shrugged.

"Does anyone else know you have this?"

"No."

"Were you ever going to tell me?" asked Mrs. Spurr.

"Yes."

"Were you going to tell Elliot?" I asked.

"Yes."

"But you never got around to it before he ... passed away?" I asked.

"Yes."

I paused, much to Mr. Z's apparent consternation as Mrs. Spurr looked quizzically at me, but I needed to think. I felt like some dots might be connecting here. Like if I were a real detective I'd be deducing something at this moment. Like realizing just in time that indeed Timmy must have fallen into a well and needed my help.

"Was there something different about the Spurrt in that particular batch?"

"YES!"

"Did it taste different?"

"Yes."

"Better?"

"Yes."

"Did it have the same refreshing, pick-me-up effect?"

"No."

"Less?"

"No."

"More?"

"YES!"

"It was a higher high, so to speak, and it lasted longer?"

"YES!"

Mrs. Spurr's eyes went wide. Mr. Z heaved what appeared to be a sigh of relief, an expression of gratitude forming on his face.

It only took a few minutes of further questioning to establish that each time Mr. Z had consumed a 12-ounce bottle of the Spurrt that had gone through the ViroBactiZap 5000 machine during the accident the pick-me-up effect was more pronounced and lasted 10-12 hours instead of the usual hour or so experienced by drinking normal Spurrt, or other soft drinks for that matter. How, I didn't know, but the malfunctioning machine must have altered the chemical makeup of the Spurrt formula in such a way as to change its physiological effects, at least on Mr. Z.

The implications were staggering. I didn't need a Wash Booker to tell me what a competitive advantage this would mean for the brand if the effects worked on everyone and could be achieved in mass production. This was revolutionary. No wonder Mr. Z didn't want Mrs. Spurr to sell the company.

Time for a few more questions.

"Does anyone else know about this effect?"

"No."

"Elliot spent a lot of time in the research lab after your accident. Did he tell you why?"

"No."

"Do you think he suspected this is what happened?"

Mr. Z shrugged as if to say, "I don't know" or "Maybe." So actually he could answer three types of questions, not just yes and no.

I imagined Fanny Spurr wondering at some point whether, if Elliot had known about the extra case, he might not have had to spend so much time in the lab. Maybe he wouldn't have died. Of course, that assumed his nocturnal lab time had anything to do with the tainted Spurrt in the first place. No one knew. I said nothing, and Mrs. Spurr moved things along.

"Dear, do you think we should run some tests with that machine to see if the effects can still be duplicated?" asked Mrs. Spurr.

"Yes," nodded Mr. Z.

I asked her if the machine had been used at all since the accident, and she repeated her previous assurance that there was a strict ban on any such thing. It hadn't been touched after the cleanup from the event.

Another thought popped into my head.

"Maybe we could use some of the product in the closet as a sort of 'control' against which to compare whatever we get from the experiments," I ventured. I guess that made it a closet case, but I didn't feel like making jokes at that point.

"That sounds liked a good idea," said Mrs. Spurr, turning to Mr. Z. "Would that be all right with you, my dear?"

"Yes."

"Thank you, Mr. Z," I said.

"Yes."

"Then it is settled," said Mrs. Spurr. "Mark, will you supervise the testing, please?"

"I'd be honored, but I'm not sure I'm qualified."

"You know more about this now than anyone, you have access to me and my husband if more questions need to be asked, you have our trust, and I believe you have leadership skills," she said.

"Well, okay then. I'll see what I can do."

"Good. I will ask Wendell Cox to have the Research and Development people actually carry out the experiments. And I will ask Trey to come and observe, and help if he can. You know he is taking chemistry over at Chapel Hill."

"Okay." I wondered briefly why she wasn't going to ask Adam for help. The big chemistry expert at Duke. But I didn't say anything.

"As soon as you leave, I am going to call Frank Sheldon and have him prepare nondisclosure agreements to be signed by anyone having any connection with this project. I will make a list, but I know it includes you, Mr. Cox, Mr. Sullivan, Mr. Booker and the R&D people to begin with. And probably some of the technicians on the bottling line who will be involved. Mr. Cox can tell me who they will be. Maybe others as well."

Smart lady.

I had another thought. A long shot maybe, but worth a try.

"I'm not sure it's appropriate to ask, but is it possible I could drink one of those bottles myself?"

Mr. and Mrs. Z exchanged glances. Mr. Z nodded.

I've tasted a lot of Spurrt, of course, and I like it, but this bottle did taste better. Unless I was simply wanting and

199

expecting it to taste better because the excitement of the day's revelations was altering my perceptions. But I didn't think so.

Then the pick-me-up kicked in, slowly at first, but perceptibly. It was nothing like a drug high (based on what I've been told about such things, never having experienced one myself, of course), but after five minutes I no longer noticed my fatigue from the tedious yes and no questioning session. Fanny and Mr. Z looked at me expectantly.

"You're right," I said. "It does taste better. And I feel pretty good. Thank you for trusting me with this. I'm not sure how, but I think it will help as we continue to sort things out." I was excited and blabbering, but it was all I could come up with right then.

I took my leave and headed out to the car with a spring in my step, wondering how long the effect would last.

Chapter 30

Tadashi Tanaka received his further orders. They came in a DHL Express envelope hand delivered to his dorm room in Mangum Hall at UNC-Chapel Hill.

He and Trey both lived in Mangum Hall, a coed dorm on the Upper Quad within 10 minutes' walk from the Carolina Coffee Shop. Both could afford to live in a more expensive house or apartment off-campus, which would require payment for utilities, etc., and sometimes bus fare if far enough away, but Trey liked the cachet of Mangum, and he liked his roommates, of whom Tanaka was not one, although they both lived on the same floor. Tanaka liked it because it was where Trey lived, and he wanted to stick close to his target for more efficient befriending and espionage.

On most days the dorm did smell like stale beer except on Tanaka's and Trey's floor. There it smelled more like stale Spurrt, a pleasant-enough aroma but which the other students on the floor didn't like. They preferred stale beer.

Unfortunately, Tanaka was not there to sign for the envelope, being at the time in the Student Center with Pamela, the British fellow student who detested being called "Pam," and of whom he found himself becoming quite fond. The after-class meetings were becoming more frequent, and he had also developed a liking for Earl Grey tea, as had Pamela for green. He had explained to her the intricacies of the time-honored Japanese tea ceremony and showed her videos of it on YouTube, and she was fascinated. The ceremony was a far cry from putting tea bags in hot water, which was as ceremonious as it ever got at the Student Center, and it appealed to her British sense of formality. This was the same sense that put Pamela a cut above typical American women he knew, though he was not familiar with that particular idiom.

Tanaka had not yet shared with Pamela his secret life of international intrigue which might have appealed to her British James Bond-ish sense of adventure, assuming she had such.

So the envelope had gone back to the local DHL distribution center and in its place, taped to his dorm room door, was a notice of attempted delivery. Tanaka saw it upon his return that afternoon, after arranging a later assignation with Pamela in the Davis Library stacks. By then it was too late that day to drive to the distribution center to claim the envelope, so he had to wait until after his early classes the next morning before driving over, his fingernails ragged from much chewing and having heard little of what was discussed in class. His evening date in the stacks with Pamela had not gone well. "You seem distant tonight," she observed. "Really?" he said, "I hadn't noticed." "Precisely," she concluded.

The DHL envelope was well-sealed and difficult to open, especially with shaky hands and stubby fingernails. Sitting in his red Honda Civic in the DHL parking lot and with the aid of the tiny Swiss Army knife he kept on his keychain, he finally got it. He pulled out one sheet of A4 paper, the size used in Japan, and England as well, oddly enough. The orders were in terse Japanese:

"You must determine whether Mark Fairley has discovered the truth. If he has, then under no circumstance is he to be allowed to communicate it to anyone. Ever. Or at least until we have successfully acquired Spurr Nutritionals."

This was scary stuff. Was Tanaka supposed to kill Mark Fairley if he discovered "the truth"? That seemed extreme. Anyway, how was Tanaka supposed to discern whether Fairley had actually discovered it? Nobody had told Tanaka what "the truth" was, so how would he recognize it, or at least recognize that Fairley had found it? And what *was* "the truth"? And what if Tanaka at some point became convinced Fairley knew the truth and then killed him, later to find out he was mistaken? What if he wasn't mistaken but Fairley had "communicated it to" someone before Tanaka killed him? Would they make him kill that person too? Or persons?

Maybe he could kidnap Fairley and keep him incommunicado before he could discover the truth, or, if he did discover it, then before he could tell anyone. At least he wouldn't have killed him, an action impossible to undo. Maybe the acquisition of Spurr Nutritionals would take place quickly so Fairley's ordeal, and Tanaka's, could be short-lived. But negotiations hadn't even gotten off the ground, and Kashimoto had been trying to get them started for years already, to no avail.

Anyway, where would he stash Fairley? Mangum dorm was out. Too many prying eyes, and he would have to bring in food, and people would wonder how he could be eating so much without gaining weight. Especially Pamela. Plus, he could never invite her up to his room. Plus, plus, could she ever fall in love with a killer, even with her British sense of James Bond-ish adventure, assuming still that she had such? No, maybe he'd have to rent a storage unit somewhere close by and keep Fairley there. But then he'd have to go to Bass Pro Shops and pick up a camp toilet and other supplies. Kitty litter wouldn't cut it.

The greenhouse effect of the Honda Civic's rolled up windows slowly heated the air until it threatened to bake him in the bright sunlight of the day. He hardly noticed.

Full ride scholarship or not, this was way beyond anything Tanaka had signed up for. He thought about it. He was a senior and would be graduating soon and could take his degree home with pride, maybe even landing a good job at Kashimoto, something that would have a career path beyond those of most Japanese "salarymen." Was there a way he could hold out here without killing anybody, just until graduation, when they would presumably have to call him back to Tokyo because his student visa would no longer be valid?

His now parboiled brain told him there was only one answer. He had more apologizing to do.

Chapter 31

My mind was reeling as I left the Spurrs' home after my surprisingly productive Q&A session with Mr. Z. Of course, we'd have to complete the testing, but if it worked—if we could replicate what Mr. Z had experienced—then Spurr Nutritionals would have a whole new lease on life, as they say. It would certainly change history, or my version of it anyway. Agnes would be ecstatic. Wash Booker could quit bugging Jim Sullivan about new products for a while.

I was already writing advertising slogans in my head as I drove back to the plant, remembering to put on my Permanent Visitor lanyard and name badge as I drove.

"Stay alert with Spurrt." "Full throttle in a bottle!" "A wink, a drink, and you're in the pink!" Not brilliant, I admit, but a lot more energetic than the current time-worn slogan: "The drink that says 'Got a Life!'"

And a catchy jingle:

> I'd like to buy the world a Spurrt
> And keep it company.
> It's otherwise a world of hurt,
> That needs a symphony.
> It's the real thing.
> Hal-leluiah, hal-leluiah,
> Hal-le-e-lu-iah!

Clearly, I was still feeling it.

A drink that kept you going for a full 10 hours was unheard of. It would set the industry on its ear. No doubt others would try to compete, to figure out the Spurrt formula and how to alter its characteristics the way the ViroBactiZap 5000 apparently did when it was stressed by having a full-grown man pulled through it. I doubted anyone would try that, exactly. We certainly weren't going to. Where would we find volunteers, after all? "You will risk bodily injury and the likelihood of becoming incoherent, unintelligible and grumpy for an indeterminate period, but just sign this waiver and collect your bonus on the way out after the experiment." Probably not.

What I was counting on was for the machine to have remained in its altered state after Mr. Z's passage through it. Support for that hope was the many bottles of altered Spurr that had followed him. Too bad he drank all but one case. If we turned the machine back on and it maintained its altered state instead of rebooting, or whatever machines do these days when they're turned back on, and if it produced enhanced Spurrt (I was no longer calling it tainted), and if we could reverse engineer the machine to build others identical to it without violating the patents of the machine's developers, then we were golden. Sales and market share would skyrocket.

A lot of ifs. But worth a try.

Then I thought of some possible downsides. Would there be side effects? Would it be like those drugs on TV where the warnings were scarier than the diseases the drugs were designed to combat? Would it be addictive? Would people forget to eat regularly because they felt so good all day and eventually suffer malnutrition? What about shelf life? Would it be significantly less than the current product? More than? Could the effect be produced in aluminum canned product as well as in plastic bottles, not just in the glass bottles? Would the bottles and cans have to display warning labels of some kind?

No doubt the coffee lobby and the soft drink lobby would pressure Congress to make the FDA ban Spurrt as harmful to health or to the environment, or to make it a controlled substance, treating it like a drug, or exercise some other form of government overreach. But that could take years, barring a dictatorial Presidential Executive Order, but at least the current Administration seemed to be pro-business and favored protection of property rights.

Since the incident of Tadashi Tanaka dangerously following me through the speed trap, I had gotten into the habit of checking my rearview mirror a lot more frequently than before. Paranoia? Maybe, but there was too much suspicious stuff going on around here. I looked. There was nobody behind me, but just then another thought hit me. Why did the Japanese company, Kashimoto, step up its efforts to woo Fanny Spurr immediately after Mr. Z's accident? Why then? And why were they so interested in the first place?

This was a question for someone with a real detective's mind. I'm not naturally suspicious, although I can be a bit cynical. But real detectives like Marshall Blue and Jake Keil were trained and paid to be suspicious. I was going to have to bring them up to date on today's developments anyway, of course. And in so doing raise the Kashimoto question. The police don't sign nondisclosure agreements, but I was sure Fanny Spurr would understand.

I hadn't left the Spurrs' house without having one more short conversation with Fanny Spurr after Mr. Z, apparently exhausted from the Q&A, retired to his bedroom. I needed help with something else that might or might not be another piece of the puzzle.

"Mrs. Spurr, I'm sorry to have to bring this up again so soon after … you know. But could you tell me a little more about the accident that killed Elliot's wife?"

"Oh, did I forget to explain about that? I am so sorry. Yes, poor Lucy was killed in an automobile accident. Right here in Spurrville. It was down where the highway comes into Lester County. She was coming out of a side street and a speeding car from out of state collided with her. She had stopped at the stop sign as she should have, but it happened anyway. She died instantly."

"And the other driver?"

"Unscathed. His car was a mess, naturally, but he was not hurt. Sheriff Belton put him in the jail, but he was out in a few days. It seems it was his first offense and there was no alcohol involved as it was only 9:00 in the morning. The judge down in Sanford let him off with a fine and a warning, and we have not seen him around here since."

"Just a fine and a warning? That doesn't seem right."

"We thought so too, but there was not much the sheriff could do about it."

"But surely the man could at least have been sued in civil court."

"I think Sheriff Belton felt that would be problematic, what with the paperwork involved in extradition requests and so forth. The man was from out of state. Nevertheless, Elliot talked to Mr. Sheldon, and Mr. Sheldon did file suit. It was still pending when Elliot passed, and I am not quite sure of its current status."

"So that's it then?"

"No. The sheriff did feel quite badly about the whole thing. Lucy and Cecil's wife, Bonnie, were good friends from church. So he did do something. That speed trap down there? I might as well call it what it is—a speed trap. Sheriff Belton set it up in Lucy's honor. No more speeding through Lester County. No, sir."

Belton continued to surprise me. There was more depth to him than I had imagined based on my first encounter. He was a man of honor and integrity. He couldn't be bought off even with a slice of lemon meringue pie, that was for certain. And now this, "The Lucy Spurr Memorial Speed Trap." I imagined a billboard: "Welcome to Lester County, a Certified Community. No Speed, No Weed. No Need. Now entering the Lucy Spurr Memorial Speed Trap Zone." I guess such a notice would defeat the purpose. Still, it was a grand and honorable gesture I couldn't help applauding silently as I gazed on Fanny Spurr's beatific face. Or her beatific silhouette, since the sunlight was streaming in behind her again. Why couldn't I have come on a rainy day?

I left feeling proud that not only had I apparently unlocked the big secret Mr. Z had been harboring since his accident, but also I had the honor of being stopped not once but twice in a memorial speed trap. Only in North Carolina? I wondered.

And, darn! Once again I had forgotten to ask Mrs. Spurr if she could fix my speeding tickets.

Chapter 32

Tadashi Tanaka was waiting for me in my little office at the plant. Agnes warned me before I went in.

"I don't know what he wants," she said, "but I understand he's a friend of Trey's so I just assumed it was all right."

"It's fine, Agnes. Thank you."

Now what? I was still feeling pretty upbeat from drinking the enhanced Spurrt, so I was ready for almost anything.

I went on in, and Tanaka rose to greet me, Visitor badge dangling and hand outstretched and with what appeared to be a slight and possibly involuntary bow.

"Excuse me," he said. "I am Tadashi Tanaka. People call me Tad."

"Yes, I think we've met. Sort of."

I never did get a good look at Tanaka in my rearview mirror or as he was sprinting away from Trey's booth at the Carolina Coffee Shop, but up close he looked a pleasant enough fellow. Short hair. Clean shaven. Dressed in better-than-average college kid clothing—chinos, untucked and unbuttoned collared shirt over an untucked tee shirt, all apparently freshly laundered. And canvas sneakers. He'd gotten dressed up for me.

I motioned him to be seated again while I took my own seat behind my desk. I didn't feel like playing "I'm just an ordinary guy" today.

"You're not from around here, are you?" I said. I couldn't help it. You take your shots where you can. Of course, it was totally unfair.

"I don't know what you mean," he answered. "I'm from Tokyo."

"Yes, sorry. It's just a local expression I seem to have picked up."

"Oh."

"What can I do for you?"

He stood up and faced me.

"I am here to apologize, Fairley-san … I mean Mr. Fairley."

"To apologize?"

"Yes. Please excuse me. I have failed. I am a disgrace. I apologize."

"Can you be more specific?"

"I was following you, dangerously closely, and I was caught, Mr. Fairley. Later, you saw me with Trey Spurr, and I ran away. There will be questions. I have lost Trey's trust."

"I see." I didn't.

"I am sorry. Very sorry. I apologize. Profusely."

"You are sorry?"

"Yes."

"Very sorry?"

"Yes, very sorry. I apologize."

"Profusely?"

"I said profusely."

"Have you learned anything from this experience?"

"I don't know."

"Then you should be sorry. Very sorry."

"I said I was sorry. Very sorry. I apologized. Profusely."

"It's okay then."

"I'm sorry."

"That's enough."

"Excuse me."

"You're excused. Now please be quiet for a minute. Let me talk."

"Yes." With a slight bow.

I had never been subjected to a Japanese apology before, although I have read about them. Any minute I was expecting him to pull out a *harikiri* knife and disembowel himself, but maybe they don't do that sort of thing anymore. Or not as much. Anyway, it affected me. In fact, it touched me deeply, even though I couldn't be sure exactly what he was apologizing for. For following me inappropriately, or for getting caught at it? Running away at the Carolina Coffee Shop? Impolite, but not worthy of such a display of contrition, at least not in my book.

"I accept your apology."

"Thank you," said Tanaka. He sat back down.

"But I must admit I'm still a little put out with you."

"Put out?"

"Uh, it means annoyed, irritated."

"I see."

"And I have a bone to pick with you."

"My English is good, I think, but I don't understand some of your sayings."

"Idioms?"

"Yes, idioms."

I decided to use more of them on purpose to keep him off balance.

"It means I have a score to settle with you."

"Is that another idiom?"

"Because of you I got a speeding ticket."

"I got one too."

"You deserved it. You should have gotten one for reckless driving too, and scaring the crap out of me—another idiom, by the way."

"I know that one."

"And forcing me to race through the speed trap hoping the

213

sheriff would stop you, which he did. But later he gave me a ticket too."

"I apologized."

"Yes, but that doesn't change the fact that I want to know what's behind your odd behavior."

"Behind?" He looked around, but of course there was nothing to see but the as yet undecorated beige back wall of my office.

"I mean, what is going on?"

"There is nothing going on."

"Have you ever heard of Kashimoto Foods?"

"No."

"In Tokyo. Big company."

"No, I don't think so."

"They want to acquire Spurr Nutritionals. To buy it. Trey's father's company."

"Yes, Trey has mentioned this, but he has never told me the name of the company."

"How do I know you're not working for them?"

"I am not working for them."

I took out my smartphone and showed Tanaka my photo of Tom Ake and Jerry Bono from General Tso's.

"Do you know these two?"

"No, I've never seen them before. Who are they?"

"Just two guys who work in a Chinese takeout place in Raleigh, but I think they may be working for Kashimoto on the side."

"I don't think so. I mean, uh, they don't look like the type who would be working for a big company like that."

"Like what?"

"You know, like Kashimoto. You said it's a big company. Besides, these men don't look very Japanese."

"You may have me on that point, since everybody knows all

Asian people look alike to us Americans, but I think you know a lot more than you're letting on."

"Letting on?"

Maybe I should dial back the idioms.

"That you know more than you're telling me.

"I don't."

"For all I know, these guys are thugs hired by the Japanese *Yukata* to soften us up so Mrs. Spurr will agree to sell the company to Kashimoto Foods."

"Excuse me, but *yukata* in Japan is a casual summer kimono. Maybe you mean *Yakuza*, the crime syndicate."

"Whatever."

"Kashimoto would never be involved with the Yakuza. They would not hire Japanese thugs."

"You just said you never heard of Kashimoto."

"A big Japanese company would not hire Japanese thugs in America."

This made sense. Japanese thugs would be too obvious anywhere, and especially in Lester County. They would point the finger directly at Kashimoto. No, if Kashimoto hired thugs they would be American thugs. But the American men who had called on Fanny Spurr last week didn't seem like thugs. Boors maybe, but not thugs.

So who were Tom and Jerry? Clearly, somebody had hired them to do what they were doing. Not salting the landscape with menus, of course. That had to be Nick Papadopoulos' doing. No, it was their appearance at the Neighborhood Watch meeting, their appearance at my house later that night, their probable but not provable being the ones who broke in and stole Mr. Z's notes from my briefcase, and their being sighted around town by Sheriff Belton and by Clara Fritts, assuming she would confirm it when he showed her their photo. Whether she did or didn't, the menus they gave her were proof enough for me.

And what exactly was the nature of their relationship to Adam Spurr? No doubt he was lying about offering to let them audit chemistry classes at Duke. I was still waiting to see if the DNA evidence would link the two of them to the gas jets from the research lab, but if it did, what did that mean? It would prove they had been in the lab at some time. Did Adam send them? But why? It wouldn't prove they had been there the night of the explosion, and surely Adam wouldn't have sent them there to murder his brother, no matter how jealous he was of him. Did he send them to the other places as well—the meeting, my house, skulking around town?

Adam knew Kashimoto wanted to buy Spurr Nutritionals. Was Adam using the Japanese-looking Tom and Jerry to cast suspicion on Kashimoto? To give Kashimoto such a bad reputation in Spurrville that they would have to give up their quest? Why would he care?

Suddenly, I thought maybe I knew.

Tanaka had been eying me warily during this extended moment of reflection.

"I'm sorry. I didn't mean to be rude, but I have a lot to think about right now. I hope you understand."

"It's okay, Mr. Fairley. I accept your apology."

"Are you mocking me now?"

"No, sir."

"Why did you run when you saw me come into the coffee house to meet Trey? And by the way, you're not a very good liar. Sheriff Belton told me he did not give you a ticket."

"I apologize."

"Let's don't start that again. Just answer my questions. Friend of Trey's or no friend of Trey's, if you don't I'll have a talk with the sheriff about you and see if he wants to change his mind."

I hoped I had him rattled pretty well now, even without any more intentional idioms.

"How do you know I am Trey's friend?"

"Sheriff Belton again. Confirmed by Trey himself after you ran off."

Tanaka took on a pensive air of his own, as if he were struggling with an inner conflict. It turned out he was.

"Mr. Fairley, I will come clean with you."

"That is a very good idiom, Tad. Congratulations."

"Thank you."

"Come clean about what?"

"You are right about me. Maybe you should be a police detective. It is true I am working for Kashimoto Foods. I was sent here to become a friend of Trey Spurr and spy on him and his family's company. I call Tokyo from time to time and tell them what I am finding out. In return, they pay my expenses to attend the university. It's like a scholarship, what some Americans call 'a full ride.'"

I must admit I was surprised. Maybe I shouldn't have been, based on his strange behavior, but I was. Apparently, my detecting skills needed some further honing.

Sitting there talking to young Tanaka, I couldn't help thinking of my son, William, also a college student who would soon be making his own life-changing decisions. It gave me some empathy for Tanaka even though William's version of a 'full ride' was limited to driving a used Ford Fiesta—dark blue, not red—I bought from my neighbor, Allan Whitbread, after his daughter graduated and joined the Peace Corps.

"What have you told them at Kashimoto?" I asked Tanaka.

"So far, it hasn't been much. That is mainly because Trey doesn't know much. He concentrates on his studies and does not go back to Spurrville very often because he is now an orphan and does not particularly enjoy living with his grandmother. She is strict. Trey has told me the company is working on some new products, but he doesn't know what they are. I know about Mr. Spurr's accident, of course, and I reported that. I know about the explosion in the research lab and the death of Trey's father. Trey was very upset. I know from Trey that his grandmother hired you as an advisor to the company and to write about it. I know you found some evidence that makes the police think Trey's father may have been murdered, and now Trey is more upset. I have reported all these things, but they keep asking for more. Sometimes I have made things up just to have something to report, and I am ashamed of that."

"You know Kashimoto has been trying to buy Spurr Nutritionals."

"Yes. It is why they sent me. Sometimes I drive representatives from the investment banking firm of Kuroibishi-Whitestone to and from the airport."

"Like the two who were here the other day?"

"Yes. Mr. Wright and Mr. Johnson."

"Mrs. Spurr sent them away."

"They deserved it."

Interesting.

"Why are they so desperate to buy Spurr?"

"There is a secret about Spurrt. Kashimoto tests all competitors' products extensively, and they discovered this secret a few years ago. They have not told me what the secret is, but I think they believe it will change the nutritional drink industry somehow and will change the value of the Spurr company."

"And so they want to buy the company before we find out what the secret is."

"Yes. They tell me they think maybe the secret was revealed when Mr. Spurr had the accident, and they want to know if anyone in the company realizes it yet. When I could not find out from Trey, they ordered me to follow you to see if you know what the secret is. If you know, then others in the company must also know."

"I do not know." It wasn't a lie, since I wasn't sure. Yet.

"I told them that."

"Did you tell them what a lousy job you did trying to follow me? How you botched it?"

"Yes. That is why I ran when you came to see Trey. I could not face you yet." Tanaka hung his head. "But what is 'botched'?"

"Screwed up."

"Oh."

"Have you told Trey about all this?"

"Yes. He understood because we are friends. That much is genuine."

Trey must have a tremendous capacity for trauma and disappointment, I thought. Maybe it's a family trait.

"Why are you telling me these things?"

"Because I am ashamed. I have been dishonest. I have betrayed a friend. I have put you in danger."

"You can say that again. I got a speeding ticket too, remember?"

"I have apologized for that."

"So you have." Tanaka was apparently good at compartmentalizing things.

"What will you do now?" I asked. "You have just betrayed Kashimoto."

"To say it the Japanese way, I have lost face because of Kashimoto. Of course it was my decision to work with them, but I was younger and more naïve when they first came to me, and it seemed like a glamorous opportunity. To go to university is very important in Japan."

"I have heard that."

"But now I want to do what is the right thing. I must tell

Kashimoto I cannot go on living a lie. I will tell them I have told you and Trey the truth."

"Even if it means losing your 'full ride'?"

"Maybe they will understand. Maybe because Trey still thinks of me as a real friend now that I have told him the truth, Kashimoto will see an opportunity for me to help represent them to Mrs. Spurr."

"Maybe, but it sounds like a long shot to me."

"I thought a shot is a very quick thing that does not last long. What is a long one?"

"Why don't you look that one up, Tad? Google it."

"Okay."

"Well, thank you for coming to me about this. It took a lot of courage."

"Yes."

"What is it you say in Japanese – *arigato*?"

"*Hai, arigato. Dō itashimashite.* You're welcome. *Dewa Sayonara*, Fairley-san."

Tanaka got up to leave. We shook hands again.

"*Sayonara*, Tanaka-san," I said.

"Or maybe I will just keep on making things up for a while."

Chapter 33

Apparently, Fanny Spurr called Wendell Cox while I was talking with Tanaka because as soon as Tanaka left Cox stuck his head in my doorway and said he needed to see me.

"Your place or mine?" I asked.

"The conference room," he said. "I've already got Jim Sullivan and Wash Booker in there waiting."

"What's up? Do you want Agnes too?" I knew he didn't, and I knew what was up, and if this was to be the start of an historic development, I had to suggest including her.

"Just come. We'll fill her in later."

The conference room wasn't fancy. Its walls, beige like those in my office, sported standard hotel-type framed pictures of bridge scenes. Maybe these were meant to complement the North Carolina lighthouse scenes found in the lobby. The Brooklyn Bridge, the Golden Gate Bridge, Tower Bridge, London Bridge (the one now crossing a canal in Lake Havasu City, Arizona), the Verrazano Narrows Bridge, Sydney Harbor Bridge, the Ponte Vecchio, and the Bridge on the River Kwai, this a still photo from the movie. What they really needed now was a Bridge over Troubled Water.

The furniture had been top of the line in its day, except for the conference table which looked solid mahogany but was only a veneer. The dark blue upholstered swivel chairs on casters were still comfortable but looked shabby. Six inches of a drop-down projection screen dangled forlornly from the ceiling at one end of the room, under which was a small lectern. A digital projector hung from the ceiling at the midpoint, aimed at where the screen would be if fully dropped down. Its remote controller lay beside a dark gray multidirectional teleconferencing phone that resembled a small beached manta ray with a round keypad in place of a spiny tail. There was a thin layer of dust on it.

No coffee. No donuts. Not even any Spurrt. Spartan. Sullivan's doing, presumably, and not unwarranted based on my reading of the financials.

Booker and Sullivan acknowledged me when I walked in, but less than enthusiastically I thought. Probably miffed that once again I might be privy to something they didn't know about yet. Cox got right down to business.

"Mrs. Spurr called. She and Mr. Z want us to run some tests using the ViroBactiZap 5000. They want us to duplicate what happened when Mr. Z fell into it and try to find out how it might have affected the products that were being bottled just then. All but one case of those bottles have been consumed already, by Mr. Z actually, so we won't have much to compare the new production to, but Mr. Z gave Mark here a clue about what to look for."

All eyes on me.

I recounted my morning with the Spurrs and what I had learned about Mr. Z's experience with what I decided on the spur of the moment to call the "accidental Spurrt" versus regular Spurrt, leaving out the fact I had tried a bottle myself and was still feeling its effects. I mentioned the last case in Mr. Z's closet and that he had agreed to make it available. Their eyes on me widened, probably not out of renewed respect for my interrogation and detection skills, but more likely as the implications of Spurrt as a 10-hour pick-me-up began to sink in.

"This means not only do we have to re-create the conditions

and run some product through the machine and then do a chemical analysis of the resulting product compared to normal product and the last remaining bottles from the accident," said Cox, "but also we'll have to test it on volunteers and record its effects on them."

"We've done taste-testing a lot, of course," said Booker, "but never anything like this."

"Never too late to learn," said Cox.

"Will we have to shut down a line to get this done?" asked Sullivan. "We can't afford to slow production right now. It was a real setback when everybody went home the other day."

"No," said Cox. "We haven't been using the line were the accident happened anyway, so there'll be no need to change regular production schedules."

"Who's going to design the test procedures?" asked Booker.

"I'll get the R&D people in here, and they'll develop the protocols, including how to select volunteers to test the experimental product and what instructions they should follow."

Everybody nodded.

"Mrs. Spurr wants Agnes to take notes and Heidi Wilton to take pictures and video as we go along. Which is fine. And don't be surprised if you see young Trey Spurr underfoot. Mrs. Spurr wants him to observe, I guess because he's a chemistry major in school."

Bemused nodding.

"What I'm not sure I understand," Cox continued, looking at me, "is she says she wants Mark to supervise."

It was obviously not a statement but a question. And a challenge. Everyone immediately adopted appropriately quizzical expressions.

"I think she only wants me to stay on top of the situation and make suggestions if I have any," I said, "since I'm the one, other than she, who spoke with Mr. Z. You are in charge, Mr. Cox, and I intend to stay out of your way."

That seemed to satisfy them.

"Okay then, I'll get started with the R&D folks in a few minutes," said Cox. "Just one more thing though. Everybody involved is going to have to sign new nondisclosure agreements. The lawyer is sending them over to me this afternoon."

The meeting was over. I had missed lunch. My watch said it was too late to get anything at the company cafeteria, and I didn't feel like driving to the Set-A-Spell or Hardees. That left the vending machines in the employee break area. Sugar, salt and fat. My favorites. But at least I remembered salt was still okay. Maybe I could find something by Kashi that didn't taste like vitamin-fortified twigs. Were they related to Kashimoto? I doubted it, but these days you never know.

About that time, "La Marseillaise" erupted in my pants again.

Chapter 34

A few hours later another meeting takes place in the ornate conference room of the plush executive office suite on the top floor of the headquarters of the Kashimoto Foods conglomerate in the Shinjuku business district of Tokyo. Only those in the inner circle attend, filling fewer than half of the chairs at the long, solid teak conference table. Kashimoto-*shachō* sits at the head, flanked by his subordinates in strict descending order of subordination.

"Today we speak English," Kashimoto begins. "Practice for our upcoming negotiations with the people from Spurr Nutritionals."

"*Hai!* English!" says a subordinate far down the line. It is Yamada.

Kashimoto looks at Yamada sternly.

"I mean, Yes! English! *Sumimasen!*"

Stern looks from everyone.

"Of course, I mean 'I am sorry.'" Yamada hangs his head in shame.

"Perhaps some of us would like some tea?" suggests Kashimoto.

"I will fetch it!" says Yamada, rising, bowing, and heading to the door.

"Thank you, Yamada-san."

The door closes behind Yamada.

"Now," continues Kashimoto, "Imamura-san, what is your report?"

"Tanaka received his further orders, Kashimoto-*shachō*," says Imamura, his voice quavering as he searches for the correct English phrasings.

Kashimoto nods approvingly.

Imamura, feeling more confident, continues. "He was very pleased with them. He has met with Mark Fairley and believes Fairley has not discovered the secret, but that he is getting close. He reports young Trey Spurr has told him he is invited to observe some testing that is being planned at the bottling plant. The testing involves the ViroBactiZap 5000 machine into which Mr. Zachariah Spurr-*Kaichō* was thrown, causing him to lose his ability to communicate. Tanaka-san does not yet know what has prompted the company to do this testing, but he feels it does not bode well for us."

"Excuse me," pipes up Ohbora from the Technical Research Division. "Tanaka is right. This is what we have feared."

"We must see to it that the machine is destroyed!" says another subordinate.

All heads nod in agreement. Except Kashimoto's.

The heads stop nodding.

"May I continue?" asks Imamura.

Kashimoto nods.

"Tanaka wishes to convey his gratitude for all we are doing for him and says that although he is unworthy he respectfully looks forward to the possibility of finding a humble entry-level position here at Kashimoto Foods where he can be of some small service upon his return to Japan after he graduates with his degree in chemistry, which he feels will be *cum laude* at least. He also wishes us to know that because of his friendship with Trey Spurr, he may be in a position to assist in the negotiations for the acquisition of the company by representing Kashimoto Foods as being honest and trustworthy."

Kashimoto looks at Ohbora.

"Perhaps we can find something for him in the Technical Research Division," says Ohbora.

Kashimoto nods. Everyone nods. Imamura resumes.

"Tanaka is aware of the unfortunate recent encounter between Mrs. Fanny Spurr- *Kaichō Fujin* and the two representatives of Kuroibishi-Whitestone of New York on our behalf, Mr. Johnson and Mr. Wright, and he suggests he may be able to be of some service in repairing the relationship."

"It would seem young Tanaka-san has grown wise beyond his years from his university experience," says Kashimoto. "We have been wise to invest in him."

"Tanaka humbly suggests Mr. Wright is an idiot and should be relieved of his assignment."

At this, Kashimoto nods gravely, as do each of the others in turn.

"Tanaka has taken the liberty of revealing to Trey Spurr his relationship with us and has apologized to him for his deceit. Profusely. And Trey Spurr has forgiven him because he has convinced Trey Spurr he had only the best interests of his friend's family's business at heart."

"Trey Spurr, on the other hand," says Kashimoto, "does not seem wise beyond his years."

"Tanaka apologizes that he may possibly not have a complete understanding of his further orders and asks how he will know when he should kill Mark Fairley."

"Tell him not to do so," says Kashimoto. "Fairley may yet be useful to us."

Imamura nods. Everyone is relieved.

"Now we must give some further consideration to how to stop the tests."

"With respect, Kashimoto-*shachō*, I agree with my colleague across the table," says another subordinate. "The ViroBactiZap 5000 machine must be destroyed."

"Is this what you all think?" says Kashimoto.

"*Hai!*" "*So desu!*" "*Hai, hai!*" All around the table.

A stern look from Kashimoto.

"We mean, Yes, yes!" they say, almost in unison.

"Very well. It is also what I believe. Imamura-san, our young Tanaka has proven to be resourceful. Instruct him to sabotage the machine before the tests can take place."

"At once, Kashimoto-*shachō*."

Kashimoto rises. Everyone rises. The meeting is over. They bow to Kashimoto and to one another. Kashimoto exits. Everyone exits. The door closes behind them.

A short time later the door reopens. Yamada enters, followed by three young women wearing Kashimoto Foods kimonos. They are carrying an elaborate tea service.

The room is empty.

"Well," says Yamada in English, which the women do not understand. "More for me then."

Chapter 35

The call was from Detective Keil, and it was the one I'd been waiting for.

"We got a match on the DNA," he said.

"Only one?"

"Well, there were two, but one was Wendell Cox."

We both knew Cox had put his mouth on the gas jet so he could blow through it to see if it was open or closed.

"So, that just leaves the other one, which is Jerry Bono," Keil continued. "He was definitely in the lab at some point."

"But not Tom Ake?"

"Nope. And I've checked them both out. Bono has an apartment in Raleigh, and Ake lives with his parents. Clean records. No priors. Apparently model citizens, born and raised here. Attended local schools and then a few classes at Durham Tech before getting jobs at that restaurant. But their grandparents were native Hawaiians, which is why everybody thinks they look Asian. They could pass for Japanese."

"Or Chinese, working in that restaurant."

"Right."

"Are you going to arrest Bono?"

"This evidence doesn't prove he was there the night of the explosion, and it doesn't prove he's the one who opened the gas jets. The only thing I could charge him with is trespassing, and then only if someone at Spurr Nutritionals wants to press charges, assuming he wasn't invited there by Elliot Spurr or somebody else."

"Not likely," I said. "But it might have been Adam, although I don't know why."

"I agree. But while I could probably convince somebody at Spurr to press charges, I think there's more to it than that, and I want to let things play out a little longer."

"What are you going to do?"

"I'm going to go question Bono. Rattle his cage and see what falls out. Tom Ake too. Especially since Sheriff Belton told me Clara Fritts recognized the two of them from the pictures we took at the Chinese place."

"Be sure and rattle them about breaking into my house and stealing papers from my briefcase. I'm convinced it was them."

"Oh, I'll do that; don't you worry."

"I have some news for you too," I said.

"I'm listening."

I told Keil what I'd learned from Mr. Z that morning and about the planned tests of more product we would run through the ViroBactiZap 5000 machine. I told him what I'd gleaned from analyzing the Spurr Nutritionals financial statements Jim Sullivan had shown me—how precarious but also how valuable the company was.

"Good motives for murder," he said.

I told him about my conversation with Tad Tanaka, which he found interesting.

"It may explain the timing of Kashimoto's stepped up efforts to convince Fanny Spurr to sell. They're afraid something about Mr. Z's accident may lead to our discovering the secret they've been guarding," I said.

Keil agreed.

"I've got one more thing for you too," Keil continued. "That professor friend of yours, Adam Spurr? Turns out he's a very rich man."

That was a surprise, sort of. But also a relief and a mystery. All in one. Another enigma.

"If money is the motive, then doesn't that take the spotlight off of him?"

"Rich people like to get richer, has been my experience," Keil said.

Keil promised to pass what I'd told him on to Sheriff Belton, the SBI and Detective Blue in Greensboro, and then he said goodbye and hung up. I pondered how much of what he told me I should tell Fanny Spurr. Probably all of it. She could handle it.

Agnes, on the other hand, could wait.

I called Fanny Spurr. I told her all of it, including Adam's apparent relationship with Ake and Bono. She was silent for a long moment and then said, "Little Adam. That poor boy. Heavens to Betsy, what could he be thinking?"

"I wonder the same thing myself, ma'am, but I'm sure Detective Keil will get to the bottom of it, and we'll find out it's something good that for some reason Adam doesn't feel comfortable sharing just yet."

"I do hope you are right, bless his heart."

It probably wasn't the best time to do it, but I went back to something I'd been forgetting to ask her for too long already. I told her about my speeding tickets from Sheriff Belton and asked if she could put in a good word for me.

"Are you asking me to 'fix' them? That is the correct terminology, is it not?"

"Yes, ma'am, to both questions."

"Well, I must agree they do not seem very fair to me either. I will certainly see what I can do."

I thanked her very much, and we ended the conversation. I was still feeling pretty good, at least as much from the effects of the enhanced Spurrt as from Mrs. Spurr's promise to fix my tickets.

I took a moment and changed my ringtone to one that sounds like an actual telephone.

Chapter 36

The drive home from Spurrville usually takes about an hour. That day it seemed to take no time at all. I found Emily in the kitchen and gave her a kiss. A big one.

"Oh my! What's gotten into you?" she said.

I told her.

Chapter 37

I needed a break.

It would take Wendell Cox several days to organize the ViroBactiZap 5000 tests and put together a team of volunteer product tasters, so I didn't have to be in Spurrville for a while. And since Trey would be present on test day, I could wait until then to continue making his acquaintance. I could work on the history project in Greensboro using material I brought home in my briefcase. Locked.

Detective Keil didn't need my help to rattle cages, and Detective Blue seemed content to await events before deciding whether to go after Ake and Bono himself for the break-in at my house, which would involve jurisdictional issues, or simply drop the case for lack of evidence.

I didn't sleep well that night even though I was safe at home with Emily snoozing softly beside me. I couldn't turn my mind off, and when I did drift into slumber I was haunted by dream snippets. Little red cars chasing me, driven by midget Shriners. Drowning in a sea of takeout menus while Clara Fritts, Agnes Smith and Fanny Spurr looked on, cackling like witches. Why them? They were the good guys. Being in a familiar building looking for a men's room and discovering someone had either removed them all or turned them into Florida rooms. The building exploding. Fortunately, I got out alive, but I still had to go to the bathroom.

I awoke at 4:00 a.m. and did go to the bathroom, happy to see it had not been turned into a Florida room. After that, I tossed and turned until finally getting up again around 6:30. My prostate was normal the last time I had a physical, so it must be the stress.

Emily was already up. Breakfast was fried eggs, bacon and pancakes, with strawberries this time. Sometimes it's banana slices. Although I had slept poorly, I didn't feel abnormally tired. However, while getting my coffee I noticed I had absent-mindedly not belted my pants tightly enough, and it felt strange.

"My pants are loose," I remarked to Emily, although why such a thing would be remarkable did not occur to me. Sometimes you just say things.

"Loose lips sink ships," I said. "I wonder what loose pants do."

"They fall down," said Emily.

Both of us burst out laughing. Maybe it was a release of the tension we'd both been under. Mine from being in the middle of the action. Hers from not being there and worrying about me instead. I tightened my belt.

Belt tightening is something I'll be thinking a lot more about if I don't find a real job soon. Or if my book doesn't sell. Or if I don't win the lottery. I'd gotten so caught up in the consulting detective thing I had gotten slack about looking at the ads in the *Wall Street Journal* and following up on résumés I had sent out. With no responses from any of them, it was as if the world had put me on hold until things got straightened out in Lester County. And except for Fanny Spurr's dazzlingly bright Florida room, Lester County was starting to remind me of a dark, ersatz amusement park where the dodge 'ems give you whiplash and the roller coaster only goes down.

For some reason I made my coffee fuzzy that morning on purpose. I'd decided I liked it that way. Sort of a poor man's cappuccino but without the cream and cinnamon.

Later, when reviewing my notes, I realized the change in my coffee tastes was an example of what we writers call "character development." According to experts, it's important that characters demonstrate development. I wondered if changing my ringtones a couple of times was another good example. Or forgetting to tighten my pants.

I spent the morning at the computer following up on contacts and doing some networking by e-mail. I made a couple of calls to headhunters I'd worked with in my previous lives and to whom I'd sent updated résumés, but they had nothing that was even a loose fit, so to speak.

Were jobs like pants? If it's a loose fit do you fall down on the job? Sorry, not funny.

I checked the *Wall Street Journal* and a few other sources of job postings and found three that looked interesting enough to act on, which I did, tailoring cover letters and e-mailing them with my résumé.

Out of curiosity, I Googled "private investigator equipment" to see what would come up. There were 16,200,000 results. I didn't have time to look at all of them that day, or in this lifetime, but one caught my eye. From this site you could order a complete private eye kit—they called it a combo deal—that looked like it had everything the aspiring gumshoe would need. Let's see …

- Personalized private eye folio with leather case in your choice of black or brown with a badge flap that folds to the outside of the case
- Private Investigator badge
- Investigator ball cap (black, white, red or blue)
- Private Investigator windshield pass
- Do it yourself ID card kit
- Your choice of Federal Eagle, Compass Rose, Lady Justice or Security Enforcement hologram for the ID card and windshield pass

All for only $90 plus tax and shipping. Almost worth it just for the cool hat.

I decided to take a pass on the private eye combo kit, at least unless and until the Spurr gig turned into a permanent calling. Then I might spring for a better one. Maybe there's a $150 version that comes with flashlight, compass and lockpicking tools. And maybe a deerstalker cap and magnifying glass. A kit with a pair of actual gumshoes was probably at least $200. But it would be deductible as a business expense.

Then, of course, there was still my detective name to think about. I'm no Sherlock, Sir Arthur Conan Doyle is long gone and last I heard Doc Watson was a bluegrass guitar player, so I was having to figure things out on my own. Jake was a good name, but taken. Dirk still had a nice ring to it. But would it go well with Fairley? Maybe I needed a new last name too. Dirk Pitt? Good, but taken by author Clive Cussler and, I suspect, with just the slightest bit of tongue-in-cheek. I've read *Dirk Gently's Holistic Detective Agency*, a funny spoof by Douglas Adams. As a detective, maybe I'm kind of a spoof myself. So why not an outrageous surname? Like Falcone, maybe. "Dirk Falcone, Private Eye. Have Intuition, Will Travel."

I'd have to sleep on it. Too soon to order new business cards anyway. After giving one to Detective Keil, I still had 249 left from my original supply of 250, the Office Depot minimum order. Keil was not likely to hire me, but maybe he could be a reference.

Besides, a name like Dirk raises expectations, if not eyebrows. The downside is people might start calling me "Dork."

My day's work done, I took Emily to lunch at Lucky 32 and spent the rest of the afternoon on my deck watching old *Magnum, P.I.* episodes on Emily's iPad. I needed some pointers. That evening, we called Lisa, Judy and William at their respective schools, which we try to do at least once a week. Fortunately, none of them asked for any money this time.

After two more days of doing domestic stuff around the house but otherwise taking it easy—although I did do some work on the history—it was time to head back to Spurrville for the big experiment. Remembering the video of Mr. Z's accident, I didn't wear a tie.

Chapter 38

Jerry Bono was nervous. And it wasn't simply because he couldn't keep straight when he should be using his fake Chinese accent and when he should be using his fake Japanese accent. That didn't seem to bother Tom, but the other problem was, Jerry couldn't tell the difference between the two accents, but he assumed there should be one, and it worried him. What if he wasn't fooling anybody?

Chinese for the restaurant or when asking permission to leave takeout menus. Japanese for field ops, as he liked to call his forays into danger and intrigue at the bidding of the shadowy figure he now knew as Professor Adam Spurr of Duke University. But sometimes leaving takeout menus was part of a field op, so he had to be prepared to gingerly switch between the two accents as circumstances demanded.

With his native Hawaiian features, he knew he looked the part, or parts, as did Tom for the same reason. And he'd heard a great many Japanese and Chinese accents on TV shows, although of course it was impossible to tell which were authentic and which were fake. He knew both the Chinese and the Japanese had trouble with the English "r" and "l" sounds and frequently confused the two or muffed them altogether. So if he put his mind to it, Jerry could confuse them on purpose. He would practice in front of the medicine cabinet mirror in the bathroom of his tiny Raleigh apartment. "I come flom Japan, and I velly happy in North Calorina." It was a tongue-twister for sure, but he worked hard at it.

241

Switching to Chinese meant not only intentionally confusing "r" and "l," but also emphasizing the halting, missing-words style he had seen in Charlie Chan movies on late night TV and saying "Ah, so" a lot with his tongue held behind his bottom teeth. Someone had told him Warner Oland, the actor who played Charlie Chan, the famous fictional Chinese detective of the Honolulu police force, was Swedish-American, but he didn't believe it.

Jerry had noticed Charlie Chan used a lot of clever philosophical sayings. He'd heard of Confucius, a famous Chinese person who was quoted a lot by smart people. Many statements containing important ideas began with, "Confucius say …" Jerry assumed Charlie Chan was quoting Confucius and thought it would be useful to salt his fake Chinese conversations with as many of these important sayings as he could remember, whether they fit the occasion or not. So along with, "You wan' wanton on top that?" and "Spling loll velly nice today" went "Aras, mouse cannot cast shadow like erephant" and "Cannot tewr where path read until leach end of load." And his favorite, "A woman not made for heavy thinking, but should arways decolate scene like brossom of prum." He'd noticed that when he tried to utter these gems, especially the last one, he was not fully understood, which Tom said was just as well or he and General Tso's Golden Chicken Pagoda might have gotten into a lot of trouble.

Once, when he Googled "Famous quotations" in order to beef up his aphorism repertoire, the first famous quotater who came up was Yogi Berra. He assumed Yogi Berra's name was an Americanized version of Yoga, which he thought was Chinese. Therefore, Yoga Berra was probably a contemporary of Confucius, and they probably competed with each other over who could come up with the cleverest sayings. "It's deja vu awr ova again." "Neva ansa anonymous retter." "Future not what it used to be." "When come to folk in load, take it." And many more. These sounded pretty good to Jerry.

Jerry wasn't trying to make fun of Chinese accents, or of Japanese. He respected Chinese and Japanese people, although he didn't know any of them personally. In fact, he felt a sort of kinship with them because of his own Polynesian heritage. He was simply doing his best to carry out the wishes of his employers, Nick Papadopoulos and the Duke professor.

Nick Papadopoulos wasn't much help as an accent coach. "When the customers come in, just try and sound Chinese, that's all. Don't worry, they'll fall for it." And they usuarry did.

It was different for Tom. The whole business of the stupid aphorisms drove him nuts because he couldn't think of any, and so he didn't talk much whether at the restaurant or in the field, leaving most of it to Jerry except when they were in a jam.

Which they were in now. Which was another reason Jerry was nervous. That detective, Keil, had just now parked his dark gray unmarked Ford Crown Victoria outside General Tso's and was on his way in.

It was mid-morning, before the lunch rush, and the place was empty, but Jerry was at his accustomed station behind the order counter. José was in the kitchen frying rice and steaming dumplings. The koi were swimming lazily in their aquarium. Tom was sweeping the floor in the dining area. It was make-work because he and Jerry had swept up carefully the night before, but he needed something to do because you never knew when Nick would pop in unannounced. All three were wearing their little paper chef hats. The koi were not.

In fact, Nick Papadopoulos was spending the morning at one of his two Italian restaurants, Mama Papadapa's, named in honor of his mother who was Greek but could pass for Italian. It was her profile on the restaurant's logo and menus, facing left, which did not feature her best side. His other Italian restaurant was Mama Papadapa's Too, and on its logo Mrs. Papadopoulos' profile faced right, which did. He'd promised Mama he would change the profile at the first restaurant, but somehow he had never gotten around to it. It would have meant buying and installing new signage and printing up new menus, which for the Italian restaurant were much more expensive than the flimsy ones he gave away by the hundreds from General Tso's. When Nick or his father took Mrs. Papadopoulos out for dinner, it was always to Mama Papadapa's Too, or sometimes to his Indian restaurant, Tandoor City.

Detective Keil opened the door and entered General Tso's as if he owned it. He paused, let his stern gaze sweep over the newly-swept room, nodded to himself, and strode to the counter.

"What's the cheapest thing on the menu?" he demanded.

"Loast pork egg lowr. One dorra," stammered Jerry.

"What?"

"Loast pork egg lowr. One dorra," tried Jerry again.

"Okay, never mind that. What's the next cheapest thing.

"Fantail shlimp. Dorra ten."

"Sounds good. How many shrimps come with that?"

"One."

"You gotta be kidding. Okay, what's after that?"

"Spling lowr, vegebal onry. Dorra twenty. Afta that, shlimp egg lowr, dorra twenty-five. Then jump up flom there."

"Okay, gimme a shlimp ... I mean shrimp egg roll, please."

"You wan' wanton on top that?"

"What?"

Tom had had enough of the charade.

"Just talk plain English, Jerry!"

"Do you want some wanton soup with that, sir?"

Somewhat taken aback, but only somewhat, Keil answered. "No, thanks."

244

"Okay, that's a dollar thirty-four with tax."

Jerry tonged a shrimp egg roll, put it into a small takeout container, put the container in a plastic grocery bag with a Food Lion logo on it, took Keil's money and gave him his change.

"Where's your boss?" asked Keil.

"He's not here today."

"Crap! A dollar thirty-four down the drain."

"But he may come back any time," said Tom. "Often does."

"Goody. Something to look forward to then."

Keil decided to leave the shrimp egg roll in the bag instead of eating it, so he'd have something to show if Papadopoulos did come back.

"Anyway, it's you two I came to see."

Jerry froze. As did José, but Keil couldn't see him in the relative darkness of the kitchen. Jerry leaned on his broom and waited.

"Come over here, Mr. Ake," Keil said.

Tom came over and stood next to Jerry behind the counter, as if it would provide him some protection from what might be coming. He leaned the broom against the wall. Keil sniffed the air quizzically, momentarily resembling a bipedal bloodhound. He grimaced.

"On second thought, Mr. Ake, maybe you should go sit over there," he said, indicating a table on the far side of the little room. He'd forgotten about Tom's cologne fetish. Tom sat.

"And take off the little hats."

Tom and Jerry took off their hats. José, still in the kitchen, took off his hat.

That settled, Keil regrouped.

"All right, you two, let me lay it out for you. We know you were in Greensboro at Mark Fairley's Neighborhood Watch meeting. Who else would leave takeout menus from this

245

restaurant and be dumb enough to leave them as far away as Greensboro? Besides, Fairley identified you right here the other day as being the ones he saw there. His wife confirmed it when we showed her your pictures. We know you've been skulking around in Spurrville pretending to be Japanese or Chinese or something because Sheriff Belton recognized your pictures, as did the waitress at the Set-A-Spell Restaurant where, again, you left some takeout menus. Not the height of tact, I might add, leaving menus at somebody else's restaurant. But that's not a crime, is it? Dumb, but not a crime. I've got to give you credit, though, for not leaving any fingerprints. Must have been wearing gloves."

Jerry was beginning to feel faint. He wanted to sit down. Maybe have a slug of warm wanton soup broth to calm his nerves. Tom sat stone still. José snuck out the back door for a smoke. Keil saw the door open and close, momentarily letting in some sunlight, but he ignored it.

"Don't plan on going anywhere, you two; there's more," Keil went on. "We know it was you two Fairley's neighbor saw lurking around Fairley's house after the meeting while he and his wife were out guarding the neighborhood. We're pretty sure it was you who broke in and stole some things from his briefcase. Can't prove it now, but when we do, you'll go away for a long time. Now, have you got anything to say?"

Tom and Jerry both shook their heads almost imperceptibly. Jerry came out from behind the counter and sat down at one of the other tables.

"I'll go on then, gentlemen, if you'll permit. Your trail of takeout menus tells us you've been in the office reception area at Spurr Nutritionals and the lobby of the research lab that blew up. Were you there by invitation, or did you just sneak in after-hours somehow?"

Keil paused to see what reaction this might elicit. There was none, although Jerry looked like he might burst into tears at any moment.

"No comment, eh?"

There was none.

"Well riddle me this then. How did your DNA, Mr. Bono, come to be found on two gas jets at the lab that were turned on so the place filled up with gas, killing Mr. Elliot Spurr before exploding in a ball of flames like an atomic bomb?"

Tom looked at Jerry.

Jerry did burst into tears.

"I didn't kill anybody!" he blubbered.

"Is that the night you were there?" asked Tom incredulously. "While I was on my date?"

"I ... I don't know. Maybe. But I swear I didn't kill anybody."

"So, Mr. Ake, you claim you weren't there with Mr. Bono, eh? I'm not surprised. A typical case of honor among thieves gone awry, or in this case among murderers."

"No, no. I really wasn't there. I had a date. I remember because she had to drive her own car because Jerry had ours that night. And also because it's the one and only date I've had in about a year."

I can't imagine why, thought Keil but didn't say so.

"A memorable occasion, I'm sure. And I suppose your date will confirm your alibi?"

"I guess so. She wasn't real happy about the car thing, but it was either that or a bus. I can't afford taxis."

"Okay, why don't you just sit quietly over there for a while, Mr. Ake," said Keil. Keil remained standing at the counter.

A customer opened the door, looked in, surveyed the situation, and quietly left. The koi in the aquarium appeared unconcerned.

"Well, it looks like you're on your own here, Mr. Bono. For the present anyway."

"I have to go to the bathroom," said Jerry with some urgency.

"You can hold it just a little longer," said Keil. "I'm almost finished."

He was used to this kind of squirming when he had a suspect dead to rights, and he liked it. Instead of continuing, Keil waited. He said nothing for almost a full minute during which he just stared at Jerry. And stared. And stared some more.

Jerry cracked.

"I didn't mean it! It was an accident! It was just a joke, a practical joke! You have to believe me!"

"Some joke!" said Keil. "You killed a man!"

"No! I was just going to let the water run so they'd have a big water bill, that's all!"

"What the crap are you talking about, Bono?"

"I just turned on a bunch of water faucets and got out of there as soon as I could. I didn't find anything, and I didn't take anything. Please!"

"Wait, you thought those were water faucets?"

"They were! I wondered why no water came out at first, but I thought it was just air in the pipes or something."

"You were going to flood the lab with water?"

"No! Not flood it. The water would just go down the drains in the sinks! That's all! How could water explode? How could it make a fire? If anything, it should have put out a fire, right?"

"You didn't smell the gas?"

"What gas? There was gas?" said Jerry.

Jerry paused and thought a moment. Difficult, considering everything that was running through his mind.

"Wait. I remember now, I had a real bad cold that night. I couldn't smell anything. Coughing and sneezing, blowing my nose, hoping nobody would hear me."

That explains the spittle and snot, thought Keil.

Two more customers looked in, held a short conference on the sidewalk, and walked away.

"So, Mr. Bono, let me see if I got this straight. You're telling me you opened a bunch of gas jets you *thought* were water faucets, and then you just left the building?"

"I guess so. Yes. Am I in trouble?"

What. A. Jerk. thought Keil.

"I'd have to say I think you're in a little trouble, yes."

"I really have to go to the bathroom."

"Me too," said Tom.

"Shut up," said Keil. "Right now, Bono, I've got you for involuntary manslaughter at least. That's good for about 25 years. Plus, trespassing, breaking and entering, reckless endangerment, destruction of property, wasting natural resources and who knows what else. Probably illegal parking too."

Keil knew involuntary manslaughter was a Class F felony in North Carolina and carried a sentence of 10 to 41 months, only 3½ years max and probably a lot less or maybe even zero for a certifiable idiot, but Jerry didn't know that.

"But if you cooperate right now, maybe I can help you. How about it?"

Jerry whimpered.

"I'll take that as a yes. Were you working for somebody? Who sent you?"

Silence.

"Was it that professor, what was his name? Adam Spurr?"

More silence. Some squirming.

"I thought so. Why did he send you?"

Tom spoke up, and this time Keil let him talk.

"All he ever told us was he wanted us to look for information about what Elliot Spurr was up to in the lab. He thought maybe Mr. Fairley might have some information, too, but we were just supposed to keep an eye on him, maybe scare him a little. Same with Elliot Spurr, except the scaring part. We weren't supposed to hurt anybody."

"I didn't even know he was in the lab that night," said Jerry.

"So you did break into Fairley's house, then?" said Keil.

"No!" said Tom, looking hard at Jerry.

Darn, he got smart for a second, thought Keil. He knows I can't prove they did it so he's denying it.

"Okay then, one more question. Why were you pretending to be Japanese, or whatever?"

"We don't know," Tom and Jerry said in unison.

Keil rolled his eyes and threw up his hands, then pulled out his handcuffs.

"Jerry Bono, you're under arrest for the murder of Elliot Spurr and for all that other stuff at the lab. Get on your feet."

Jerry got up, and Keil handcuffed him.

"I still have to go to the bathroom."

Keil sighed and removed the handcuffs.

"Go ahead then, but don't try anything. I can see the back door from here. If you don't come back in two minutes, I'm taking Mr. Ake in instead. And be sure and wash your hands!"

Jerry went. José opened the back door and looked in, then closed the door again.

Jerry was back in under two minutes. The cuffs went back on. Keil read him his rights, picked up the bag with the shrimp egg roll, and marched Jerry to the door.

"Wait! The keys!" cried Tom. "The car keys!"

Jerry looked at Keil. Keil removed the handcuffs. Jerry fumbled for the keys to the Tercel, fished them out of his pants pocket and tossed them to Tom. Keil put the handcuffs back on.

"Journey of thousand miwr start with first step!" yelled Jerry.

Then they were out the door and gone.

José returned. He put his little paper chef hat back on. Tom sat dumbfounded for a moment before finally putting his hat back on too, standing up, going to the bathroom, washing his hands thoroughly and then taking up his station behind the counter. It was almost time for the lunch crowd, a few of whom appeared to be milling around uncertainly on the sidewalk.

Suddenly, Nick Papadopoulos was among them, enthusiastically motioning for them all to come on in. Nick followed them through the door. He looked around. The place was clean. Good. There were customers. Good. The koi looked content. Good, but who cares? José was in the kitchen. Good. Tom was on duty. Good.

"Where's Jerry?" he said.

"That Detective Keil was here. He arrested Jerry and took him away."

"The detective, huh? I hope he ordered something."

Chapter 39

The scene surrounding the ViroBactiZap 5000 machine on the botting line was quite the tableaux. The key players were assembled and ready: Wendell Cox; the bottling line operator and a shift foreman; two technicians; a representative from R&D; Jim Sullivan; Wash Booker; Heidi Wilton with her video camera on a tripod and a still camera on a strap around her neck; me; and Trey Spurr who had unexpectedly brought Tad Tanaka along as a friendly observer. Cox seemed uneasy about that, as was I, but it was Trey Spurr, after all, son of the late Elliot Spurr and grandson of the great Mr. Z, so what could we say?

We were all wearing kudzu-green construction-type hard hats with a stylized, energetic-looking red "S" on the front. Our cell phones were silenced.

The area was cordoned off to a wide distance with Caution tape, and a security guard patrolled the perimeter so curious onlookers could neither interfere nor know exactly what we were up to. They could easily guess the what, I supposed, but not the why.

As in the video I'd watched, the gray, boxlike ViroBactiZap 5000 straddled the bottling line between the filling operation and the bottle capping station, forming a bridge for the bottles to pass under. I couldn't see if there were any moving parts, and it looked like the bottles wouldn't be touched as they passed. The only marking on the machine that stood out to me today was a sign saying "Danger, High Voltage."

Not having heard from Detective Keil for a couple of days,

253

I had called him from home the previous afternoon to see how his cage rattling had gone. Apparently, it had gone well. Jerry Bono had confessed to being in the lab the night of the explosion. Tom, it seemed, had an alibi, but Keil had arrested Jerry at General Tso's and taken him to jail.

"These guys are unbelievably dumb, if you ask me," Keil said. "I don't think Bono realized he was opening gas jets or even that he was at the lab the same night as the explosion until I connected the dots for him. I'm convinced nobody intentionally killed Elliot Spurr."

"I guess that's good to know."

"Yeah, and I've told Sheriff Belton and Marshall Blue over your way, and Belton tells me he's relieved and so is Fanny Spurr that at least now we know nobody's out to get them. Still, nobody can figure out why these guys were pretending to be Japanese or whatever. They say they don't know either, which makes no sense at all. All the way to the station, Bono kept saying things like, 'It gets late early out here. It ain't over till it's over. Humility only defense against rightful blame. Man who ride tiger cannot dismount.' Stuff like that. In that stupid Chinese accent. I couldn't get him to shut up."

"Sounds like a combination of Yogi Berra and Charlie Chan," I said. "Strange."

"You can say that again. They also fingered Adam Spurr as their boss in all this, but they don't seem to have a clue why or what he was up to. But I'll find out."

I had my suspicions about Adam but decided it was premature to tell Keil about them.

"I must say, you don't seem very pleased about arresting Bono."

"You're right, I'm not. Still too many unanswered questions. And, sure, I'm glad we got to the bottom of who's responsible for the explosion and all, but it wasn't a very satisfying bust."

"Because?"

"I like my criminals hard-boiled, Mr. Fairley. Mean and nasty and arrogant, even if a little short-changed in the brains department. I like it when I can have some fun crackin' 'em. You know, knocking them off their tough guy horses. But these two guys are just idiots, especially Bono. No attitudes to break. Just unadulterated stupidity. No law against that, unfortunately. But they're such transparent dimwits I'm surprised those pictures we took of them on our smartphones even came out. It'll be a miracle if either one of them does any jail time."

"What about the break-in at my house?" I asked.

"No, they didn't confess to the break-in, but you can bet I'm going to sweat Bono some more, and we'll see what pops out."

Wendell Cox was about to start the ball rolling at the test site so I stopped thinking about Keil and paid attention to his instructions.

"Listen up, everybody! First of all, you'll need your ear protection," said Cox, clearly unhappy there was such a crowd gathered around.

He handed out foam earplugs which we squeezed and rolled up tightly in our fingers and inserted into our ears.

"There's really not much to see, but here's what's going to happen. As before, when Mr. Z had his accident, we're going to run a small test batch of 10 cases of regular Spurrt, or 240 12 oz. bottles. As soon as the line starts up, I'll push this green button which activates the ViroBactiZap 5000. If there's any problem, I'll hit the red shutoff button. Everybody okay with that?"

Everybody was.

"When we're done, the R&D folks will collect the bottles and take them away for testing. Nobody but them is to touch those bottles. Okay? Now make sure you stand well clear of the line."

Heidi Wilton turned on her video camera.

At a nod from Cox, the line operator removed the safety cover from a control box and flipped a toggle switch. The conveyor belt noisily came to life. Then Cox pushed the green button. Bottles proceeded rapidly through the new machine.

"Nothing's happening!" shouted Tanaka, edging closer to the line. "Is it working? I don't see anything!"

"There's nothing to see!" yelled Cox over the din of the machinery. "The beam is invisible. Now please back away!"

"Then how do you know if it's working?"

Tanaka moved closer to the ViroBactiZap 5000. From where I stood it looked like he had something in his hand that he had just dug out of his pocket. Was it a rock? He bent over as if to get a better look at the bottles whizzing into the machine.

As Cox reached to take Tanaka by the shoulder and coax him away, Tanaka's Visitor badge and lanyard fell loose and wrapped itself around one of the bottles hurtling into the tunnel. Before anyone could react, Tanaka plunged head first on to the bottling line and through the ViroBactiZap 5000. He shot out the other side, landing in a heap on the floor at the feet of one of the technicians.

"Tad!" yelled Trey, too late.

Red warning lights flashed and safety klaxons sounded. The bottling line did not shut down. An eerie bluish glow enveloped the ViroBactiZap 5000, and inside it thousands of mini-lightning sparks played on the bottles as they continued to pass through, like a Tesla coil experiment, accompanied by a continuous zapping sound that rivaled the decibels of the line itself.

Quickly, Cox sprang to the line controls and flipped the "off" switch. Almost simultaneously, a technician thrust a clipboard through the bluish glow and hit the red button on the ViroBactiZap 5000. The sounds died away. The blue glow faded. There was deathly silence.

On the floor, shoeless, his shirt in shreds, Tanaka moaned softly, held up a trembling right hand, waving it gently from side to side, and whispered, "*Dai jobu desu.*"

Heidi Wilton remained transfixed behind the still-running video camera. Later, the slowed-down video would show the same barest hint of a bluish glow fading from Tanaka's head as the one that had enveloped Mr. Z's on the previous occasion. Tanaka raised his head once, briefly, before passing out.

Chapter 40

Tom Ake was angry. Royally PO'ed.

Once the initial shock and surprise of Jerry's sudden arrest had worn off, Tom realized he felt no real emotion about it. He didn't care. But then he thought he was supposed to care. So then he started to feel guilty that he didn't care. So he decided he would care. A lot. And now he did. And now he also felt anger over the guilt of not having cared before. And that had him PO'ed. Mostly at that meddler, Mark Fairley.

If only Fairley hadn't gotten involved, all the way from Greensboro, for Pete's sake. If only he hadn't been there for Jerry and him to chase around looking for whatever they could find that might interest the professor, they wouldn't have had to break into his house and his briefcase. To find what? Just some old illegible notes. And only copies at that. Although one of them did seem to please the professor. Who, when it came to it, which might be very soon, would leave them hanging out to dry because, as he'd reminded them, he'd never asked them to break into Fairley's house. And it was the professor who kept sending them back to that research lab at the company. Over and over again, until something bad happened. Through no fault of Jerry's. Maybe he should be angry at the professor. But he was paying them good money for their work. No, if it hadn't been for Fairley finding those gas jets with Jerry's DNA everything would still be okay. Except Elliot Spurr would still be dead, of course, but that couldn't be helped.

Tom was very, very angry. He had to do something. Fairley had to pay.

But how?

I won't really hurt him, Tom thought, remembering the professor's earlier admonition. I'll just scare him half to death. But, again, how?

Tom thought and thought. And he thought some more. Then it hit him. His dad had a gun, and Tom knew where he kept it. It wouldn't be too hard to borrow it, just once, without his dad finding out.

Tom had never fired his dad's gun, or any gun for that matter. His dad wasn't the type for teaching his son guy stuff like baseball, football, fishing or hunting. Or cigar smoking or beer drinking, although he was good at those. Or how to talk to women. Tom had pretty much been on his own in those departments since he was a little boy. His mom had tried teaching him things once in a while, but she was more into cooking and decorating and gardening, and these days even more into her bridge club. All wonderful things Tom appreciated, but they weren't guy things. She was definitely never a soccer mom. No matter. What could be hard about shooting a gun?

Finding the right ammunition, for one thing. As far as Tom knew, his dad didn't have any in the house. The gun was a Walther PPQ, similar in Tom's mind to the Walther PPK favored by James Bond, so it must be a good one. It was a nine millimeter semi-automatic pistol with a magazine that held 12 bullets. Or was it 15? Who cared? He wouldn't be counting his shots like Clint Eastwood, and he didn't expect anybody to be shooting back.

So at least Tom knew what size bullets to look for. He went to a Field & Stream store in Raleigh. He couldn't believe the selection! So many choices! Lead round nose, wad cutter (whatever that was—sounded more like something used on chewing tobacco), semi wad cutter, full metal jacket, semi jacket, full jacket hollow point, semi jacket hollow point, and more. And so many brands!

Tom was tempted to ask a store clerk for help, but he knew the clerk would have to ask a lot of questions in order to help Tom narrow down his selection options. He couldn't have that. "What do you recommend if I only want to scare somebody?" was not likely to get him where he wanted to go. So again he was on his own. He figured blanks would be the safest thing, but what was the fun in that? Would it scare Fairley? No, for that he needed something that was still reasonably safe but produced the satisfying sounds of ricochet. Bang! -whang-ang-ang-ang-ang. He could hear it in his head. He finally settled on a box of semi jacket hollow points. Being hollow, they were probably the next best thing to blanks.

Gun. Bullets. A little extra cologne as a confidence builder. He was ready.

Chapter 41

"*Dai jobu desu,*" which I later found out means something like "I'm okay," were the last coherent words spoken by Tadashi Tanaka for a long time. And they were a lie, as were so many other things in his young life. The only things about him I believed were true were he was working for Kashimoto Foods and he was genuinely Trey Spurr's friend. The fact that those two truths were largely incompatible was clearly having an effect on him, as evidenced by his leveraging the friendship to gain access to the ViroBactiZap 5000 machine so he could sabotage it. The rock lying beside him on the floor after the commotion had died down was proof enough.

But why? Evidently, as Tanaka had admitted to me in my office, the people at Kashimoto knew something the rest of us didn't know or weren't supposed to know, and they didn't want us to find out. Obviously, it had something to do with what we might discover as a result of our test of the machine. To me it seemed they had sent Tanaka on a fool's errand. They must have figured out we had at least a theory about what we would learn in the testing. Otherwise, why test? Surely it must have occurred to someone at Kashimoto that if the ViroBactiZap 5000 were destroyed it would only be a setback, that we would simply get another one and run more tests, even if we had to throw a life-size dummy or something through it to duplicate the conditions of the previous two unfortunate incidents, and that we would be all the more determined because of what their futile gesture had told us about the importance of doing so.

But maybe they were trying to buy time by delaying things, hoping somehow they could repair their current rift with Fanny Spurr over the two gentlemen from New York who had so offended her—and now this, of course—and finally achieve success in their increasingly lucrative bids to buy out Spurr Nutritionals. Maybe they weren't as smart and sophisticated as they made themselves out to be. Certainly not on as low a level as were Tom and Jerry, the two fake Japanese guys, but low enough. Sending a boy with a rock in his pocket to sabotage an experiment at a big corporation spoke of desperation, not finesse.

Tanaka was hustled off to the company infirmary where the security guard kept an eye on him until Sheriff Belton came to arrest him. Trey Spurr and the company nurse were the only ones allowed in to see him.

Talking to Wendell Cox later, I resisted the urge to say, "It must have been like déjà vu all over again," but it was not lost on either of us how events had conspired to create test conditions almost identical to those that had started all this in the first place. Not that anyone wished harm on poor Tanaka, but they couldn't very well have been more ideal. Was it fate? Good living? Kashimoto getting their just desserts? Who knows?

While everyone rushed to unsilence their cell phones and begin making calls or resume video games—you couldn't tell—including me except I didn't make any calls, Cox supervised the transfer of the test bottles to the R&D people. With his approval, they had carved out a small space in an unused section of the shipping dock area for a makeshift combination lab and clinic, and the employees who had been carefully selected as "tasters" were assembled and ready for their instructions. Basically, they were to record their going-in feelings and emotional state on a detailed questionnaire, and the three company nurses—who were getting a full workout today between this job and giving first aid to Tanaka—would take their blood pressure and other vitals, plus blood and urine samples—all to provide a baseline. Then half the subjects would be given normal regular Spurrt. This was the control group. The other half would get the test Spurrt from this morning's run. All would be directed to drink a bottle at pre-determined intervals for the next several days. None of the volunteers, or "subjects," was told which kind of Spurrt they were getting. After each imbibing, a nurse would check them again, and they would again record their feelings and state of mind. It was going to get tedious pretty quickly for them, but they were all in line for nice bonuses, so they would probably tolerate it well enough. The repeated peeing and bloodletting might become a literal pain very soon, however, and no one would want to be stopped by Sheriff Belton or a deputy with needle tracks in their arms, but it couldn't be helped. Each volunteer was given an official card stating they were participating in a test, which they could show if necessary. The whole thing was well thought out and administered, as far as I could tell.

Before carting Tanaka away, Sheriff Belton commandeered a copy of the video file on a thumb drive from Heidi Wilton and then questioned everyone who had witnessed the bizarre incident. He used my little office to interrogate each witness separately. He asked me to sit in, as sort of a super-witness, I guess. That was okay with me, but it got pretty boring after a while, listening to the same story over and over with only a few inconsistencies. This time, instead of blind men describing an elephant, everybody had seen the whole scene wide-eyed, although, like the blind men, from different vantage points.

Agnes Smith, who had not been at the scene, was only too happy to take notes for Belton as he plowed through the group.

She sat on the edge of my desk, which was disconcerting to Belton at first, but he eventually got used to it. He started with Trey Spurr and then interviewed Wendell Cox and all the others in turn, working his way down the list and saving me for last.

"Well, Mr. Fairley, the suspects, if that's what they are, seem to drop like flies when you're around," he said, clearly referring to Ake, Bono and Tanaka.

"I don't know what you mean, Sheriff," I said.

"Of course you don't."

He was very thorough with me.

By the time Belton had questioned everyone, the whole ordeal had taken all morning and part of the afternoon, with lunch only a short break for sandwiches brought in from the company cafeteria. I'm sure it was more tiring for him than for the rest of us, but that was his job, and I thought he was doing it well. Of course, I didn't forget he needed to look good for Fanny Spurr and the SBI.

"I heard what Trey Spurr told you, but I wonder what he really thinks about all this?" I said to him when we were finished.

"I s'pose he's kind of in shock. Trusted friend and all that, you know. It'll be interesting to see where that goes from here."

I agreed. I could only imagine what grandma Fanny Spurr would have to say about it. I assumed Trey would be the one to break this latest news to her, if Wendell Cox or Jim Sullivan didn't do it first. I wasn't going to call her right away myself and say, "Gee, the test went really well this morning. Couldn't have been better!" It was the truth, but somehow it didn't seem appropriate to present it quite that way in view of the drama involved. Let Sullivan and Cox handle it. I'm just the history guy.

"That poor boy," said Agnes.

"Yeah, right," said Belton.

"What are you going to do with Tanaka?" I asked.

"Turn him over to Jake Keil as soon as he can get here. I've already called him. Tanaka looks like he should go to a hospital, and we don't have a proper one here in Lester County. And I don't have enough deputies to keep a 24/7 watch on him if he's not in my jail. I'm not sure how, but all this is tied into the cases Keil is working on already, so it makes sense jurisdictionally too."

"That poor boy," said Agnes.

"Yeah."

Chapter 42

Things were falling into place nicely. Or "dropping like flies," if you went with Sheriff Belton's take on it. That is, at least as far as those of us in the real world were concerned. By the next day in the fantasy world where some of the media lives, it was literally a different story.

Arrest in Spurrville Bombing

Raleigh, N.C. (UP)—Early yesterday police arrested Mr. Gerald O. Bono, 25, of Raleigh on suspicion of murder in the recent explosion and fire at the Spurr Nutritionals company in Spurrville, NC, that killed Elliot Spurr, 52, president of the company and scion of the prominent Spurr family, as he apparently slept in the research laboratory where the nighttime fire took place. It is not known why Mr. Spurr, a widower with a son attending The University of North Carolina at Chapel Hill, was in the lab at the time of the blast and not sleeping at home with his dog, Jack Russell. No drugs or alcohol were found at the scene, according to sources close to the case, although the fire was so intense that any such evidence might have been destroyed.

This was the first alleged murder in Lester County since records started being kept in 1866. Mr. Bono was arrested at his place of employment, Colonel Chicken's Chinese Pagoda in the Airedale Shopping Center in Raleigh. Mike

Padoplis, owner of Colonel Chicken's, described Bono as "a dependable worker. I didn't know him that well as he only worked here about five years. After all, I own seven other restaurants too. But he seemed nice." Co-workers, friends and neighbors at his apartment complex expressed surprise over the arrest, describing Bono as "a pleasant young man, quiet, and not the type to do anything like this, but these days you never know."

Police would not divulge what evidence led them to suspect Mr. Bono, who lived alone. No drugs, alcohol, firearms or computer were found at his apartment, according to sources. No motive has been determined, but earlier reports indicate police suspected revenge for something Mr. Spurr might have done while on a cruise. Unnamed sources close to the investigation say the police have subpoenaed cruise ship passenger records for the time period in question. Mr. Bono is being held on $100,000 bond and is expected to be arraigned on Thursday.

One account had him listed as Gerry O'Bono, which gave him yet a third fake nationality to add to his résumé, although with his features I doubted he could pass for Irish so easily. I'd love to hear him try the fake accent. "Top o' the marnin' to ya! Faith and begorrah it is, y'know!" No, and anyway Jerry probably thought Faith and Begorrah were Bible characters.

Seeing we were apparently finished with the round of interrogations, crime scene photos and evidence gathering, I asked Sheriff Belton if I could leave.

"Aren't you going to answer your phone first?" he said.

I thought I'd been hearing a phone ring, but I assumed it was coming from another office and that whoever was supposed to answer it was out. But it was mine. Done in once again by my own ringtone. I pulled it out of my pocket and discovered I had four missed calls and three voicemails. They were from Emily. She would not be happy.

I called her back, ready to apologize. Profusely.

"They called again," she said. Before I had a chance to get very profuse.

"Who called again?"

"Those people, or whoever it was who called before and then hung up."

It took me a moment to remember the incident.

"You mean the call with the odd sounds in the background? Like traffic going by?"

"Yes, and that thing that goes 'ding' when you pull into a gas station."

"Did they say anything this time, or was it just heavy breathing?"

"He said he needed to meet with you."

"Who needed to meet with me?"

"Tom somebody. At the Set-A-Spell Restaurant."

"Tom Ake?" It was the only Tom I could think of at the moment.

"Maybe. Something like that."

Why on earth would Tom Ake want to meet with me? To explain himself? Apologize? Confess to breaking into my house? Reveal his true relationship with Adam Spurr? Ask for a reference so he could get a better job? None of those made any sense. I would have thought he'd want to steer as clear of me as possible. And why pick a place in Spurrville, so near the scene of the crime, as it were? I was reasonably sure it wasn't to check on whether Clara Fritts still had the takeout menus he and Jerry had left.

"What else did he say?"

"Just that he wanted to meet and give you some information about the Spurrt company. At 3 p.m."

"At the Set-A-Spell?"

"Yes."

"I can do that, I guess. He didn't say, 'Come alone,' or 'No cops,' or anything strange like that, did he?"

"Not funny. Isn't he one of those oriental-looking men who showed up at the Neighborhood Watch meeting, and they arrested the other one for murder?"

"Suspicion of murder, but yes."

"Then I don't want you to meet with him!"

"I'm not so sure I want to meet with him either, but the Set-A-Spell is pretty safe. Neutral ground. And I think the head waitress there likes me."

That didn't reassure Emily much (or me either), but I promised her I'd ask Sheriff Belton to come with me as backup—I'm getting into the detective jargon, apparently—and she reluctantly agreed to let me go as long as I promised to call her when it was over and then come straight home.

I thought it might not be wise just then to mention what had happened that morning with Tanaka, so I didn't.

By then it was almost 2:45 so I headed out to the car and drove to the Set-A-Spell, parking on the street in front again, behind an ancient brown Toyota Tercel with a mismatched front fender and a missing wheel cover. I know I should have told Belton where I was going, like I'd promised Emily, but in my haste and confusion over what Ake could possibly want with me, I had simply forgotten. I tried to call Belton after I parked. No luck. The dispatcher said he was still at the Spurrt company and couldn't be disturbed. "No, sir, not even for you." What about Deputy P.D. Rivers? Off today. And the other part-time deputy was at Myrtle Beach, presumably not on official business. I was on my own. Except, of course, for Clara Fritts.

I fed the parking meter and went into the Set-A-Spell, remembering to say "Hello" at the door.

"Hello, hon!" came Clara's unmistakable voice from somewhere in the back. "Go ahead and seat yourself!"

It was obvious right away Tom Ake had gotten there ahead of me. I smelled him before I saw him. He was sitting at a table in a relatively dark spot far from the window. Obviously, he had seated himself too. Clara would never have put him way back there. Other than Ake and me, the place was empty, as it would be at this hour. We nodded to each other. I sat down across the table from him. No takeout menus were in evidence. He looked terrible. He looked like he hadn't shaved in four or five days. I know that's a popular macho style for young men currently, but on him it was more of a homeless look. I couldn't tell if he'd bathed in that time, but even if he hadn't, the cologne would have masked any body odor. Which is the main point of cologne anyway, when you think about it. Before we could speak to each other, Clara was upon us.

"You boys are just in time! We close up for an hour in a few minutes, you know. What can I getcha that won't take very long?"

"Hello, Clara," I said. "Just coffee please. And this is my, uh … friend, Tom Ake."

"Pleased to meetcha, hon. What for you?"

"Coffee."

Obviously, Clara didn't recognize Ake in his clever five-day beard disguise. Even with the cologne. A point for him.

Clara whisked herself away to the kitchen.

Ake said in a low voice, "I have a gun. Let's go outside."

Just like that. Another point for him. A big one.

"Can I write a note to the waitress—tell her we'll be right back?"

Ake nodded.

I grabbed a napkin, took out my pen and scribbled "Call 911" and tossed it on the table in hopes he wouldn't take time

273

to try to read it. He didn't. We went outside. He motioned me into the driveway beside the building, where the dumpster was still partially blocking the way. I didn't see the gun until he fumbled it out of his pants pocket, almost dropping it. It looked very big.

There's a running gag in the movie *The Princess Bride* where the character Montoya confronts the evil Count Rugen and says, "Hello. My name is Inigo Montoya. You killed my father. Prepare to die." That is what flashed through my mind as I faced the shaky-gunned Tom Ake. I was expecting him to say, "Hello. My name is Thomas Ake. You had my friend arrested. Prepare to die."

What he did say was, "I don't like you very much." And then he fired once in the air.

Ake looked almost as shocked as I probably did. Did the gun go off by accident? Was it the first time he'd ever fired a pistol? What the hell was the matter with him? Would he fire again?

Bang! -whang-ang-ang-ang-ang.

Yes.

The bullet ricocheted off the dumpster and the walls on either side of the driveway. I felt something tug at my foot but no pain.

Now Ake looked pleased with himself.

No time for further analysis. I did the first thing that came to mind. I jumped into the dumpster and closed the lid over me. Fortunately, it was almost empty (what day was this?). Some light streamed in because the lid was bent from years of use and didn't fit snugly. As my eyes adjusted, I noticed three General Tso's takeout menus wedged into a seam at the bottom of the dumpster, apparently stuck there through several collection cycles. I had missed them.

Bang! -whang-ang-ang-ang-ang. Lots of ricocheting.

Followed by, "Come out of there you meddling rat!"

All Ake had to do was open the lid and start firing blindly, and my goose would be cooked, so I held on for dear life to the edge of the lid, keeping it down with my weight and hoping he wouldn't have the leverage to get it open if it occurred to him to try. I prayed he wouldn't aim at my exposed fingers. I checked my foot. A bullet had grazed my shoe.

For a moment, it was as if I left my body and was viewing the scene from several feet above the action, but I could somehow see myself through the dumpster lid. My life passed in front of my eyes. Not my whole life. Only this part. The one where I'm just a middle-aged management consultant innocently trying to write the history of a troubled soft drink company but instead surveying the bullet-ruined upper of my left down-at-heel Bally loafer and wondering why I'm hiding in a Dumpster hoping a fake Japanese guy with a gun doesn't make me the star of the final chapter. Then I thought, I think I just wrote the hook line for this novel.

BANG! -WHANG-ANG-ang-ang-ang.

From inside the dumpster, to which I had returned after the momentary vision, the sound was deafening.

BANG! -whang-ang-ang-ang-ang. "Ouch!! Oww! I'm hit!"

Who said that? I felt around. No pain, no missing parts. Fingers intact. It must have been Ake. A ricochet. Sure enough, I could hear him moaning. I lifted the lid a little.

"Don't you dare come out of there. No, I mean, yes, you come out of there, you coward!"

Bang! -whang-ang-ang-ang-ang. "AAAgh!!!"

I was witnessing the definition of insanity. He'd shot himself twice now. Yes, but on second thought, was the insanity only Ake's or was it mine too?

Then a new voice.

"What the Sam Hill is going on here??" It sounded like

275

Sheriff Belton. "Put the gun down, you little twerp, or I'll tie you up in a bow!"

Good old Clara had come through!

"You! You there in the dumpster! Come on out with your hands where I can see them!"

It proved to be a lot harder to climb out of the dumpster than it had been to jump in, especially keeping my hands where Belton could see them.

"Well, well, if it's not the peripatetic Mr. Mark Fairley. The proverbial bad penny turns up again. Are you all right?" The expression of concern seemed an afterthought, but it probably wasn't.

Belton was standing there, arms akimbo, no gun drawn. Ake was slumped against the wall on the other side of the driveway, whimpering, the gun on the ground beside him. He didn't seem to be hurt badly. Wounded pride more than anything, I supposed, although there was a small amount of blood. I checked again and was happy to find myself unscathed except for my shoe. Close call.

Belton took Ake's gun, got him to his feet, snapped handcuffs on him, checked his identification, read him his rights and started walking him toward Old Betsy.

"I thought you looked familiar there, Mr. Ake," said Belton. "I almost didn't recognize you, you know, what with that rug you're wearing on your face."

Evidently, Sheriff Belton had never before gotten close enough to Ake for the cologne to have made an impression.

"I just wanted to scare him. Just wanted to scare him," was all Ake kept saying until Belton told him to shut up.

Just then, Clara Fritts appeared from around the corner.

"You boys know your coffee's getting cold. And we're about to close. Oh, hi, Seedy. I didn't see you drive up. You know we're about to close, hon. Say, is everything okay out here?"

"Just fine, Clara. Just fine," said Belton.

"Thanks for calling the sheriff, Clara," I said. "Probably saved my life."

She looked bewildered. "But I didn't."

"The napkin?" I said. "'Call 911'?"

"Didn't see any napkin. Are you sure you're okay?"

"I only used hollow point bullets!" called Tom Ake.

"I told you to shut up!" countered Belton.

"Well then, Sheriff," I said, "how did you know to show up here like the cavalry?"

"Didn't. I had some unfinished business with you I forgot about in all the confusion at the Spurrt plant today, but I overheard you on the phone telling whoever it was that you were going to be at the Set-A-Spell, so here I came. I've got a warrant for your arrest in connection with two unpaid speeding tickets."

"You've got to be kidding."

Clara looked askance at me.

"You know me, Mr. Fairley," said Belton. "I don't kid. I'm going to need you to come down and give me your statement after I book this guy anyway, and maybe I'll book you too if we can't get this settled."

I had never been sure if Fanny Spurr had "fixed" those tickets for me or not. I guess not. All of a sudden, my wallet was feeling a lot lighter.

Belton cordoned off the area with yellow crime scene tape, interviewed the witness (Clara), and took many photographs with a fancy Nikon. Then he put on a pair of surgical gloves and started picking up shell casings, putting each into an evidence bag and labeling it.

"I could use a little help finding bullet fragments," he said.

"You seriously want me to help?"

He produced another pair of gloves and a few more bags,

handing them to me along with another marker. I couldn't believe it. Here I was, the victim of a vicious, if stupid, attack, asked to police the area of my own ordeal.

"I'd ask Wild Bill Hickok over there," he said, referring to Ake, "but I'm afraid he'd try to swallow the evidence or something."

"Aren't you at least going to deputize me for this very sensitive assignment?" I asked. "I think I deserve it."

"Okay, Zap! you're a deputy for the next 30 minutes. Sorry I forgot my royal sword, or I'd knight you too. Don't let it go to your head."

It almost made up for not investing in the private eye combo kit. I didn't bother asking him for a badge. One thing sure, Dirk Falcone wouldn't have put up with this.

By the time we finished bagging as many bullet fragments as we could find, removed the crime scene tape and tossed it in the dumpster, all the while listening to Tom Ake's repeated cries of "I have to go to the bathroom!" from Old Betsy, my parking meter had expired. There was a ticket on my windshield. Evidently, even though the town of Spurrville has no police force other than the Sheriff's office, they do have a meter maid.

I went inside and paid Clara for two coffees, plus a tip. Hard to believe I was buying coffee for a guy who "just wanted to scare" me by firing a 9mm pistol wildly in an alley I was occupying. There was a parking ticket on the Tercel's windshield too. I deduced it was Tom Ake's and left it there. Enough was enough.

Chapter 43

News 16 Alert: Group Protests Jailing of Hawaiian Suspects

Transcript (Click to see video report)

(Male reporter in studio) Protesters gathered for a second day outside the Raleigh jail where two men are being held on charges ranging from trespassing to murder. In the most serious of the charges, Thomas O. Ake is accused in the attempted murder of Mr. Mark Fairley of Greensboro outside a restaurant in Spurrville, and Gerald O. Bono is accused of involuntary manslaughter in an explosion and fire at the Spurr Nutritionals, Inc., plant, also in Spurrville, that took the life of Mr. Elliot Spurr, president of that company. The two accused men are Raleigh residents and co-workers at The General Chinese Restaurant here in Raleigh. Both men have native Hawaiian roots although they were born and raised in Raleigh and, as far as this reporter can determine, have never traveled outside North Carolina except for Myrtle Beach occasionally, much less to Hawaii.

The dozen or so protesters are upset over what they claim is police discrimination because both of the men being held are Hawaiian, whom they view as a minority. Earlier today, I visited the scene of the demonstration to interview a few of the protesters.

(Scene on street: Demonstrators displaying hand-lettered signs with such slogans as "Free the Hawaiian Two!" "Free the Hawaiian too!" and "Free Too Hawaians!" [sic] are seen while a small crowd of bystanders mill around.)

Reporter: Hi, I'm Roberto Quinoa from News 16. May I speak to you for a moment, ma'am?

Protester: It's about time you guys showed up! We've been Tweeting for hours!

Rep: Yes, I'm sure. Would you mind telling me your name and why you're here?

Pro: My name is Rhoada Beatwix, and I'm here because this is all just so-o-o unfair! These two heroic men are being singled out solely because they are a minority.

Rep: Hawaiians are a minority?

Pro: Look around you. How many Hawaiians do you see?

Rep: Well, none that I can be sure of, but …

Pro: My point exactly. And the few that are here are mostly locked up in that jail. (to the crowd) Free the Hawaiians!

Rep: And you, sir. Your name?

Pro: Algernon Wu. And with a name like mine, it's a wonder I'm not in that same jail on some trumped up charge too.

280

Rep: But the county prosecutor assures me the charges these men face are genuine.

Pro: (another woman) What does he know? Besides, it doesn't matter what they're charged with. They're a minority, and that's patently de facto unfair discrimination, pure and simple.

Rep: And you are …?

Pro: Myra Gribble, thank you very much. (to the crowd) Police discrimination! Profiling! Let us see the body camera footage! We have a right!

(crowd starts chanting: "Free them! Free them! Free them all!")

Rep: And how about you, ma'am? Your name?

Pro: Miranda Melenkampf. What's your question?

Rep: I hardly know where to begin. Uh, but aren't there a lot of Hawaiians in Hawaii? They're hardly a minority there.

Pro: There are a lot of Chinese in China too, but in North Carolina they're a minority! Like Algernon here. What did you say your name was again?

Rep: Roberto Quinoa.

Pro: Hispanic, right?

281

Rep: Yes. Well, Peruvian, actually.

Pro: Then you should know. Welcome, my brother! And watch your back.

Rep: But Hawaii is a state. You know, in The United States.

Pro: All the more reason we should all be ashamed of ourselves. In fact, we need to be calling them Hawaiian-Americans! (to the crowd) They're oppressing the Hawaiian-Americans!

(The crowd takes up the chant) "Free the Hawaiian-American Two!"

Rep: But what if they were from North Dakota, for example?

Pro: Wait, you say they're from North Dakota?

Rep: No, but …

Pro: (to crowd) Free the North Dakotans! Free the North-Dakotan-Americans!

(The crowd takes up the chant. People are seen rewriting their signs.)

Rep: This is Peruvian-American Roberto Quinoa reporting.

Chapter 44

If ever Detective Jake Keil was going to rattle Adam Spurr's cage, now was the time to do it, in my opinion.

Instead, he chose to rattle mine.

"You're the one common denominator in all this," he said.

"That's absurd!"

Actually, he and Sheriff Belton were double-teaming me, Belton as the good cop and Keil the bad one. It was two days after the Shoot-Out at the Set-A-Spell Corral, and we were seated in my little office at Spurr Nutritionals, Belton in a chair and Keil on the edge of my desk where Agnes Smith usually sat. Keil and Belton had summoned themselves here on the pretense of bringing me some new information about the case. The door was closed, and Agnes was not present. Probably sitting on her own desk down the hall.

The meeting started out innocently enough, with Sheriff Belton recounting highlights of his arrest of Tom Ake.

"It took all day with the doors open and the windows rolled down to air out Old Betsy after I drove Ake to the jail in her. I made him take a shower and slap on a couple Band-Aids before I turned him over to Jake here."

"For which I thank you very much," said Keil.

It quickly moved to finger pointing from there. Their fingers, pointed at me.

I had paid my not inconsiderable speeding ticket fines and the smaller but still substantial parking fine with a credit card (not American Express) at the Sheriff's Office. Unfortunately, these would not be deductible as business expenses. I dictated a statement about my encounter with Tom Ake to the Sheriff's "day girl" cum dispatcher, who typed it up and had me sign it. And I went home feeling Belton and I were all square. Maybe I was wrong, unless, as I suspected, Keil had talked him into participating in today's little charade. I couldn't figure Keil's motives because I didn't know him as well, but I had observed Belton had a sense of humor. Twisted, but there nevertheless. And it was nice of him to take time away from his speed trap duties.

It took a while for Emily to calm down after I told her what happened outside the Set-A-Spell. I emphasized how quickly Sheriff Belton had showed up, that Tom Ake wasn't trying to hurt me, that it was he who got hurt, but only slightly, and that the dumpster was a very safe hiding place. I repeated all this to Lisa, Judy and William when they called, having seen newspaper accounts of my adventure. I did not show Emily my shot shoe. She will read about it right now in this book. And I will be in trouble again, but probably not nearly as much.

I also told her about how the ViroBactiZap 5000 test session had gone, including Tadashi Tanaka's misguided and unsuccessful attempt to sabotage it, injuring himself in the process while inadvertently creating ideal test conditions. Her anger at me, assuaged only a little by her relief that I hadn't been hurt, was diluted only slightly more by sympathy for Tanaka, which I didn't share, but I was happy to take what I could get in the way of a reduced level of heat. And silence.

Because early in our marriage we had agreed never to let the sun go down on our anger, she did relent enough to say "I love you" before the lights went out at bedtime. I know she was still unhappy with me, and I resolved never to let anything like this happen again. Anyway, it's not that I look for trouble or that I enjoy it. On the contrary. It just seems to find me.

Especially if I ignore common sense suggestions like, "Make sure you take Sheriff Belton with you," which Emily mentioned more than once before we got our relationship back to some semblance of normal.

Another thing that helped was all the known perpetrators of mayhem in this case were now locked up in a Raleigh jail. So maybe the mean streets of Spurrville and the sanctity of our Greensboro home-as-castle were safe once again.

On the other hand, it still wasn't clear what was behind all this. This was not a simple case of Colonel Mustard in the library with the wrench. Ake, Bono and Tanaka were only agents, pawns really, in a larger game. Yes, maybe Kashimoto's motives were clear enough—divert Spurr's attention from the secret of the enhanced product long enough to buy out the company—but there had to be more. And as far as I was concerned, it had to be a vindictive Adam Spurr who was smack dab in the middle of the more.

So that's what I had hoped to explain to Keil and Belton there in my office.

They were pretending to have none of it.

"And you're a notorious scofflaw too," added Belton, apparently trying to reverse roles and play bad cop now but doing a poor job of it.

"Did I break into my own house and steal papers from my own briefcase?" I asked.

"There's no proof that break-in ever happened, you know," said Keil.

"Did you find *my* DNA on the gas jets at the lab?"

"We found your fingerprints."

"Of course you did. My apologies for not blowing my nose on one of those gas jets too while I was at it. And by the way, have you traced the rock I gave Tadashi Tanaka back to the quarry I stole it from?"

285

"No need for sarcasm, Mr. Fairley," said Belton.

"You keep saying that," I retorted, "but your own actions make it seem ever so necessary from time to time. How much do you think I paid Tom Ake to let me hide in a dumpster while he used it for target practice?"

"That's a good question. I wish I'd thought of it myself," said Belton.

I'd had enough. "If you really had anything on me, you'd have arrested me by now," I said, resorting to the time-honored ploy of the sneering perp in the precinct interrogation room of a TV cop show.

"Now, now, Mr. Fairley, there's no need to resort to the tired old ploy of the sneering perp in the precinct interrogation room in a TV cop show," said Keil, apparently reading my mind.

"To what must I resort, then, to get you gentlemen to end this farce?"

"Whaddaya think, Seedy?"

"Oh, I don't know. What do you think?" said Belton.

Keil turned to me. "I think we're just having some fun with you, Mr. Fairley," he said. "You being the amateur detective and all. We just thought we'd give you a taste of how it's really done."

"Said the crack investigators who missed the critical evidence of the open gas jets."

"You got me there," admitted Belton.

"Though I must say the thing with the chopsticks was pretty clever," I allowed, nodding at Keil.

"Thank you. Seems we can learn from each other. Which is what we really came here to do. Maybe a little brainstorming, since we're all looking at this from different angles."

"Like the blind men and the elephant," I said.

"The what?" said Belton.

"Never mind. I'm just glad you're finished with your little entertainment for the morning. Does this mean I'm in the Detective's Club now so we can get on with the real case? After all, let me remind you I am a former Deputy Sheriff in this county, and for that I deserve a little professional courtesy."

Belton looked at Keil and shrugged. "It was a moment of weakness I'll regret for the rest of my life."

Keil laughed.

"Or are you going to let me go with a warning and then put a tail on me, like on TV, to see if I will lead you to the real culprits?"

"Gosh darn, I hadn't thought of that," said Belton with a slight twinkle in his eye. "What about you, Jake?'

"Me neither, Seedy."

"All right then, what's this 'new information' you say you have? Or was that just a way of getting me to agree to this meeting?"

Keil spoke first. "No, we really wanted the meeting. Thought maybe you might have some ideas. Truth is, we've got squat, although we can do some more digging and rattling here and there. Ake and Bono admit Adam Spurr hired them to skulk around, but Spurr denies it and sticks to the story he first told us at the Chinese place—they're just casual acquaintances he's taken a fatherly interest in. Which is more BS in one week than I usually see in a month."

"So you have talked to him again, I take it?" I said.

"Oh, you bet I have, but he's a cool one. He's smart enough to know we have no proof of his involvement in anything connected to this case other than the claims of those two goofballs. It's his word against theirs, and who do you think a jury would be more likely to believe? Especially if he has a good lawyer, which he would. And anyway, why would he hire people to snoop around you and the company in the first place? Seems like he could come and go anytime he wanted, as a family member, if he wanted to know what was going on."

"Maybe he has some other reason to keep his interest hidden, or he just doesn't feel welcome even if he is a family member," I offered. "They don't seem to see a role for him in the company's future."

Belton nodded agreement. "No head for the business, according to Mrs. Spurr."

"And the Japanese guy, Tanaka, just sort of came out of left field with that rock, apparently acting on orders from the high muckety-mucks at that company in Japan. I believe Adam Spurr when he says he'd never heard of Tanaka, and I can't find any connection between Tanaka and the other two guys.

"I think we've dealt with a bunch of symptoms, but we don't know what the root cause of the illness is yet," Keil concluded.

"Do you think there is an illness, as you put it?" I asked.

"People don't show up at Neighborhood Watch meetings 90 miles from home, steal stuff from a briefcase inside somebody's house, leave takeout menus from a restaurant too far away to get to on a lunch hour, use fake Japanese accents and blow up a research lab—even if it was a dumb-ass practical joke gone wrong—for no reason. Ake, Bono and Tanaka are just the guppies in a tank full of sharks. There's a bigger game here."

"So, Mr. Fairley," said Sheriff Belton, "or should I call you Mark now, seeing as how you're in the Club?"

"Only if I can call you Seedy."

He thought about it. And thought about it. And finally said, "Okay."

Followed by, "So, Mark, do you have a theory?"

"It so happens I do, Seedy, and I'll be happy to tell you."

Which I did, for the next half hour.

Chapter 45

"You're probably wondering why I called this meeting," I heard myself saying in front of the mirror in my bathroom at home as I prepared to sally forth to yet another encounter in Fanny Spurr's Florida room. It sounded more lame than "It was a dark and stormy night." I didn't like it. I confess I was nervous about what this day would hold. I needed to come up with something better.

Ready or not, I finished my morning ablutions, gulped down the last dregs of my fuzzy instant coffee, kissed Emily goodbye with a promise to keep her informed, backed the Acura out of the garage and down the driveway, checked both sides of the street for lurking little red cars and, seeing none, drove the 50 miles to Fanny Spurr's house, slowing only for the unmanned Lucy Spurr Memorial Speed Trap which formed the gateway to Lester County.

Two weeks had gone by since the strange meeting with Belton and Keil in my office—long enough for Wendell Cox and his R&D people to complete their tests, for me to complete most of the company history, or at least as much as I could complete without knowing the outcome of the tests and their possible aftermath. Bail had been set and trial dates calendared for Tanaka and the Hawaiian Two, as the media were calling Ake and Bono. As none of them could make bail (both Kashimoto and Papadopoulos seemingly unwilling to help their employees in need), they were all three still in custody.

The circular drive in front of the Spurrs' Georgian mansion

was full of parked cars, but I nosed mine into a small space between Old Betsy and what I assumed was Jake Keil's unmarked Ford Crown Victoria, leaving no room for a delivery vehicle in case somebody wanted to order a pizza. Or Chinese. I hoped there would be coffee and donuts, which would have arrived before most of the cars got there to block the way, but it was more likely Fanny Spurr would be offering tea in exquisite little demitasse cups along with air sandwiches prepared by whoever answers the phone and feeds the dog. I got a picture in my head of Sheriff Seedy Belton and Detective Jake Keil holding dainty little teacups, pinkies raised politely. It made me smile.

With Mrs. Spurr's cooperation and that of the prosecutor in Raleigh, she, Belton and Keil had assembled a group of people I thought might be helpful in clearing things up once and for all. When I rang the doorbell, Mrs. Spurr herself opened the door.

"Everyone's here," she said simply, leading me back to the Florida room, my designated venue for the gathering. Actually, the Florida room wasn't quite big enough, and some of the attendees had spilled out into the adjoining living room. Most were standing around talking quietly, but a few were seated in the wicker Florida room furniture, leaving empty a large number of folding chairs that looked like they had been borrowed from a church. All were wearing "HELLO my name is" sticky-back paper name badges and presumably had had a chance to introduce themselves to one another.

All had little teacups. Evidently, the air sandwiches had not yet been served. Perhaps they were awaiting my arrival. I gratefully accepted my name badge and a teacup proffered by Mrs. Spurr.

As I nodded to everyone and received their nods in return, I performed a mental roll call. Mr. Z was there in a wheelchair, although I knew he could walk, unless he'd taken a turn for the worse that I hadn't heard about. Mrs. Spurr sat beside him. Belton and Keil were there, of course, standing. The others included Duke University Distinguished Professor of Chemistry Dr. Adam Spurr, young Trey Spurr, Jim Sullivan, Wash Booker, and Wendell Cox. Also Tad Tanaka, Tom Ake, Jerry Bono, two uniformed Raleigh police officers keeping an eye on Ake, Bono and Tanaka along with a pleasant looking man in a deputy sheriff uniform who I assumed was Pee Dee Rivers on duty for once, Agnes Smith, Heidi Wilton without her video camera, Frank Sheldon, Esq., and a tall, balding man with a briefcase named Fred Landis (the man, not the briefcase) who was Ake's, Bono's and Tanaka's court-appointed attorney. And me. Twenty in all. Who knew there could be that many demitasse cups in the world, and all right here in Spurrville?

Absent were Detective Marshall Blue from Greensboro, Lonnie the gatehouse guard, Connie the receptionist, Clara Fritts, and Nick Papadopoulos, none of whom had been invited. And Elliot Spurr, who was dead.

"Please find a seat, if you're so inclined," I said, "and thank you for coming."

There was some shuffling about, reminiscent of musical chairs but without the music, until those who wanted to sit had done so. I was grateful for the crowd because even with most of them seated they blocked much of the sunlight streaming through the Florida room windows, which meant I wouldn't have to squint while talking to silhouettes today.

It was time to begin.

"You're probably wondering why I called this meeting."

They stared at me in silence. Jake Keil rolled his eyes.

"That's supposed to be a joke, folks, to break the ice, because I know most of you are indeed wondering why you're here.

And maybe this is too serious an occasion for joking, but I do want everyone to feel comfortable and relaxed, at least here at the beginning."

A few of them smiled, and some glanced up as if to see if they had permission from the real authority figures—Fanny Spurr, and Detective Keil—to relax. Mrs. Spurr smiled broadly, but Keil didn't betray any emotion, and I knew that meant Ake, Bono and Tanaka would still be wound up tighter than guitar strings about to break. So far, so good.

"For those who don't know, although I think most of you do, my name is Mark Fairley. I live in Greensboro. I've worked in a number of big companies, and Mrs. Spurr hired me to write a history of Spurr Nutritionals. With the gracious help of Agnes Smith here, I am almost finished with that assignment, and let me say it is an honorable history of a great company with an almost fairy tale beginning, outstanding leadership over the years, an enviable team of loyal employees, quality products that have brought pleasure to millions, and a legacy all of you who are part of it can be justly proud of."

I had them now, I thought.

"But as with any good story, there is tragedy along with the comedy and drama. I refer, of course, to the untimely death of Mr. Elliot Spurr, the president, and before that, his wife, Lucy, as well as the unfortunate accident that has kept Mr. Zachariah Spurr from his daily involvement in the affairs of the business."

I purposely ignored Tanaka's current plight—in custody for attempted sabotage of the ViroBactiZap 5000 machine and in danger of losing face with Kashimoto foods and his full ride at Carolina, not to mention Trey Spurr's friendship—and gave them all a moment for respectful, head-bowed silence before continuing. I was tempted to mention my house being broken into, being shot at in a dumpster, a major argument with my wife, and my speeding and parking tickets, but I didn't think those particular personal tragedies rose to the level of the ones experienced by the Spurr family.

"So therefore, I might have started this meeting by saying, 'It was the best of times, it was the worst of times.'"

"Aren't you supposed to put 'Confucius say' at the beginning of that?" piped up Jerry Bono, who I guess wasn't as tightly wound as I thought. Or maybe his string broke a long time ago. Keil glared at him.

"Well, aren't you??" said Jerry, genuinely puzzled.

"No, in this case it's 'Charles Dickens say," I said. "But never mind that. What some of you may not know is Mrs. Spurr and Mr. Z also asked me, as part of my history assignment, to be on the lookout for evidence that might further explain some of these misfortunes, especially as they might be connected to attempts to acquire Spurr Nutritionals by third parties."

In other words, they'd asked me to spy on everybody, but I didn't want it to come out sounding like that. I looked around to see if anybody appeared surprised or offended. Nobody did.

"And with the invaluable guidance and help of Sheriff Belton, Detective Jake Keil, the SBI and Detective Marshall Blue from Greensboro, who couldn't be with us today, I believe I've been able to accomplish that in a small way. Now, as a result of our combined efforts, whether that history ends with the final chapter I have to write this week or continues indefinitely into an even brighter future may well be determined by what takes place here today."

You could have heard a pin drop, as they say. Instead, we heard a pen drop. It was Heidi Wilton's.

"Sorry," she whispered, retrieving it.

"This is absurd!" said Adam Spurr, rising from his folding chair. "I don't see what this is going to accomplish any more than if you had convened a company picnic, which is what this looks like except for the criminals you've invited. I have better things to do with my time."

"Please stay, Adam," Fanny Spurr said quietly.

He slowly sat back down, with a disgusted look on his face. All eyes were on me again.

"We will get to you in due course, Professor," I said. "No pun intended. But first, let me paint a picture of the current situation at Spurr Nutritionals. This company has a lot going for it, but right now it's between a rock and a hard place."

I glanced at Tanaka to see if he had any reaction to this idiom, but he didn't. Nor did Jerry Bono.

"To put it bluntly, the business has stagnated. Operations are efficient, but the lack of new products, coupled with a failure to expand internationally, is causing it to fall behind competitively. Elliot Spurr and Jim Sullivan wisely invested in state of the art equipment, processes and computerized systems over the years, including a modern if modest research laboratory, but in so doing borrowed heavily, putting the company deeply in debt. The balance sheet is upside down because there hasn't been money left to invest in marketing, new products and expansion to increase sales and revenue enough to service and pay down the debt. Spurr Nutritionals is drowning in debt. However, there may be a lifeline. I'll come to that in a moment.

"Other companies have made overtures to acquire Spurr, to buy it out. Among these, one in particular, Kashimoto Foods of Japan, has been particularly aggressive, sending representatives from their New York investment banking firm, Kuroibishi-Whitestone, to make repeated offers—very attractive offers—to buy Spurr. However, Mr. and Mrs. Spurr here have been reluctant to sell out, and certainly not to just anybody. Justifiable pride in the company name and heritage is one reason, and another of equal or greater importance is concern over what would happen to the employees and the traditions they've established over several generations.

"Why Kashimoto's unusual interest, you might ask? Our friend, Mr. Tanaka here, can tell us, and has told me and Detective Keil. It turns out he has been secretly working for Kashimoto, who paid his tuition and expenses at Chapel Hill for him to befriend young Mr. Trey Spurr and report back to Kashimoto the goings on at the company."

Gasps could be heard throughout the room, which I noticed was becoming warmer as the greenhouse effect kicked in. Tanaka hung his head.

"Please tell all of us what you know, Mr. Tanaka," I said. Keil told me Tanaka had regained his ability to talk after a few days, possibly owing to his youth and better physical condition than Mr. Z's at the times of their respective trips through the ViroBactiZap 5000 machine. Score one for pizza and beer. Or more likely green tea, raw fish, seaweed and exercise.

Tanaka stood up. Haltingly at first, and after getting a nod from his attorney, Mr. Landis, he spoke. "I am sorry about everything. I have betrayed my friend, Trey. I have now betrayed my employer. I don't deserve to live. I have betrayed everyone. I apologize. Profusely. *Sumimasen*! *Owabishimasu*!"

"Yes, we've been through all that, Mr. Tanaka," I said, "but I asked you to tell us what you know." I was afraid maybe he'd concealed another rock on his person and was going to bash himself in the head with it.

"I have learned that Trey is a true friend and that he doesn't know very much about what is going on at the company," he continued. "This was a disappointment to my employers. However, I learned from my employers that they know a secret about the product, Spurrt, and have known it for years. They seem to believe this secret, when discovered, would make Spurr Nutritionals much more valuable than it now appears to be, and that is why they want to buy it. Apparently, they cannot duplicate the secret with their own products in order to compete, and they have not been successful in working out the exact formula for Spurrt in order to successfully duplicate the secret with a copied product. When Mr. Spurr had his accident with the new machine, Kashimoto became afraid Spurr might learn the secret, which I presume has something to do with the machine. It was their desire to prevent Spurr from discovering this secret before they could buy the company that led to my being ordered to sabotage it."

Very articulate for a frightened college kid, I thought.

"And what exactly is that secret, Mr. Tanaka?"

"I don't know. They never told me."

"Thank you, Mr. Tanaka. You may sit down. Now before we delve further into that, I would like us to hear from Mr. Sullivan, the VP of Finance. Mr. Sullivan, exactly how valuable is Spurr Nutritionals?"

"You know very well I'm not at liberty to comment on that!" he said, rather defiantly, although I suspected it was as much to impress Mr. and Mrs. Spurr as to try to thwart me.

"Sorry, Jim," I said. "I should have announced at the beginning that today we're going to put all our cards on the table."

Again no reaction from Bono or Tanaka to the idiom, but Fanny Spurr gave Sullivan a subtle nod.

"All right, if you must know. The company isn't very valuable at all right now. If you take away taxes and interest on the debt, our EBIT looks great, but in reality there's no hiding the debt."

"Isn't it true, Jim," I said, "that if it weren't for how important the company is to the banks and the local economy, the banks would have foreclosed long ago? Spurr Nutritionals would be shuttered and empty like so many other industries in North Carolina."

"Yes, unless somebody would buy us out. But the kicker is there's a balloon payment coming due soon. It will take a miracle to meet it, and it's hard to imagine any buyer willing to take on that obligation."

"Was Elliot Spurr aware of all this?" I asked.

"Fully aware. As are Mr. and Mrs. Spurr, of course."

Sullivan then mentioned a figure for the balloon payment, and many people winced. Sad frowns were beginning to be displayed around the room. Heidi Wilton looked especially sad, but Fanny and Mr. Z maintained stone faces. Adam Spurr was frowning but did not look very sad.

"And yet Kashimoto maintains a strong interest," I said. "So strong that only recently Mrs. Spurr had to banish two men from Kuroibishi-Whitestone who appeared at her door unannounced. Isn't that right, ma'am?"

"Yes, Mark, that is correct."

"So naturally we wonder why that would be. Mr. Tanaka says it's about a secret they've discovered. Which doesn't directly bring us to Mr. Wash Booker, VP of Sales and Marketing, but nevertheless I would like us to hear from him briefly."

"About what?" said Booker.

"About your new product plans, please."

"Well, as I've told you, the destruction of the research lab was a major setback, and of course the loss of Elliot was even more so. He was very interested in developing new products, as I think I've also told you before. In any case, we do in fact have some exciting things on the drawing board. Unfortunately, as you and Jim have said, we can't afford to bring them forward."

"Specifics?"

"Can't we just agree to leave those particular cards face down for now?"

"Okay, fair enough," I said. "Do you, or does anyone here, have any idea why Elliot Spurr made nighttime trips to the lab? Did he confide in anyone here?"

"No," said Booker. "He never said anything to me even though I did ask him about it. He just shrugged it off as if it weren't important."

"Anyone else?"

No one spoke up, and their mostly neutral or quizzical expressions betrayed nothing.

It was getting hotter in the Florida room, but I wanted to press on. No one else seemed to be uncomfortable, so maybe it was just me. I wasn't used to being on stage, and this Agatha Christie case wrap-up act was a new and daunting experience.

"Now Mr. Wendell Cox, VP of Manufacturing and R&D, could you bring us up to date on your area, please?"

Cox was about to speak when, apparently in response to some unseen signal, Fanny Spurr rose and said, "Excuse me, Mark, but perhaps now would be a good time to take a short break?"

The air sandwiches had arrived.

Chapter 46

Agatha Christie's Hercule Poirot never made small talk during a break in a case wrap-up, and I found it hard to do so myself. "Nice weather we're having," "I'm sorry to hear about your aunt, and I hope she gets better soon" and "How 'bout those Panthers?" doesn't measure up to "So you, Monsieur Weathersby, stole back into the victim's bedroom in the dark of night to recover the murder weapon most deadly and cruel that you hid so cleverly in the bottom seam of the window drapery before your escape most cowardly, but which I show to you now! You, you turn *l'estomac*, monsieur!"

Poirot probably did eat air sandwiches and drink tea on occasion, but they were not his favorites.

The interruption in the flow of questions and responses was bad enough, but taking polite turns to use the tiny guest bathroom was worse. "After you." "No, no, you were here first." (But never "and you look like you need to go more than I do.")

After asking Mrs. Spurr if she might be feeling a bit warm in the Florida room, hoping it would encourage her to have someone adjust the air conditioning, I stepped into the foyer to call Emily on my smartphone. She answered immediately.

"How's it going?" she asked.

"Making progress," I responded, "but we're taking potty break right now so I thought I'd see how things were going with you."

"Nothing to report."

"No calls, no e-mails inviting me to interviews?"

"Not a one."

Now that this case was looking like it might be about over and with only a few loose ends to tie up in my history writing assignment, this was disappointing news. Again. I'd tried everything I could think of to get a job, but to no avail. It was like I went to sleep and woke up in a world where there were no jobs except for other people, Emily still looked like Emily but wasn't, and my key no longer fit in my front door.

My severance and healthcare benefits would run out soon, and workman's comp, assuming I even qualified for it, wouldn't hold us for long.

I confess I even contemplated a life of crime. But I couldn't come up with a list of crimes I'd be any good at. In a nutshell, I'm just too honest. We will simply have to starve or rely upon the charity of others. Maybe a GoFundMe page? In my case, just a sophisticated way to be a panhandler. Or Emily will have to get a job. Now there's an idea.

Chapter 47

It was noticeably cooler in the Florida room by the time we reconvened and Wendell Cox had explained about testing the new batch of enhanced Spurrt we'd run through the original ViroBactiZap 5000 machine, along with Tanaka. He was standing, talking from notes.

"The taste tests went about as we expected, according to the R&D folks," he was saying. "For people in the control group drinking regular Spurrt from a normal bottling line, their pick-me-up lasted anywhere from one to two hours depending on their weight, their other physiological characteristics, how much they'd had to eat before or while drinking the Spurrt and the time of day or night. For the test group who received the 'enhanced' product, the effect lasted 10 to 12 hours, again varying by those same factors. My understanding is this is similar to what Mr. Spurr experienced when drinking the enhanced Spurrt after his accident. Is that correct, sir?"

Mr. Z nodded emphatically, and Cox continued.

"An added benefit is the test product reportedly tastes better than the normal product. I have to admit I snuck some for myself, and I'd have to agree. Neither group experienced any weight gain or loss over the test period, which was 10 days, and there were no side effects. With Mr. Z's permission, we used a few bottles he had saved from the first accident some months ago, and we saw the same effects as in the test group. That is, a marked increase in the duration of the pick-me-up. This indicated the effect doesn't diminish if the product isn't

301

used for a while. I would say the shelf life of the test product is about the same as normal product."

Heidi Wilton was looking less sad now, as were others in the room.

"And what do you think causes this effect?" I asked.

"Frankly, we don't know. We have no good idea why the human body responds physiologically to the enhanced product the way it does. We will need to bring in some medical people to help us with that."

"Anything else?"

"Yes. While the taste tests were going on, we acquired a second ViroBactiZap 5000 on loan from the manufacturer. When we ran product through the second machine without the, uh, help, shall we say, of Mr. Z or Mr. Tanaka, the effect did not present itself. The product did taste better, but the pick-me-up duration was the same as always. In other words, the machine did exactly what it was designed to do, no more and no less. How it works is the machine shoots a precisely generated and continuously monitored beam or ray of combined ultraviolet light and electrical energy through the bottles as they pass through. Apparently, the presence of a foreign body, uh, so to speak and no offense to Mr. Tanaka, is required in order to alter the beam in such a way as to create the new effect. We haven't analyzed the beam to determine what it is that changes. We will need the cooperation of the machine's manufacturer to do that, and we haven't felt it wise to mention anything about this to them yet."

Jim Sullivan and Frank Sheldon nodded their approval of this, as did Fanny Spurr, Mr. Z, and Adam, who I hadn't thought was paying that much attention until just then.

Cox went on. "We also took the first ViroBactiZap 5000 and ran some new product through it without, uh, introducing any foreign bodies, which is what we had intended to do all along, before Mr. Tanaka's unexpected, shall we say, participation. That product showed the same enhanced effects as did the original batch that ran at the time of Mr. Z's accident. Better taste, *and* the much longer pick-me-up duration. So apparently, once the beam has been changed it stays changed. It looks like we only have to run a foreign body through these machines once to achieve a permanent adjustment.

"The obvious next step was to see if we could replicate the effect using the second machine. But to do it, we would need an appropriate foreign body to put through the machine."

"And?"

"You can bet we had some interesting brainstorming sessions over that."

"I presume you didn't feel it would be right to ask Mr. Tanaka to volunteer," I ventured.

"Of course not. Though it did cross our minds." Looking at Tanaka.

Some mild chuckling from the assembly, not including Tanaka.

"So, what would be a good substitute for a live human body?" Cox went on, "presumably preferably male? First we tried suspending a sack of potatoes in the machine as the bottles passed through. No offense, Mr. Z."

Mr. Z smiled.

"That didn't work. Nor did tomatoes. Or a stuffed deer we borrowed from a taxidermist. We're still working on that problem, but I'm confident we'll come up with something soon."

"Knowing you, I'm sure you will," I said. "Thank you, Mr. Cox."

Cox sat down. Belton and Keil were getting fidgety, so I knew it was time for some more crime talk.

"Detective Keil, if I may question Mr. Ake and Mr. Bono please?"

"Be my guest."

"Thank you. Tom and Jerry, we know what you've been charged with. Now how about telling us what you were really up to?"

"Is this off the record?" asked Tom.

"No, it's not," interjected Keil. "I read you your rights, remember? Anything you say can and will be used against you in a court of law."

Lawyer Fred Landis started to say something, but Tom waved him off.

"We have nothing to hide," said Tom. "We were working for Professor Spurr. He hired us to do what we did."

"That's preposterous, and you know it!" said Adam, rising again from his seat.

"Please sit down, sir," I said. "I told you we would get to you soon."

"Maybe not soon enough to preempt these lies you're about to hear!" But he sat back down.

"All right, Tom," I continued, "Did the professor hire you to crash our Neighborhood Watch meeting?"

"Yes."

"To break into my house?"

A long pause. "No."

"To skulk around Spurrville, raising suspicions?"

"What is 'skulk'?" said Jerry.

"To sneak around looking suspicious."

"Yes," said Tom. Jerry nodded.

"To leave takeout menus everywhere you went?"

"No, that was part of our job at the restaurant."

"But you must admit, it did make for pretty good cover, didn't it, helping you gain access to buildings and offices, and churches even, and other places you would otherwise have no business in?"

"Yes."

"But why? Why did the professor hire you to do these things?"

"We don't know," Tom and Jerry said, almost in unison. "He never told us," continued Tom. "He just said to show up at these places or move around in Spurrville from time to time and to use Japanese accents whenever we talked to anybody. And to wear gloves."

"Yeah, wear gloves," chimed in Jerry.

"He said to tell him about anything we saw, but he never told us what he was looking for, so after a while it was frustrating, and we wanted to stop. But he was paying us, so we didn't."

"How much was he paying you?"

"At first it was $25 for each trip, which we split, but we finally got him up to $40 at the end," answered Tom, looking proud of himself.

There were ill-concealed smirks around the room.

"What??" said Tom. "It was plus gas money too!"

More smirks. Some eye rolling from Keil and Belton. A smile formed on attorney Fred Landis' face. I suspect it was in that moment he settled upon what his defense strategy was going to be.

"Did you break into my house and steal documents from my briefcase?"

Jerry looked imploringly at Tom, who said, "No!"

Summoning my most accusatory tone, I struck back. "If the professor didn't hire you to do it, then why did you blow up the research lab and kill Elliot Spurr!?"

"It was just supposed to be a practical joke!" cried Tom. "Jerry didn't know what he was doing. He thought the gas jets were water faucets. He was going to let the water run and make the company pay a big water bill. To get back at 'The Man,' you know? And he didn't know anybody was in there with him."

There were gasps from those who hadn't heard this part of their story before.

"Is that true, Jerry?" I asked.

"Yes."

"Do you believe him, Detective Keil?"

"Oh yes."

"I have to go to the bathroom," said Jerry.

Chapter 48

We took another short break, but this time most people stayed in the room, maybe sensing something even more earthshaking was about to come. Fanny Spurr spoke quietly to her husband, who alternately nodded or shook his head. Trey and Frank Sheldon joined them but didn't say anything. Booker, Sullivan and Cox chatted amiably. Heidi and Agnes made a pair, both looking over the notes they had taken. The two uniformed policemen had bathroom duty with the prisoners, accompanied by Landis, while Keil, Belton and Rivers conferred, presumably over official police-type business. Only Adam remained by himself, seated, speaking to no one, not even his parents. I didn't know what to make of his behavior, but I hoped for the best.

When everybody resumed their places, I resumed my line of inquiry.

"Professor Adam Spurr, I said we would come to you, and now we have. The obvious first question is, why did you hire Tom Ake and Jerry Bono?"

"Assuming I actually did," Adam retorted. "All you have is their say so, and I'm sure everyone here today has made some judgement about their credibility."

"So you deny it?"

"Not exactly, but before I speak, is there anything else you'd like to accuse me of?" This while looking from me to Keil and back to me, his gaze also falling ever so briefly on his mother.

"No, I'll leave that to you yourself if you're so inclined," I said.

"Very funny."

I thought Keil would like that even if Adam didn't, and his expression told me I was right.

"Rather than ask Detective Keil to question you, as I believe he has already done on more than one occasion, why don't you just tell us what's on your mind, Professor."

"All right, I will." He glared at me as he rose from his chair. "Yes, Mr. Keil has indeed questioned me, but even to this very day he has found no evidence of wrongdoing on my part. Isn't that right, Mr. Keil?"

"It's true," said Keil. "Other than being an accessory to trespassing, which isn't a crime yet, and contributing to the delinquency of mental minors, which isn't either. But we're not through yet."

"I think you will be through very soon," said Adam. "Yes, I did hire Tom Ake and Jerry Bono to go skulking about, as you put it, wearing gloves, using fake Japanese accents and filling the world with takeout menus from their pitiful Chinese restaurant. And I truly cannot tell you how sorry I am and how grieved that this has led to the death of my brother. It was not something I wanted, and you must believe me on this. In my wildest dreams I could not have conceived of it happening. I have lost much sleep over it—not as much as my dear parents and nephew Trey, I know, not nearly as much—but much indeed. Mr. Fairley, if in fact these two did break into your house, it was on their own initiative. I never asked them to do such a thing. I never would."

"That's right. He never asked us to," said Jerry.

"Shut up," said Tom.

"And while I did send them to the offices and reception areas at the company and to the research lab and other locations on more than one occasion, it was always to be during business hours. Never at night. They broke no laws on my instructions. Again, this was something done on Jerry Bono's initiative. Ordinarily, one applauds initiative, but in this case one obviously would not."

Jerry hid his face in his hands.

"As for their 30 or 40 pieces of silver, if anyone here chooses to associate this with that infinitely greater crime, I paid them only what they were worth, as it turns out. More, in fact. It was a hard lesson, and I am ashamed, but I learned never again to hire an imbecile to do a moron's job. Or a 'mentally challenged' person, if you prefer to be politically correct, which I don't."

A few people didn't know whether to be amused by this or not, but furtive glances at the somber faces of Fanny and Mr. Z quickly guided then toward a more suitably serious attitude.

"And why did I do it, you ask? Yes, why? That's the question of the hour. Do you like chemistry?"

Uh oh, where was this going?

"Do you?" Adam's eyes swept the room. "You should. As I once reminded Mr. Fairley here, it is the stuff of life. It is everywhere. From your waking moments until you drift off to sleep, and even after. From birth to death, it is with us. It is certainly the stuff of Spurr Nutritionals. What is Spurrt itself but a brilliant mixture of chemicals? A splendid concoction, to be sure, but one of chemicals nevertheless. And it is apparently the stuff of whatever is causing the enhanced Spurrt to behave as it does. All your livelihoods depend upon it here in Spurrville and may do so even more in the future if what Mr. Cox has reported is any indication.

"Ah, but there comes a time in life when we understand 'chemistry' is not just about a chemical formula. About valences and acids and bases. Protons, neutrons and boiling points. Solutions and reactions. No, there is much more. In our relationships with one another, for example, we often refer to that effortless rapport and connection that can exist between two people or two or more groups of people as 'good chemistry.' Isn't that right? There's chemistry in a love affair. Chemistry in inviting someone to join your club or your fraternity or sorority. Or what you look for when you hire someone for an important job on your team at work.

"I don't have the pleasure of teaching that kind of chemistry, and do you know why? It's because I've rarely experienced it myself. Not since middle school at any rate. Apparently, there was a dearth of chemistry that somehow developed between me and my family. Yes, I loved my brother Elliot, and he loved me. And don't misunderstand, my parents were good parents. I know they loved me, and they love me now. But somehow a chasm slowly opened up. Maybe it was based on misunderstanding. Maybe misplaced aspirations for a son who had interests unlike those of his father and grandfather before him. Maybe because my name is Adam, but I'm not the first-born!"

At this, Adam looked directly at his father, who winced. Fanny put her hand to her mouth.

"Whatever the cause, the chemistry died. Maybe it was just easier for me to bury myself in my work and pretend there was no problem. Easier to lick my wounds in private, making no attempt to reach out and heal the rift. Maybe it was easier for Mother and Father to rationalize, 'Poor Adam, bless his heart, he has no head for business, but we're happy he's so successful as a teacher at the college.' Well, you've now seen the result. A relational chemistry experiment gone horribly wrong."

I had sat down when Adam stood because I sensed something important was about to happen. Also, I wanted to observe the reactions on various faces without being obvious. All eyes were on Adam throughout his whole monologue, and everyone was paying rapt attention. Even Keil and Belton seemed impressed. Trey's jaw had dropped. I couldn't read

Fanny and Mr. Z, who remained stone-faced, although I thought I saw the glint of a teardrop forming in one of Fanny's eyes. No dog barked, no phone rang and no air sandwiches arrived, as if God were providing the perfect conditions for what was taking place.

"I am here today," Adam went on, "to ask if that long-lost chemistry can somehow be restored."

He was addressing his mother and father directly now, although everyone at Spurr Nutritionals was understood to be included in the question.

"I know the dire condition of the company, as Mr. Sullivan has so capably described it. I know you don't really want to have to sell it, least of all to the people Mr. Tanaka represents. My sole aim in hiring these two men, Mr. Ake and Mr. Bono, was to have them mistaken for Japanese thugs and thereby put you off from acceding to the ever more lucrative offers you have been receiving from Kashimoto Foods while I made certain arrangements. That they provided me with valuable information from time to time was a side benefit, almost serendipitous, and I may have steered them to be at certain places at certain times where I thought they might make observations that might interest me."

"That's right, but he never told us what he was looking for," said Tom. "We wanted to quit!"

Keil and Landis shushed him with hand gestures.

"I was deceitful, yes, but as I said, I never asked them to break the law," Adam said. "It turns out Kashimoto Foods has acted less honorably than I in that regard, and I wish that to be recognized publicly."

"Where are you going with this, Professor?" I asked. I hated to interrupt him, but a part of me felt I still had to assert my control of the meeting. Just as Hercule Poirot would have done, but he would have done it more forcefully. Adam gave me a pained look, then a more imperious one, as if suddenly realizing the meeting was now rightfully his and his alone. Which at that point, I think it was.

"I have a proposal," he said. "Here it is. Oh, and by the way, this is not a negotiation. Of course, there will be details to work out, and maybe some compromises, but in the main this is a simple yes or no proposal."

It was deathly quiet. No pins dropped. Or pens. It seemed almost everyone had stopped breathing.

"I will cover the balloon payment. By dint of hard work and smart investments, I have the wherewithal to do so."

Gasping was heard around the room.

"In addition, I will assume most of the company's long term debt. Not the working capital debt, only the long term. In return, I require a controlling interest in the company. That is, a majority of the stock, 51%, which I will amass by assessing its value using my own formula and paying each current stockholder on a pro rata basis at a substantial discount. This is called a leveraged buyout, or an LBO. I will have a seat on the Board of Directors and by virtue of my holdings I will be de facto chairman, although you, Father, will retain the title of Chairman Emeritus. Call me whatever you want—President, CEO, or whatever—as long as it sounds good to the investment community. Why do I care what the investment community thinks? Because as soon as I am satisfied with Mr. Booker's new product plans, including the plans for introducing the enhanced Spurrt—that is, the new and improved superior Spurrt—to the market, which will result in skyrocketing sales and profits with which to pay off the debt I will be holding, we will conduct an IPO, or what I'm sure you know is called an initial public offering of stock, in order to raise the funds necessary to execute the new product and expansion plans. And rebuild the research laboratory, of course, making it a world-class facility. Which, it just now occurred to me, we can name The Elliot and Lucy Spurr Family Nutritional Research Laboratory.

"The competitive advantage afforded by the new Spurrt will make the stock very attractive. You will become rich. Richer than you already are, Father. Then, assuming success with that, the longer term plan is to buy back the stock at a profit to the shareholders, in the process of which we will all become even richer, but more importantly we will take the company back into private ownership.

"That's about it. Do you think you can agree to that?"

Chapter 49

They did agree to it, naturally. Fanny Spurr couldn't stop crying, and Mr. Z was so moved he started talking intelligibly again. Doctors later said it was the shock.

Adam said he planned to keep his position at Duke unless and until he couldn't spread himself between there and the company anymore, but since he felt comfortable with the team of Sullivan, Booker and Cox running things at Spurr, he didn't think it would come to that.

Adam said, too, he felt badly that he had essentially bought his way back into the family, which was true in a big way, but he was also grateful to have been in a position to help. I wasn't privy to their family conversations, but apparently they all came to terms with his indirect role in Elliot's death and forgave him.

I won't say there was dancing in the streets of Spurrville, but that evening there was a hot time at the Set-A-Spell Family Restaurant and Nite Club as scores of employees and townspeople engaged in hearty eating, drinking, backslapping, and general merriment, accompanied by some pretty good pickin' and grinnin' by local musicians, even though it wasn't a Friday or Saturday. Belton and Rivers left their breathalyzers at the Sheriff's office and joined in the fun. Even Bill Lester closed up his dry goods and hardware stores early and celebrated with the crowd. Jake Keil and his band, The Cops, stopped by and played a set, to the delight of all. Fanny and Mr. Z showed up in Mr. Z's Cadillac DeVille. Mr. Lester and

Mr. Z were seen shaking hands. After 30 minutes, which was enough time for Mr. Z to toss down two beers and Fanny to enjoy a tad more than a demitasse of chardonnay, they were driven home by Sheriff Belton in Old Betsy.

Adam didn't come.

I had one draft beer with the revelers and then drove home myself, exhausted but happy. Only to discover it was Emily's and my night for Neighborhood Watch duty again. We tried to get Don Bledsole to switch with us, but he was too busy doing important chairman things, and he refused. I slept through most of our watch period, leaving Emily and the neighborhood easy prey in case any more fake Japanese people showed up to wreak havoc or to leave useless Chinese takeout menus.

Trey Spurr moved in with Adam, his uncle, who agreed to take care of him until he graduated and went out on his own or went to grad school, maybe followed by a job at Spurr Nutritionals or maybe not. It was enough that he was a chemistry major, so the last I heard they were getting along well. For Trey it had to be a whole lot less restrictive an environment than living with his grandparents.

Because it now looked like the end of the road for Spurr Nutritionals was a lot further off than Fanny Spurr had thought, there was a lot less pressure to get the history finished. It now seemed there was going to be a lot more of it to come. I turned over what I had done to Agnes Smith, who took on the project with great enthusiasm because it was right up her alley, and it kept her from having to retire anytime soon.

I was paid well for my efforts, including a generous and unexpected bonus for "performance above and beyond," as Fanny and Mr. Z put it. Equally unexpectedly, with Adam's approval they awarded me a modest block of stock. Jim

Sullivan says I'll make a lot of money from it when they do the IPO. Which will be soon, I hope. Otherwise, when the bonus runs out I may have to become a greeter at Walmart.

Even though I'm kidding about being a greeter at Walmart, it will be a while before you and I can find enhanced Spurtt at the supermarket. Testing, refining, package design, advertising, distribution—all these things take time, even when you're in a hurry. But it will happen. Meanwhile, as part of my bonus, Fanny Spurr slipped me two more bottles from Mr. Z's stash, and Emily and I shared them on a special occasion. Like the next day.

The Spurrs declined to press charges against Tad Tanaka in the attempted sabotage of the ViroBactiZap 5000 (or "vandalism," as they chose to call it), because of all he'd been through, so to speak, because of the way Kashimoto Foods had taken advantage of his naïveté and because there was nothing to be gained by it. He graduated from Carolina and went back to Tokyo where, according to Trey who has kept in touch, Kashimoto welcomed him as a kind of hero because of the way he "threw himself into his work." It was a good way for everyone there to save face. At the same time, Kashimoto stepped up its efforts to prevent Spurrt from being imported into Japan. Trey told me Pamela visited Tanaka there once, and even met his parents, but I don't know if their relationship has progressed beyond that.

Shortly after Tanaka was released from jail, I noticed the "hateful" Facebook page was taken down. I had chosen not to ask him about it during the wrap-up meeting, and I never found out if it was because Facebook administrators did it at the request of the police or because it had been Tanaka's work all along and he no longer needed it. It made me wonder who authored the phony mouse parts claims too.

Because of a lenient judge, Tom Ake and Jerry Bono are

serving short jail sentences which will be followed by probation and community service, much to the chagrin of Detective Keil. But he says it is what he expected, given their inherent proclivity for dumbness. I don't know if their jobs will be waiting for them at General Tso's Golden Chicken Pagoda when they get out of jail. Nick Papadopoulos doesn't seem capable of much empathy, but where else will he find a pair as loyal and dependable who are willing to work for fried rice, wonton and the occasional cashew? And can pass for Chinese.

Frank Sheldon's suit against the out of state man who rammed Lucy Spurr's car is still pending.

Detective Marshall Blue and I keep in touch, but there isn't much to talk about.

I never did meet any of the people from the SBI.

Oh, you may recall Sheriff Belton telling me Clara Fritts and some of her friends are on the Lester County Board of Elections. Did I happen to mention that Lonnie the gatehouse guard is also the mayor of Spurrville?

I keep asking lawyer Sheldon, Esq., if he has any other clients who might need my special services, but he says not, although he'll keep an eye out.

I haven't bothered to go back and change what I wrote earlier about hoping this book will bring in some money. I still do. Maybe if I publish it under the pen name Dirk Falcone it will have more appeal. Anyway, if you enjoyed reading this, whether it's by Mark or Dirk (but not Dork), please tell your friends and write five-star reviews on Amazon and Goodreads. And please "Like" and Share the Facebook page I will have created for it.

Nobody ever did figure out what Elliot Spurr had been doing all those late nights in the lab. Most assume he was running experiments to discover the secret of the enhanced

Spurrt, but there was no evidence of that. Maybe he was using the lab as a sort of sanctuary within which to pray for a miracle that would save the company. If so, I'd say the prayers were answered. Sort of.

What's your theory?

The End

If you have enjoyed this book, please consider leaving a review for Walt on Amazon, Goodreads or at the Fantastic Books Store to let him know what you thought of his work.

You can find out more about Walt below and on his author page on the Fantastic Books Store website. While you're there, why not browse Walt's other works and the rest of our literary offering?

www.FantasticBooksStore.com

About the Author

Walt Pilcher is a former CEO of L'eggs®, the pantyhose in the plastic eggs. His comic writing career coincides with his business writing career, and it was often impossible to tell them apart. Himself a two-time victim of corporate downsizing long before it was cool, he eventually became president of two major apparel companies in the U.S. and one in Japan, although not at the same time, and lived in Tokyo for 14 months during which two comedians were elected as governors of Japan's biggest cities. We are not making this up.

He is the author of *On Shallowed Ground, including Dr. Barker's Scientific Metamorphical Prostate Health Formula® and other Stories, Poems, Comedy and Dark Matter from the Center of the Universe* and the satirical novel, *Everybody Shrugged*, both from Fantastic Books Publishing. His non-fiction book, *The Five-fold Effect: Unlocking Power Leadership for Amazing Results in Your Organization* (WestBow Press), was a First Horizon Award finalist in the 2015 Eric Hoffer Book Award competition.

Walt holds a BA from Wesleyan University and an MBA from Stanford University. Currently, he ghostwrites book cover blurbs from his home in Greensboro, North Carolina, where he lives with his wife, Carol, an artist.

Also by Walt Pilcher published by Fantastic Books Publishing

On Shallowed Ground
Everybody Shrugged

Made in the USA
Lexington, KY
03 November 2019

56268093R00186